"It's obvious everyone is stonewalling and lying through their teeth, but what can I do about it? This is the President of the United States. I can't throw him in jail. Hell, look what happened when I just cited him for contempt. What am I supposed to do? Send some of those troops he so thoughtfully provided for us down to Earth to slap him on the wrist?"

"The Russian troops might be more willing to undertake that assignment," Furakawa said with a slight smile.

"I can't believe this is *my* country," Cab said quietly. "We have the most enlightened political and legal system ever designed. This can't be happening."

"But it is, Cab. There are wicked and evil men at work here, keeping themselves safe and powerful by manipulating that system. And I ask you, once more—what *are* you going to do?"

MELINDA M. SNODGRASS
CIRCUIT

BERKLEY BOOKS, NEW YORK

CIRCUIT

A Berkley Book/published by arrangement with
the author

PRINTING HISTORY
Berkley edition/April 1986

ISBN: 0-425-08736-0

Acknowledgments

A number of people helped me create this book. They deserve mention. First Fred Ragsdale, a brilliant lawyer and law professor, who was there with advice, encouragement, and an occasional put-down just to keep me humble; my agent, Patrick Delahunt, for believing in me; my editor, Ginjer Buchanan, for having the courage to take a chance on a newcomer; and above all my thanks to Dr. Gerrold L. Walden, my brilliant and eccentric professor of Constitutional Law who taught me to love the scholarship, the glory and the wonder of the law.

Dedication

This book is for Victor Milán—best friend and dearest companion—without whose assistance and encouragement it couldn't have been done. And more than just this book; thank you for the love, support and guidance that freed me and opened up this new world.

Prologue

Harsh breathing, his own and Gregori's, filled Evgeni Feodorovitch Renko's ears. The air in his suit was so replete with the stale odor of sweat that it seemed as if he were breathing molasses. He would try to repair the filter, and nurse the suit through a few more hours. It was all he could do. Clearly no replacements were coming from the processing center in Omsk. He had asked five times without success. Evgeni made fast the tow line, and chinned on his radio.

"That's it, she's ready." A taciturn grunt was his only response, but that was typical of Gregori, and Evgeni didn't take it personally. The big man had his hands full trying to fly the balky jump booster which kept their ore moving from the mine to the kick point.

Behind Evgeni squatted the three domes of the Garmoncya Mining Collective. The colony had been backed up against a lunar mountain, with sharp outcropping of rock wrapped on either side of the domes like a stone embrace. In front of him was featureless plain lacking even a decent impact crater to break the monotony.

"Nessa says something is wrong with the stove," Gregori remarked as he and the booster floated away with five tons of ore swinging beneath it.

"She's told Omsk?"

"Of course, and naturally we have heard nothing. It will be a cold day in hell before we see a replacement." Gregori broke contact, and Evgeni, realizing the pilot had nothing more to say, started back toward the collective in long, ground-skimming leaps.

For Evgeni Renko this new socialist frontier was a bitter disappointment. He had hoped that volunteering to be a dirt miner on Luna would carry more status than a similar position in the Ukraine or Siberia, but it had proved to be no different. The shortages were much the same, worse in fact, for the distances to be covered were much greater, and life on the Moon was just as gray and drab as life in Novgorod—and potentially a lot more deadly.

Depression pulled him down to a dragging walk. Why, he wondered as he sucked at the water nipple, was he breaking his body to dig rock out of an airless waste so the Minister of Space Utilization could have an additional dacha on the Black Sea? There was no good answer to that one.

Far above him there was a glitter as the sun reflected off the gleaming curve of the U.S. Steel smelting station. Or perhaps what he had seen was the fierce glow from the solar blast furnace. Virtually next door, by System standards, the third largest metal ore processing plant in the System orbited. They bought iron ore from the asteroids, titanium and zirconium from the Moon, and they paid—paid well for the ore they received. Their suppliers got something far more tangible for their work then Evgeni, who had only the glory of the socialist revolution for his reward. He wondered again what it would be like to take that money to the shops and stores of Serenity Base or EnerSun I, and buy. For a moment a fantasy of books, and toys, and jewelry rioted through his mind.

He shook his head, jerking himself from useless dreams, and resumed his run. Too many times during the past months he had indulged in such vagrant daydreams only to stop short of real action. It was a lifetime of obedience which always pulled him back, that and fear of the anger that would be generated groundside. And more than anger there was the threat of retaliation—there were soldiers at the Lenin Base.

But they would have to cross American-held territory to reach the Collective, and the super powers were very possessive of their territorial rights. Would the government risk such a confrontation with the Americans over one small mining colony? Maybe—maybe not.

More important than the conjectural reactions of faceless bureaucrats groundside were the reactions of his people should he try to lead them in this act of rebellion. Was it worth risking the fifteen people of the Collective in a mad gamble? He thought of Irina, his wife, with her soft brown hair and doe's eyes, fashioning a doll from scraps of material for Analisa.

Analisa. The image of his daughter lingered in his mind; wide brown eyes beneath arching brows, set in a face of such elfin beauty that it squeezed his heart each time he gazed down into it. It still amazed him that such a child had been born to him—plain Evgeni Renko. Surely the father of such a child was destined for greater things, and such a child deserved better than a life in this barren waste without wealth and opportunity to smooth her way.

It was this more than any other consideration which hardened his resolve and pushed him past that mental sticking point. He stopped and gazed once more at the gleaming nimbus of the station.

Yes, he decided. I will do it.

He momentarily considered the others; Gregori, Boris, Sergei. Would they agree to his wild scheme? He thought they would. He had been their de facto leader for three years now. They would be frightened, but they would follow.

Free enterprise, the open market, capitalist exploitation.

He rolled the phrases about in his mind, inspecting them critically, and decided that he liked them. There was a risk, of course, in what he was about to attempt, but the rewards to be gained were far too great to allow fear to immobilize him. It might take a little time before he would be comfortable with his plunge into capitalism, but he thought with practice he could get used to the idea.

Probably even grow to enjoy it.

Chapter One

"Shuttle will be docking soon," Florence Wandall said from the office door.

Lydia Kim Nu, manager of EnerSun I, glanced up from a report, her pen poised in midair. "So?"

"Huntington's on board."

"I know."

"And you're still determined not to meet him at the shuttle?" Flo asked. Her hands kept clasping and unclasping, the fingers twisting through one another like thin brown worms.

She was a thin, washed-out woman of some sixty years. With her perpetually agitated expression and nervous gestures, she reminded Lydia of some exotic species of long-legged bird. The resemblance was always heightened when Flo was nervous, and in her present state Lydia fully expected Flo to unfurl a pair of wings and begin pecking at the floor.

The manager threw the pen onto the clear plastic surface of her desk, and sighed. Clearly Flo was not going to drop it, and would remain in her office until she supplied an explanation.

"No, I have not changed my mind since last night. This man has been forced upon us. The fact that I've accepted him is concession enough. I'll not be forced to be courteous as well. I'll get there when I get there."

"Oh, Lydia!" Flo took an agitated step, putting herself directly in line of the sliding door. "Do you think it's wise to provoke them?"

"While he was on Earth I had to be polite to him. He could have gone howling to the board, and I didn't need that kind of grief. But now"—she paused, her lips drawing back in an anticipatory smile—"now he'll be in my territory, and I want him to know he's got a fight on his hands. This has to be stopped here or the System will lose everything we've spent fifty years building."

"Do you and Joe have a plan?" There was a subtle emphasis on the final word, and Flo's hands fluttered in a comprehensive gesture about her head as if a plan were an object which could be materialized for her inspection.

She was still hovering nervously in the doorway, and her position, neither in nor out of the room, was causing the automatic sensing device to whine in protest. Lydia bit back a sharp remark. She reminded herself that there was no point in blowing up over a minor thing like the door. Especially since she would only be using it as an excuse to take out her frustrations over Flo's continuing naggings about presenting a conciliatory face to the Earth authorities. Lydia hadn't made a scene during committee meetings, and she wasn't going to make one now.

She scraped her hand through her long silver-gray hair, pushing it back from her face. "No, we don't. This is going to be one of those times for creative improvisation and inspiration."

"I would feel so much better if it weren't the federal government that you were improvising with."

"Why? Do you think they're any better prepared than we are?"

"Yes, and I think it's time that we stopped baiting our representatives. We've gotten as much as we can reasonably expect."

"Forgive me, Flo, but I can't agree. Our *representatives* have never given the slightest heed to our needs or desires, but have continued to pass legislation designed to limit our growth and options." Florence's mouth opened and closed several times, and Lydia, seeing a long and, no doubt, repetitive rebuttal coming, quickly headed her off. "But enough of this. I'm not meeting the shuttle, but I do have to finish this report, so if you please." She glanced pointedly at the door.

Flo looked mulish, but nodded and stepped back into the

hall. The door sighed shut behind her, and Lydia punched up a picture from outside the station. She then swung around in her chair to watch the large screen that backed her desk. A shuttle was sweeping in toward the hub for docking. She stretched back and hit the button, and one of the new SDS satellites that were under construction came into view. A final touch and stars appeared, glittering like a dusting of diamonds against the black of space. While she watched, the rotation of the station brought Earth into view. It glowed blue-green and beautiful against the vastness of space, but Kim Nu was not charmed by its fertile loveliness. Recently it had come to represent only a threat—a threat that she was no longer certain they were capable of withstanding. She grimaced slightly and, swinging back to her desk, returned to work.

Set against the icy darkness, the great wheel beckoned. Its silver beauty glowed with incandescence where the sunlight struck the outer radiation shield.

Heaven is above all yet; there sits a judge, that no king can corrupt. Justice Cabot Huntington shifted in the acceleration couch, and rested his forehead wearily against the cool surface of the shuttle's port. The lines had been running ceaselessly through his head ever since their liftoff from the Cape earlier that day. *Heaven is above all yet.* The concept disturbed him, jangling along his already taut nerves, for wasn't that the problem he had been sent to solve?

There was no doubt who the judge would be. But was it arrogance and blasphemy to set himself in such a role? He had a feeling Shakespeare was not referring to a mortal jurist. And the king? Tomas perhaps? No, that wasn't a good thought.

For better or worse he, President Tomas C. deBaca, and the rest of the powers Earthside were in this together. Weeks ago he had committed to this job, and it was a little late to be questioning the President's motives now. He closed his eyes, seeking to escape the glittering vision beyond the port.

The subdued murmur of the other passengers was an irritating drone, making it difficult for him to concentrate. He wondered if he should have taken the President up on his offer of military transport to the station. It would have provided him with greater privacy, but it might have been a tad heavy-handed, considering the way he had been foisted upon the colonists.

No, there would be time enough to begin reasserting control. No need to take up on the reins too quickly.

"Cab, if you're going to sleep, could we trade places? I'd like to watch the docking."

He opened his eyes and looked into the excited face of his law clerk, Jennifer McBride. Long red hair framed her piquant and triangular face, and intensified the deep green of her eyes. She looked scarcely old enough to be out of college, much less a licensed attorney and his former law partner.

He wondered again if he had done the right thing by offering her the position as his law clerk. The Justice Department had wanted someone with a little more political savvy, and he was beginning to think they had been right, though not for the reasons they had advanced. His was a far more selfish and personal worry. Over the past five years he had grown accustomed to Jenny's unwavering respect and devotion, and he rather feared that the upcoming months might reveal to her that he could indulge in political gamesmanship with the best of them. He knew this would not sit well with Jenny, given her contemptuous view of politicians. Her possible disillusionment was not something that he viewed with any degree of equanimity, but he didn't see what he could do about it.

He forced a smile to his lips. "I'm not sleeping, I'm thinking, but if you want to watch go ahead." Their magnetized boots helped, but it was still an interesting maneuver to switch seats. As Jenny's slim body brushed past his, Cabot questioned again whether it had been wise to include her, for purely personal reasons. On Earth it had been easy to maintain a discreet distance. It might become more difficult out here.

"Aren't you the least bit interested in our new surroundings?" Jenny asked, glancing back over her shoulder.

"Not really, no."

"You sound as if you're dreading this position. I thought you wanted to be a judge."

He busied himself with the buckle of his seat belt. "Maybe I didn't want to be a judge out here."

Jenny gave him an odd glance, then shrugged and looked out the port once more.

He wished he could share her interest in the rapidly approaching station, but memory tugged at him drawing him out of the white, sterile interior of the shuttle. Huntington closed his eyes and once more contemplated the events that had led to his current presence between Earth and Moon rather than home in California.

"Congratulations, Cab," President Tomas C. deBaca had said. The door to the Oval Office whispered shut behind Huntington after its sensitive mechanisms had determined he carried no weapons. "You've just been appointed to the Fifteenth Circuit, or rather you will be as soon as I push it through Congress."

Huntington stared. "Fifteenth Circuit? There is no Fifteenth Circuit."

His pale cheeks burned at the President's hearty laughter. "Don't be dense, Cab. Of course there's no Fifteenth Circuit— yet. But there will be by the time your appointment goes through."

"If you're referring to Argentina, no thanks." He moved smoothly to one of the armchairs that were ranged before the heavy desk. Seating himself on the edge of the chair, he planted his feet firmly on the eagle-embossed carpet, and waited, back erect, almost military in his tense, upright bearing. "I'm not ready to get blown up in my swimming pool like that poor sot from the State Department."

"It's nothing South American, I promise. We've had more trouble down there than we expected so we've pulled back for the time being."

"Congress on your back?"

"Yeah, it's like something out of the seventies." DeBaca ran a hand across his face. It was a fine, soft hand, expensively manicured.

Huntington quietly arranged his hands in his lap and inspected his thumb nails. He knew that Tomas was aware of his desire to be a judge, but he wasn't going to give the President the satisfaction of seeming too eager. The silence stretched between the two men, and Huntington could feel the impatience radiating from the large man behind the desk.

At last deBaca capitulated. "Ah, yes, the Fifteenth Circuit. It's right over your head." He grinned at Huntington's look of amazement. "That's right, Cab. You're going into space."

Cabot rose from the chair and began to pace the room. He always thought better on his feet when he was agitated, and there was no doubt that the President's revelation was unsettling news.

"I've got a quarter of a million dollar law practice. What makes you think I'd trade it for a position on the bench? Especially one off-Earth."

"Because I've known you since Harvard, my friend." He smiled. It was a smug, contented expression.

Cabot halted his nervous pacing and studied deBaca's round face. He felt a stab of resentment at the smile, for it reminded him too much of those early days when Tomas had been his undergraduate adviser. He liked the man, but sometimes Tomas could be unbearably complacent and condescending.

"Okay, assuming you're correct, why me? There are older, more qualified men."

"Your age is in your favor. It's going to be rough out there, particularly in the asteroids. And as for qualified, hell, Cab, you're one of the foremost constitutionalists in the country, and you're not locked into some law school."

"Come now, Tomas," Huntington said, crossing to the desk and perching on one corner. "You've never done anything in your life out of a love of scholarship. Also, my family is still something of an influence on the East Coast so I haven't exactly lost touch with what's happening in Washington. What do you want out there, and why do you need me to do it?"

The President frowned at the welter of papers on his desk, and absently tugged at the shaggy ends of his gray-flecked hair. The ticking of the eighteenth-century clock on the mantel was loud in the still room. Suddenly deBaca reached out and began flipping a crystal paperweight over and over in his hand. Occasionally he missed, and the faceted crystal landed with a thud on the desk.

Huntington waited, knowing how Tomas loved to be prompted. He also knew, after years of acquaintance, that by keeping silent he would force the older man to speak, avoiding several layers of political hyperbole.

"I need a constitutionalist so that he can do some creative decision writing for me," deBaca said at last. Huntington waited, but the President was once more silent except for the monotonous *slap-thud* of the paperweight.

Huntington reached out and caught the paperweight at the apex of the toss. "Don't try to weasel on me," he said softly.

"You know I'll be very upset if you send me into something I'm not prepared for."

DeBaca heaved his bulk out of the chair, and walked to the French doors with their view of the rain-soaked rose garden. It's the whole damn situation out"—the President waved vaguely skyward with one plump hand—"there." He turned back to face Cab, clasped his hands behind his back, and bounced slightly on the balls of his feet. It was very reminiscent of old Dabney, the legal historian back at Harvard, and Cab knew he was going to get a lecture. He was also damned if he was going to sit still for it.

"Cab, the System is the most vital sphere of influence today."

"I agree, but what in hell is this 'System' business. You make it sound like an autonomous unit. It's just a string of stations and some raggedy-assed miners." Cabot swung one leg and stared at the reflected sheen on the toe of his boot.

"True, but they're a very powerful string of stations and raggedy-assed miners, and they're the ones who've begun to call themselves the System. Frankly that's the whole problem. They don't need us, Cab, but without them, their energy, and their raw materials, our entire society would grind to a halt. Dammit, we're scared of them!" His hand came down heavily on the desk punctuating the remark.

"Who's *we?*"

"All the space-capable nations. We're all losing control up there." There was silence for several moments while Cab studied the choleric color that had infused the President's face.

DeBaca aimlessly shuffled papers, like an old man searching vainly for some misplaced item, then looked up and asked, "How did we end up in this mess, and why did it have to happen in my administration?" His tone was plaintive.

More out of intuition than any real sense of what the "mess" might be, Cabot spoke up. "The government lost interest in the space program. The politicians were more concerned with votes than space, and as is always the case when a vacuum is created, something came in to fill it. The private sector saw its chance and moved in." It seemed he had guessed correctly for deBaca picked up on his comment and continued.

"If only we'd agreed to the UN treaties limiting the private use of space." The President stroked at his cheeks pulling the soft folds of flesh into a caricature of heatfelt misery and worry.

"It wouldn't have made any difference. You've seen how useful the few that were passed have been. Possession is nine-tenths of the law, and once the stations and colonies were in place who was to dispute them?"

"The shuttle. If only we'd kept control of the shuttle," deBaca interjected in a startling shift of topic. He bobbed his head with excitement and for emphasis. "We could have controlled the flow of people."

Cabot shifted uncomfortably on the desk. The sharp edge of the corner was beginning to dig into his buttocks, and Tomas, unfortunately, didn't seem any closer to an explanation than he had been minutes ago.

"Tomas this is useless. It's no use rehashing what should have been done over fifty years ago. I want to know what the problem is now, and where I fit into all of this."

"They're drifting away from us, Cab, ignoring our needs and rights. With all of the heavy industry moved off-world we've just got to hold on to them. Shit!" His broad, soft hand swept the papers furiously from his desk. They fluttered to the floor. "We can't even light a Christmas tree without them."

"Where are the real trouble spots?" Cab slid from the desk, and began to gather up the scattered sheets.

"Well, the near-Earth stations are still pretty much tied to us," deBaca said as he returned to his chair. "There are one or two exceptions like that damn Reichart, but most of the big companies need us as much as we need them. The people on the stations may not like the changes we want to institute, but the boards groundside know how to play the game. They'll implement whatever we tell them to." He smiled but the momentary flicker of pleasure faded quickly.

"The real separationist tendencies are farther out, on Mars and in the asteroids." DeBaca shook his head. "I don't know how the Japanese or the Russians intend to handle the problem, but I'm going to try an old-fashioned dose of big government."

"And I'm going to be the representative of this 'big government'?" Cab placed the stack of papers back on the desk. DeBaca didn't acknowledge the action.

"We've got to establish control, Cab. The advent of a decent judicial system has always been the taming of any frontier."

"But what am I going to be replacing? They must have been using something out there."

"Some sort of quasi-judicial bodies made up of people selected from the various communities."

"Those will have to go."

"You're talking like a man who's taken the job," deBaca murmured slyly.

Huntington paused and chewed thoughtfully on the pad of his thumb. It was true, he *had* taken the job, but not for the reasons he or Tomas would have expected. A phalanx of historic, constitutional decisions seemed to be marching away from him like an army in some lawyer's fevered dream. *Marbury, Ogden, Brown, Miranda*. Great decisions, decisions of national and societal import. Maybe out in this final frontier he too would be able to make such landmark decisions. Like a John Marshall riding circuit in the early days of the Supreme Court. He reined in his imagination and looked at the President.

"Yes, I am. And why not? It sounds to me like you need a stubborn, stiff-necked constitutionalist—"

"And you certainly fit the bill. More than that, you'll come through for me, Cab. Won't you?" the President asked earnestly, exerting his not insubstantial charm.

"You know I will, Tomas," Huntington said, shaking deBaca's hand.

The President leaped up, and rushing around the desk, pounded the smaller man on the shoulder. "Goddamn, I'm glad! Now I can start to breathe again."

"It's been that bad?" He gripped deBaca's beefy forearm giving support with the contact.

"Worse. But I've got you on my team now, and I know you'll get the job done."

Get the job done. The words echoed ominously through his mind, and the judge smiled humorlessly. Faced with the immensity of space stretching away on all sides of the fragile shuttle, it seemed a gargantuan task.

Jenny's grasp brought him back to the present. He peered past her head out the port and gasped as well.

A lake of fire blazed before him. *An explosion?* he wondered wildly, and then realized what he was looking at. It was the great collecting mirror, a circle over a mile across, tipped to catch the sun. They swept over the top of the stanford torus, and Cab stared with curiosity at the rough-looking outer tire that enclosed the living habitat. He vaguely remembered some-one at the Cape telling him how ten million tons of slag and Moon dust had been compacted and placed around the station to act as a radiation shield. He could now see the hub, attached by six giant spokes to the torus. As he watched, he became aware that the spokes were rotating, but the outer shield didn't seem to be moving. By narrowing his eyes and peering back toward the rim, he was able to distinguish that the habitat was rotating within the protective shield. He grudgingly admitted to himself that it was quite an engineering feat.

A rush of sound, windlike, transmitted itself up to Hun-tington's arms and through the soles of his booted feet.

"We're braking for docking," Jenny said unnecessarily. The other passengers broke into a staccato of busy conversation.

Like stately silver whales, a line of freighters swam toward the station ahead of them. Others broke away with brief blos-soming jets, beginning the long, looping journey home to the Cape, the Sands, or the Saudi complex, bearing biochemicals, processed ore, rocket parts.

As he craned to peer out of the port, Huntington noted with disappointment and a touch of disdain that, even though the station itself was a model of engineering beauty, the surround-ing area of space was a mess. Clustered near the station were numerous Solar Power Satellites beaming their precious mi-crowaves back to rectennas across the Earth, feeding human-ity's seemingly insatiable need for power. In addition to these large arrays of photovoltaic cells were pieces of floating debris. Abandoned machinery, discarded fuel tanks from old-style shuttles, and great hunks of floating rock, gifts from the asteroid mining belt, mingled in a space-age junk pile. He wondered what the environmentalists groundside would make of it.

The shuttle slowed, then began maneuvering into the dock-ing area. With bored ease the pilot put them into a slip next to a shuttle whose marking showed it had come from the Rei-chart Industries private launching base in New Mexico.

Huntington frowned momentarily, for Reichart was likely to be a problem for the new circuit. The company had been a maverick from the early days of space industrialization. This reminder of his coming task did not improve his mood.

"Come on, your honor. Time to go." Jenny sprang to her feet, her magnetic boots held her swaying with the force of her movement.

"No regrets?" Huntington asked as he rose somewhat more cautiously.

"No, why should I have?"

"You could have made a lot of money if you'd assumed the partnership rather than taking me up on my offer." He paused and considered. "Also, if I get run out of the System on a rail, I would have an office to come back to."

Jenny lifted a slender forefinger. "First, I wouldn't have missed this for the world. I've been a space junky since childhood. And second"—a second finger rose next to its companion—"I think my feelings are hurt. It's apparent you weren't motivated by concern for my advancement and well-being. You just didn't want to break up that lovely money machine."

Huntington winced at Jenny's forthright remark. In some circles her honesty would have been lauded, but in the world of the legal brotherhood it was a drawback. She had never learned how to close one eye, and go along to get along. Brains and ability she had, but she didn't fit in, and she constantly rubbed her associates the wrong way. Sometimes Cabot wondered why she had become a lawyer, and why she stuck with it now that she knew what that world was like. More to the point he wondered why he had ever hired her, and now found her so indispensable.

They passed through a pressure lock, and into the passenger's lobby. Low-slung cushioned chairs with restraining belts and bright plastic tables bolted to the floor dotted the carpeted room. The only sounds came from the faint hum of machinery and the murmur of conversation. The decor reminded Cabot forcibly of a fast-food restaurant. He was grateful for the lack of Muzak.

He looked about the room, but no one showed any interest in their arrival. The other passengers who had been on their shuttle were hurrying out of the lobby or exchanging greetings with friends or relatives. It only served to point out Cabot and Jenny's isolation.

"Do you have any idea what we do now?" Jenny asked

quietly after five minutes had passed. "I mean, this is a big place. We could get old fast wandering around looking for where we belong."

Huntington's thin, upswept brows drew together over the bridge of his nose. "I'd assumed we'd be met but apparently they don't consider our arrival important enough to merit taking time out from their schedules. Damn the impudence," he added under his breath.

Ten more minutes passed. Jenny gave Cabot a look of growing puzzlement. "They did know when we were arriving?"

"Of course they knew."

"Then why haven't they—"

"How should I know?" He immediately regretted his lack of control for Jenny stiffened, walked to a chair, and proceeded to ignore him.

He tried out a few well-choosen oaths as he crossed to one of the courtesy com booths set against the wall. He picked up a directory, and was trying to determine who among the labyrinth of names he ought to contact when he heard Jenny call.

He turned to see her standing with a tall, elegantly dressed older woman whose hair floated about her shoulders like a silver cloud. He walked slowly back, carefully evaluating the woman from beneath half-closed lids. He realized with surprise that he was being subjected to the same careful scrutiny from a pair of fine black eyes whose delicate slant gave testimony to the woman's mixed ancestry.

"Lydia Kim Nu," she said without preamble as she thrust out her hand.

"Cabot Huntington."

So this was the powerful and autocratic manager of EnerSun I, he thought as they shook hands. The Justice Department had warned him that the operations manager of the station was one of the more influential figures in near-Earth orbit. She was also a close friend of Joseph Reichart, the wealthy and eccentric owner of Reichart Industries. Together, he and Kim Nu had blocked or simply ignored a number of federal regulations designed to exert a measure of control over the stations. This was one of the reasons EnerSun I had been choosen as the site for the Fifteenth Circuit. The President had wanted to start cracking the whip in a very obvious fashion. He couldn't reach

Reichart Industries since that station was totally private, but EnerSun was licensed by the federal government, and held a number of federal contacts.

Huntington was still smarting from the slight Kim Nu had dealt him by not bothering to be on hand to meet the shuttle. He had hoped that a modicum of politeness would be maintained during the transition from the local boards to the Fifteenth Circuit, but apparently that was not to be the case.

"I hope nothing *serious* occurred to keep you from meeting us." He followed the comment with a smile, but there was an angry glitter in his gray eyes.

"No, nothing in particular," she replied, not even bothering to take the out he had offered her. "Now, if you'll come this way I'll show you to your quarters." She turned to move away.

"I don't particularly like your attitude, Ms. Kim Nu," Huntington said, holding his position.

She glanced back and raised one eyebrow. "And I wasn't aware that I'd asked you to, Justice Huntington."

"It was extremely rude of you to fail to meet our shuttle."

"When and if I want a lecture from you on manners, I'll ask. Now, shall we go?"

"I can do this with or without your help, but it would be easier if I had your support. So why don't we discuss why you saw fit to keep us cooling our heels for twenty minutes?"

"Cab, for God's sake," Jenny muttered, embarrassed. "It's not worth this kind of attention. Why don't you just drop it?"

Kim Nu shot an approving look at Jenny. "That sounds like an excellent suggestion. But we're all forgetting our manners," she added with a sidelong glance to Huntington. "We've never formally met."

"Jennifer McBride. I'm pleased to meet you," Jenny said extending her hand.

"Likewise. I've arranged for your luggage to be sent to your apartment. I expect you'd like to freshen up."

"That would be nice, yes."

"I think you'll like your apartment. My daughter lived there for several years before moving out to Mars."

"You have children?"

"Four, all grown now."

Huntington was beginning to feel, at best, like a piece of furniture, and at worst like an unruly little boy who was being chastised by his elders by being ignored. He cleared his throat, and the two women looked at him.

"Well," he said, his eyes shifting away from Kim Nu's level glance, "if we're going, let's go, but I'd like to see my courtroom first."

"Fine."

Kim Nu led them to a doorway, and they passed from the shuttle lobby into one of the levels of the hub. "We are now in the central hub of the station," the manager explained. "This area houses our warehouses and recreational facilities, as well as docking for the shuttle."

They moved on to an AVC stop, and within moments a low white bullet train had pulled into the stop with a whisper.

"The AVC's are the easiest way to travel about the station," she said as they settled into comfortably upholstered seats. She paused at their blank looks, then explained, "This is an AVC, Automatic Vehicular Conveyance. Engineers have this passion for alphabet-soup phrases. At any rate, they make a circuit of the rim, and move through the spokes."

"Oh," Huntington said.

They rode in silence for several moments, then Lydia began, in a half-bored tour-guide voice that she reserved for high-level visitors, to talk about the station.

"EnerSun I is an operating closed system. The only things we buy from Earth are luxury items. All the necessities we make ourselves. Air, water, food, everything is available here. The hub you've seen. The five supporting spokes hold various cables and pipes, and the administrative offices. The rim houses the farms, living quarters, and laboratory space for the various companies. The heavy industry is performed outside the station."

"So that's why the area surrounding the station looks so cluttered," Huntington said in a neutral tone.

"Perhaps you'd prefer to have slag heaps in Wyoming again?" Lydia said tartly, and immediately regretted her defensiveness. The judge's tone had been low-key. She had overreacted.

Huntington seemed to withdraw behind an ice barrier, while Jenny glanced nervously from Lydia to her boss and back again.

"How many people live on the station?" Jenny asked. It was an awkward turning of the subject, but Lydia was grateful to her.

"Ten thousand. We're at top capacity right now, with a waiting list that's twice as long."

"I had no notion. When I thought about the stations I always assumed the only people out here were engineers or scientists who left their families on Earth."

"Sort of super—long-range commuters?" Lydia asked with a smile.

"Yes, something like that."

"No, we've got all types up here, and the farther out you go the more 'ordinary' they become—fewer scientists and more independent miners." She glanced at the station number. "Our stop."

Lydia led them out of the spoke and onto one of the second-level rim balconies. She then stepped back to enjoy their reactions. No one was ever prepared for their first sight of the rim. Terraced levels held multistoried buildings. It was easy to forget the presence of the curving roof hundreds of feet above their heads, and periodic groves of fruit trees gave an even greater sense of openness and freedom. Green grass and walkways mingled, ending at a large empty cut in the center of the rim's hundred-foot width.

"What's that?" Jenny asked, pointing at the cut.

"Eventually it's going to be a river, but we haven't gotten around to it yet. Filling it comes up at every council meeting, but there's always something that people would rather do first."

"It is spectacular," Huntington admitted reluctantly.

"What are we looking at?" Jenny asked.

"The residential district. There, beyond that curve, is the business district, and beyond that are the farms. I'll take you to Mercury now, and you can see your court."

They walked down a flight of stairs to the ground level, and caught another AVC. It was a shorter ride than the last one, and the courtroom was only a short distance down the Mercury spoke. Kim Nu slipped a card into the electronic lock, and the door slid quietly aside.

There was a high bench with three chairs behind it, tables for opposing counsel, and a jury box. To either side of the bench stood two flags. One was the familiar stars and stripes, but the other was a deep midnight blue. Huntington moved behind the bench, and fanned out the flag. Emblazoned across the dark blue background was a star field and the solar system.

"And this is?"

"The flag of the System."

"Interesting." He dropped the material. "I wasn't aware that *the System* had become a state."

"I take it you want it removed."

"Oh, by no means. I just don't want the people who enter this courtroom to forget which flag takes precedence."

"I doubt they could ever manage to forget." Their eyes locked. "I just hope that whoever holds court in this room continues to dispense *justice*."

"Are you doubting my integrity?"

"I don't know anything about your integrity, Mr. Huntington. I do doubt your motives."

"Why?" Jenny asked, stepping between the two combatants. "Cab is a fine lawyer, and he'll be a brilliant jurist."

Lydia's eyes flickered over to Jenny. "Fine. I just wish he could be brilliant somewhere where he was wanted."

Jenny glanced at Cab, seeking some guidance. His expression remained neutral. She looked back to Kim Nu. "What is going on here? We've just arrived, and all we've gotten is suspicion and innuendo. You know nothing about us yet you seem to be judging us very harshly."

"I know who sent you." She stepped up to the bench and ran a hand gently along its length. "And tell me, wouldn't you be hostile if outsiders were first forced upon you, and then outlawed your institutions?"

"Did you serve on one of the arbitration boards?" Huntington asked.

"Hearing boards," Lydia corrected him. "And yes, I was frequently chosen to serve."

"No wonder you're irritated. Such a sudden loss of income must have been upsetting."

"Cab!"

"Not now, Jenny." His words cut across hers like a whip.

Lydia flushed, both for herself and the law clerk. She decided to shake that complacent veneer of groundside superiority. "Before you congratulate yourself on the demise of the Hearing Boards, you might consider how many people are actually going to enter this room now."

Huntington took two hurried steps down from the bench. "What do you mean? This is now the court of justice for the System."

"True, on paper, but whether people want to use it is their business. Not all the powers groundside can force them into this court. At best they'll just ignore it; at worst they'll go back to the old vigilante actions that passed for justice before Joe Reichart began to assemble the hearing boards thirty years ago."

"None of this is surprising to me," Huntington said. "But I'd advise you to remember the old adage about water and stones. Anything can be worn down given enough time."

"Except people, judge. They tend to be amazingly resilient to pressure. Now, if you have seen all you need, I have a station to run."

"Yes, I'm satisfied."

They rode in silence back to the residential area. The lawyers had been housed in a small two-story building near the dry river bed. Kim Nu handed them a pair of disc card keys, told them where to find the nearest grocery store, and departed. She wanted to talk with the other members of the council, and she also wanted to locate the extraordinarily handsome young man who worked for Tina Duvall on the solar grids. It was apparent that Jennifer McBride was unaware of the Fifteenth Circuit's true purpose in the System. If she could somehow be wooed from her boss, Lydia had a feeling that she might become a powerful ally. And there was no doubt that the man she had in mind could be a very potent wooer.

As soon as the door closed behind the manager, Jenny rounded on Huntington. Her expression was white and stiff.

"How dare you give me a snub like that in front of a perfect stranger! I'm not some second-year law student you can bully and browbeat. I was your *partner*, for Christ's sake."

Huntington lifted his hands, holding them placatingly in front of him. "I know, I know, and I'm sorry. That woman just got under my skin. What arrogance!"

"You're a fine one to talk. Do you know how unbearable you are when you draw yourself up and put on that freezing politeness? Also, I may be slow, but I'm not stupid. I gather that we're not exactly welcome out here."

"Something like that," Huntington murmured as he dropped onto an overstuffed modular green sofa, and propped his feet on the low, clear crystal table before it.

"Something like *what?* Why aren't we welcome? What are these people afraid of?"

"I'm not sure. Change maybe."

"Well, you must have some idea. After all, you are the one who had all those briefings by the Justice Department."

"Look, Jenny, I've never been out here before either, so how can I be expected to know what's going on in these people's heads? We'll just have to watch and listen, find out what's bothering them, and put their fears to rest."

"Sounds like a great game plan, but you've hardly been following it. I mean, my God, Cab, we're not going to improve the situation by riding roughshod over these people."

Huntington thoughtfully regarded his hands for several moments, then looked up. "Jenny, sometimes in order to reach a desirable result we have to take actions that are a little less pristine than we would like."

Jenny stared at him in silence for several moments. "I don't like this, Cab. I don't like the hostility up here, and I especially don't like what you are saying. These people are Americans with the same rights as any other American citizen."

"Precisely." He dropped his feet to the floor, and leaned forward intently. "They are entitled to the *same* rights. Not more, not less, and definitely not different. Besides, this is a territory and. . . ." He bit off the rest of the sentence deciding that a reference to the insular cases at this juncture would not be politic.

"You're talking in circles. If you've got something to say, something to tell me about this assignment that I don't know, please just lay it out."

He studied her angry, beautiful face, and decided this wasn't the time to reveal the President's real hopes and desires for the Fifteenth Circuit. He stretched, and laced his fingers behind his head.

"No, no, there's nothing. I'm probably just overreacting because Kim Nu and I rubbed each other the wrong way."

"Fine, but you won't mind if I reserve judgment until I've had time to evaluate things for myself?"

"No, of course not."

"Good. Then I'm going out for a walk." The door whispered shut behind her.

Huntington paced to a window, hands locked tightly behind his back, and gazed out at the empty river bed. Perhaps Tomas had been right; he should have brought someone from the Justice Department. They would at least have understood the political realities. But he knew Jenny, respected her work, and more importantly he liked her—quixotic notions notwithstanding.

He only hoped he wouldn't have cause to regret it.

Chapter Two

"Cream and sugar?" Flo Wandall asked as she handed the cup to Tina Duvall, who sprawled in a low body-hugging chair.

"Something a little stronger, I think," Tina replied, and reached for the open bottle of bourbon that stood on the coffee table. Flo looked pained as Tina poured a liberal dollop into her steaming cup.

"Now there's a white woman I can relate to." Muhammid Ali Elija's rugged and broked-nosed face stretched into a wide grin, which heightened his ugliness and accentuated the warmth in his brown eyes.

Tina grinned back, and ran her hand affectionately across his smooth pate. "Whoops, time for you to shave again, old friend."

"Hey, if you need a shave, too, maybe we can do it together," he suggested as he tried to lift the edge of Tina's calf-length skirt for a look at her muscular leg.

"Pervert." She laughed and gave a him a light slap.

"Can't help it, lady. You bring out the male in a man."

Tina widened her brown eyes, and gave him a look of innocence, which was at total variance with her tigress body. She was medium built, but muscles rippled beneath her rose-colored silk blouse as she leaned forward for her coffee cup. Tina was addicted to the art of body building, and off-hours she could be found in one of the gyms, sweating and straining with the men.

The door to the apartment whispered open, and Trevor Martin entered with Artis Barnes. The thin, balding chemist was red to his eyebrows, and Artis was laughing up at him with bawdy good humor. Muhammid wondered what Artis had said now that had put old Trevor into such a taking.

Small, rotund, and vivacious, Artis owned the most popular bar and nightspot on the station. Her boys and girls were the prettiest, brightest, and friendliest, and a lonely shuttle pilot, a researcher in from Mars, or a single colonist on the prowl for a night of fun was never disappointed.

"Lydia's not here yet?" Artis asked, her brows rising in surprise. Flo shook her head. "Goodness, this judge must be worse than we thought."

"Let's hope not," Flo said in her soft voice. "I'm not as eager for trouble as the rest of you."

"We're not *eager* for trouble either," Tina corrected, looking thoughtfully up at a large batik wall hanging. "We're simply certain that it can't be avoided, and you're still hoping it can."

Flo shrugged, a tight little gesture. "I guess I'm just an optimist."

"Yes," Trevor agreed, helping himself to a cup of coffee. "And you have too much faith in the groundside governments."

"My, we're a cynical lot, aren't we," Artis stated as she settled herself into a chair with a flourish of her pink ruffled skirt. The color was disastrous with her sallow skin, but she was like a magpie about bright, shiny colors.

"A drink, Artis?" Tina asked.

"Yes, dear, but please don't mix it with any of that hot black stuff."

"Drinking my booze again, are you?" Lydia called from the doorway. They all turned to look at her.

"Of course, dear, you always have better quality than I'll buy."

"How did it go?" Trevor asked, rising politely to his feet at the manager's entrance.

"Not good, not bad. We sparred a bit, and we both have tender snouts, but no blood was drawn—yet."

"What's he like?" Tina asked.

Lydia accepted half a cup of coffee from Flo, and filled it the rest of the way with cream. She stared thoughtfully off into space, slowly stirring the coffee. "Small, slight build, fine eyes, and beautiful skin," she said at last. "Early forties, looks to be in good shape, and an elegant dresser." She paused to take a sip of coffee. "He's also one arrogant son of a bitch."

"I take it he didn't like you?" Trevor asked dryly.

"Quite true. But worse is that I don't think he likes any of us. He has decided that we're all wicked anarchists, and he's quite determined to fit us back into the mold."

Muhammid shifted back in his chair, and stared disgustedly up at the ceiling. "Then he's a government goon just as we suspected."

"I'm afraid so. Still, I don't know if we should lose all hope. He's not stupid, just closed-minded. Maybe we can pry it open." She paused again for a sip, then with a grimace set aside the cup. "Also, we may have an ace."

"Oh?" Artis inquired.

"He has an assistant with him. A stunningly beautiful little redhead who's as eager as a pup about being out here. Unlike her boss and me, *we* hit it off."

"None of use would ever deny your obvious charms, Lydia," Trevor said, "but I don't see how that alone is going to help us."

"Forgive me, I suppose I didn't make myself very clear. The girl has no idea that she is out here to strip us of our rights and institutions. She thinks she's come up to serve truth, beauty, and the American way. If she finds out differently she might begin to see things our way."

"But will she be able to influence her boss?"

Lydia glanced at Tina. "Who can say? But it's worth a try, and frankly, it may be the only chance we have."

"So what do we do? Haul her in and talk with her?" Muhammid asked.

"God God, no! The last thing we want to do is scare her and make her think we're fomenting a revolution out there."

"Why, who could ever think that of us?" Muhammid murmured, and his lips drew back revealing an expanse of white teeth. It was a little like the yawning mouth of a wolf cub.

Trevor eyed the black man. "No, better not bring her in. One look at this crew would quell even the most stouthearted."

"Tina," Lydia said, ignoring the chemist. "What's the name of the gorgeous young engineer you have on your grid crew?"

"Peter Traub?"

"That's the one. Tell him I have a very pleasant and not at all arduous task for him, and he's to call me as soon as possible."

"Will do."

"Now, is there anything else that has to be dealt with?"

Artis set her cup onto its saucer with a sharp snap. "Yes, Lydia, there is. I've had two people come to me about hearings for various problems, as well as calls from several lawyers. No one wants to go to this new court, but they know we've been outlawed, so what do they do?"

"Tell them to hang on for a few weeks until we see how things are going to shake down. And let's hope a major problem doesn't arise. I suppose we could try to hold some hearings in secret, but I have a feeling that Huntington is going to be watching for that kind of thing, and we'll all be in shit up to our eyebrows if he catches us. That reminds me . . . I think our weekly coffee klatch had better disband for a while.

"I can meet with each of you individually given my position, but all of us gathering each week could cause comment with our new guests. Let's not disabuse them of the notion that EnerSun, Inc., is running this station. As our cautious Flo would say"—she glanced over at the school teacher, who was staring tight-lipped into her coffee cup—"'let's not ask for trouble.'" She looked around the circle of unsmiling faces. "Good. Then we'll lay low, watch, listen, and start our own infiltration." She shrugged and gave a funny little smile. "And if worse comes to worst we can comfort ourselves that he'll only be here a short time, and then he'll go off to bedevil Mars. It'll be a year before his circuit brings him back here again."

"Somehow I'm not overwhelmingly comforted by that," Trevor said, gesturing with his cup. "If he were just one man, that sort of wait-him-out ploy might work. But we all know he's just the first volley in the battle to bring us back under government control."

"But which government?" Muhammid asked. "The Congressional committee that approved him said he also had power to deal with major problems arising under all current UN space treaties. Now you better believe the Nips, the Commies and the Saudis have all given their approval to this court or he wouldn't have that kind of power."

"I didn't know about that," Tina said, chewing nervously on a hangnail.

Artis glanced at an ornately jeweled watch that hung from a chain about her neck. "Well, it's getting to be that time of the day. I've got to get back to the bar. Anybody want to offer me some company on my way?" The question was casually presented, but her eyes raked suggestively across Trevor's long, lean body. The chemist blushed and fidgeted, but he was a pile of sand before her bulldozerlike personality. He reluctantly nodded.

Artis rose and shook out her skirt. "Then I'll see all you darlings for drinks during the next few days. Faith," she said seeing Lydia's grim expression. "Things could be worse."

"Name how," Muhammid grumbled.

"Life support could go out."

He bristled. "As if my department could ever be so inept."

She shrugged. "You asked for worse."

Tina patted Lydia on the shoulder as she headed for the door. "I'll have Peter give you a call right away. No sense wasting time."

"Thanks."

The group muttered and mumbled its way into the corridor outside Lydia's apartment. The door sighed shut behind them, and the silence was almost startling after the babble. Lydia shivered with a sudden chill. It was irrational since the room was maintained at a steady seventy-five degrees.

Nerves, she thought, and picked up the silver tray loaded with dirty cups and her precious silver coffee pot that had come down to her from grandmother Mei Ling. She was certain that the old lady had never expected it to travel so far from her home in San Francisco.

She was still feeling jittery, and she decided that what she needed was a sight of the stars, and Joe Reichart. Depositing the tray in the kitchen, she crossed to her com and punched in the signal for the Reichart station.

While she waited for her call to go through, she worried at the problem that confronted her. She felt like a sexist pig for sending Peter Traub after little McBride, and she wasn't even certain if the ploy would work. McBride had behaved like the perfect assistant, but there was something in her eyes when she gazed at her boss, and Lydia feared the girl might one day realize what she felt for the man.

"Well, maybe she and Peter can just be good friends," she said aloud.

"When you start talking to yourself it's a sign of encroaching senility," came the gravelly voice of Joseph Reichart. She jerked her head up, and looked into the brown eyes of the owner of Reichart Industries. His neatly trimmed beard and curly brown hair were heavily streaked with gray, and deep lines were etched about his eyes and mouth, encouraged by a humorously cynical view of the universe and by many years in space. Lydia felt an inordinate amount of pleasure at just seeing him. She bit her lip, feeling foolish.

"The bastards getting you down?"

"'Fraid so, and they just arrived."

"What you need, my dear, is dinner aboard my shuttle while we orbit majestically about the Earth. I'll be over in a few hours."

"You always have the right medicine."

"Of course, and I promise we won't talk business until after coffee is served."

"I'll be waiting." She felt somewhat better for the conversation, and the anticipation of seeing Joe, but there was still an uncomfortable churning in the pit of her stomach, and her stomach was an infallible indicator. Somewhere all hell was about to break loose, and she feared she and her station were going to be at the center of it.

Jenny eyed the AVC speculatively, then decided that the walk would do her good. Her anger with Cabot had faded to a dull ache, and a brisk walk would no doubt banish it entirely.

Actually, she had probably overreacted. She was off balance from the hostile reception they had received from Lydia Kim Nu, and that strange little exchange back at the apartment hadn't helped matters. She knew from oblique remarks, overheard while in Washington that the Earthside governments were worried. The question was why?

An ever bigger question was what exactly was the function of the Fifteenth Circuit to be. It was apparent that they were replacing a legal system that to all indications had been working well for thirty years. So why replace it at all? An answer didn't immediately present itself.

Her thoughts rambled on, tumbling over each other in no particular order. *Van Clive v. Odell*. The case came whispering through her mind like a puff of air through a partially opened window. Her mind snapped down on the fleeting thought holding it in place.

Heard before the Supreme Court in 2020, the case had arisen out of the Kuwait Emergency. In an effort to monitor Soviet/ Saudi actions both on the ground and in space, Air Force General Cottrell had moved personnel aboard Van Clive I to use the station as a base against Soviet/Middle East intervention. When the manager, Alice Poldeski, protested the seizure she was thrown into a makeshift brig. After the crisis ended, Neville van Clive, then president of the company, brought suit against the Secretary of Defense and the Secretary of the Air Force.

The van Clive decision rested upon Article III of the Bill of Rights. That poor old, oft-forgotten amendment had demolished the government's case, and established the principle that the rights of the people to be free from military quartering and military law extended even to the new frontier. It had established forever, one presumed, the question of authority in space—and it did not rest with the military.

So why had her subconscious kicked up the case now? There could be no comparison between the arrival of the Fifteenth Circuit on EnerSun I and the occupying troops who had held the van Clive station. Unless of course she and Cab weren't bringing the glories of Anglo-American law to the benighted spacers, but were rather the front-runners of a more subtle form of government intervention.

She shook her head to drive out the hateful suspicions that were creeping through her mind. There could be no comparison between the Fifteenth Circuit and the extra-legal actions taken by the Air Force thirty years ago!

But the new circuit had replaced the local hearing boards, and was that right? she wondered. Didn't the colonists have the right to establish whatever kind of structure they thought would be most useful to them?

She stopped and stood frowning at the fruit trees that lined the central park. No, she decided. Cab was right. They were Americans and as such they had to be subject to the same laws that governed their brethern groundside.

There was something in the argument that left her feeling faintly disquieted. She probed at it for a few more minutes, then gave up in disgust. She didn't have enough information to make a decision right now. Better to put it off until later. She settled into a quick, mile-eating walk, determined to outrun her doubts and worries if she couldn't banish them.

Jenny rambled for several hours. She discovered a large rose garden surrounding a playground, where a bevy of small children romped, climbed, swung, and shouted. It gave her a strange feeling to think that the pleasantly scruffy kids playing before her had probably been born in space, and for an instant she could understand why some of the fundamentalist religious groups were so terrified by the new space generation. Man seemed to possess a primeval fear of the new, and in the past seventy years technological advances had raced forward like a roller coaster gone mad. Without a capacity to remain flexible, one could easily be flung aside, left battered and frightened on the sidelines while the ride raced on.

Farther around the rim she discovered the business district. Terraced buildings climbed up the walls of the torus, most filled with small shops containing luxury items from Earth. She easily resisted the impulse to buy because the costs were three times what they would have been on Earth. She found she was faintly disappointed that everything was so homelike. She wished something would indicate to her that she was in space.

Her eye was caught by a jeweler's window, and she drifted over to browse. A piece of black cloth lay in the window, its surface studded with star stones. The artificially created gems had been an accident during the early days of space industrialization, made by scientists experimenting with crystal growth. They had soon become the rage Earthside.

Jenny pressed her nose against the window, and gasped when she saw the price on one of the unset jewels.

"A little beyond the average person's touch, wouldn't you say," said a softly British voice at her elbow.

Jenny jumped and whirled, and found herself staring at the front of a man's shirt. Lifting her eyes she stared up at the most handsome man she had ever seen. His eyes were a brilliant midnight-blue, and they seemed to glow in his deeply tanned face. Dark brown hair, elegantly cut, curled about the nape of his neck. He smiled, and Jenny decided it wasn't necessary for her to give him a lecture on manners. This man could accost her on the street anytime he wanted to.

He held out his hand. "Peter Traub. Do forgive me for so rudely approaching you, but you're obviously a new face, and I was curious to know who you are."

"Jennifer McBride. I'm law clerk to Justice Cabot Huntington of the Fifteen Circuit." After Kim Nu's hostility, Jenny braced herself for a similar reaction, but the man just smiled politely.

"Your first trip into space?" he asked, pulling her arm through his and strolling down the arcade.

"Uh . . . yes." She glanced pointedly at her arm. He ignored the glance.

"Do you like it?"

She surrendered, deciding that it wasn't worth a battle for possession of her person. "Yes, very much. I loved the shuttle flight up. My only disappointment is that the station is so much like Earth. This could be any shopping mall, in any city, anywhere on the planet. Only the prices set it apart."

"Ah, an adventuresome lady who likes to rough it. But won't you have a chance? I thought this new court of yours was going to make a swing through the entire System."

"Yes, we are. We're going to Mars next, and then out to the asteroids."

"You'll have a jolly time there."

"Is it very rough out there?"

"Very."

"So, what are you doing on the station?" She inwardly winced at the banality of the question, but she really didn't know any better way for two strangers to exchange information about themselves.

"I'm an SDS grid engineer. I've been here for five years, and I love it."

"Why?"

"The adventure and the freedom."

There had been a subtle emphasis on the word *freedom.* Jenny studied her companion's profile, wondering if she ought to pursue the remark. She plucked at the ends of her hair where it fell over her shoulder, then decided that if she really wanted answers to the hostility she had met on the station, she would ask.

"How do you mean freedom? I should think living inside a metal skin with only cold space outside would have rather the reverse effect."

He stopped walking and looked down at her. She looked back with almost a challenge in her green eyes. "We could talk more comfortably sitting down. May I buy you a drink?"

Jenny nodded, and Traub led her down several levels, then turned into a secluded cul-de-sac. Laughter and loud voices spilled from an open door, along with a number of tantalizing odors. Above the door hung a large white owl, and clutched in his talons were the words, THE WHITE OWL.

"Good God, a bar?"

"Yes, and the best on the station."

"I had somehow expected a model city in space to be free from such vices," Jenny said. She gave him a quick smile to remove any sting from the words.

"We are free from what I consider real vices, such as slums, pollution, and overcrowding, but do you want to be the person to tell five or six dirt miners in from the Moon that they can't have a drink?"

"I see your point."

"This is part of what I meant about the freedom up here. People basically do what they want just do long as they don't do any physical or financial damage to anyone else."

"Then you don't recognize a victimless crime as a crime?" Jenny asked as they stepped into the dimly lit bar.

"Exactly."

"I think I could get used to that idea, but I'm not sure how the authorities Earthside would regard it."

Peter placed a hand on the small of her back, then guided her across the intricately tiled floor to one of the alcove tables screened by a shimmering beaded curtain. As Jenny stepped through the tinkling crystals, she noticed that the voices from the bar had faded to a faint murmur.

"Frankly," Peter said, dropping into one of the large cushions that surrounded the table, and picking up the conversation, "What business is it of theirs?"

Jenny settled somewhat more warily into the yielding cushion, and rested her back against the tiled wall. "It's best to have as uniform a legal system as possible."

"Why?"

Startled, Jenny retreated deeper into her nest of pillows. "Well, because . . . because . . ." She stopped, realizing she didn't have a satisfactory answer.

"Look, Jennifer, most of the blue laws are on the books because a handful of people with rigid religious or moral beliefs want them there. And why they should be allowed to impose their attitudes on everyone else is beyond me. The other reason for blue laws is because the government finds them highly lucrative. Take a look at the drug laws."

"I'd rather not. I know what you're going to say, and frankly, I haven't got a single argument that would successfully rebut it." She dropped her head to contemplate the beaten brass surface of the table, fingers playing unconsciously across the intricate pattern.

Peter flagged a passing waiter. "What will you have?"

"What's available?"

"Virtually everything for a price. Wine is an import, but our home-brewed beer isn't bad."

"A beer then." Peter ordered the same, and the waiter vanished.

Jenny squared her shoulders. "You people up here do a nice job of giving me pointed lectures under the guise of conversation. And being a bright, quick-on-my-feet lawyer, I'm also beginning to catch on to the fact that Cab and I are not precisely welcome." She paused and looked at Traub, who seemed impassive. "What I would really like to know is why."

"You've disbanded our courts, and most of us believe that you threaten our institutions."

"But we represent institutions that have worked well for almost three hundred years. We bring you a level of continuity and precedent that your ad hoc hearing boards could never provide."

"You know that for a fact?"

"My boss says . . ." she began, then abruptly stopped.

He ignored her heightened color and continued. "I agree that our 'judges' weren't approved by the brotherhood Earthside, but I consider that to be a virtue. The complainants in our cases were able to select who would hear their disputes, based on their belief in those persons' honesty and integrity. We didn't have political hacks thrust upon us—" He bit off the final word, but Jenny could finish the rest of the sentence.

"Until now?" she suggested quietly.

"You said it, not I." He paused, and frowned down at the table. As Jenny had done earlier he traced the hammered pattern in the brass table with a long forefinger. Then he leaned in and gazed at her. "Look, Jenny, we have lawyers to argue for the plaintiffs, and we do take some things from your precious Anglo-American legal system. The Bill of Rights is a thing of beauty, but what about all the rest of the baggage?"

"What do you mean?"

He gestured, his hand making a quick circle in the air between them. "The Constitution proper, the agencies, the federal regulations. All that mess that we have no control over, nor any say in the process that generates it."

"Peter, a coherent legal system is the foundation of a civilization. Without it you have anarchy."

"I agree, but what made you think you were going to fill a vacuum out here? The System has built its own form of judicial process over the past seventy years, and it's worked fine for much of that time. Then you and your judge arrive, and tell us it's no good so out it goes, and we're going to have to do what you say because you have the awesome might of the federal government to back you up. Disbanding our institutions, and then holding a club over our heads to make us accept yours is not exactly the way to win our affection."

"We are not holding a club over your head. You're . . . well, most of the colonists, are American citizens. They are guaranteed the rights of all American citizens. There is no reason to view the Earthside authorities with such suspicion."

"But we're colonists, right?" She nodded, not certain where he was heading, but distrusting the half smile that played about his lips. "So what about the insular cases?"

"I'm not familiar with them."

"*Hawaii versus Mankichi* in 1903. It basically said that the constitution does not follow the flag. The Court acquiesced in the seeming need for Congress to determine what rights should be extended to a colonial territory. In short, the federal government can deny us any rights they choose because we are colonials, dependencies."

"You continue to amaze me. I thought you were an engineer."

"I am. I only know about the case because of Joe Reichart. He uses it as an example of why we need our own rights and institutions."

The drinks arrived, and Traub lifted his beer. "Only one final word, and then we'll drop it and talk about something else." He took a deep pull on the beer and deliberately wiped away the foam that adorned his upper lip. "If it comes to a confrontation between your Constitution and us, who's going to be forced to bend? The people or the paper?"

Jenny's eyes flicked away from his face. What he was saying was dangerously near to sedition, and she was beginning to feel acutely uncomfortable with the whole situation.

She leaned in until their eyes were only inches apart. "I can't answer that, but I can say that I think you're wronging Cab."

"I hope I am. And I'm sorry for upsetting you, but you seem like a nice person, and I'd hate to see you blunder into something without having your eyes open. But enough of this political wrangling. Tell me how you came to be a lawyer, and how you acquired such a prestigious position at such a tender age."

She exhaled and leaned back against the cushions. A great deal of tension had blown off with that exhalation, and her voice had returned to a more conversational level.

"First, I'm leaning toward the tough side of twenty-nine. As for how 'prestigious' this position is ..." She shrugged, and took a sip of beer. She then looked down at the dark brew and saluted Peter with the mug, giving a nod of approval. "That is open to debate. I could have stayed home on Earth and taken over the partnership that I shared with Cab, but a chance to go into space was irresistible, so I took the cut in pay, rented my house, and here I am."

"Was it just the lure of space?"

"Not entirely, no. Cab is one of the most brilliant men I've ever known. This was a whole new undertaking, and I wanted to be in on it. I wanted to see how he handled it."

"And how's he doing so far?"

"We're back on that subject."

"I know. So how is he doing?"

"It's a little early to say. We've just arrived." They drank in silence, measuring each other over the rims of their mugs. "And what about you?" she asked. "How did a Brit like you end up on an American station?"

"My mother was an American, so I spent a good deal of time in the States, and I have a soft spot for my American cousins. I took my engineering degrees in Scotland and France, but there wasn't as much opportunity aboard the west European stations. There are only two, and they tend to be more experimental in nature. I wanted real experience, not endless testing of some new alloy. I applied for the job, and mercifully Tina hired me."

Jenny opened her mouth, but before she could speak Artis bustled through the hanging curtain, sending the beads dancing with her tanklike advance. Her eyes consumed Jenny, quickly sorting and evaluating. She noted the swanlike neck, the etching of the breastbone which could be seen above the low-cut neck of her jumpsuit, and the graceful way the girl held herself. Dancer, Artis decided with approval, for she had a soft spot for creative people. If the girl had been a technocrat, she feared she wouldn't have been able to deal with her. She had frequently told Peter that he was bearable only because he was so handsome.

Jenny looked up, and Artis stared straight into her eyes, searching for hesitation or an unwillingness to meet Artis's piercing gaze. Jenny stared back, and Artis felt a surge of satisfaction. A fine bonny lass, she decided, and with that fiery coloring she was one of those mystic Celts who were so dear to Artis's heart.

"Trust Peter to find the loveliest woman on the station first." She threw him an arch look then returned to Jenny. "But you're obviously new, or I'd have tried to hire you by now."

Peter laughed and introduced the two women. "I doubt she's going to have time to work for you, Artis, and beware, this lady represents the awesome might of the federal government. She might find you a bit too off-color, and try to do something about you."

"Nonsense. She looks to be a perfectly sensible woman who understands that what occurs between two or more consenting adults is nobody's business."

"Thank you," Jenny said with a smile.

"Good heavens, child!" Artis placed one hand on her breast, and held the other out palm up as if to ward off the young lawyer. "Please don't do that again! A man hasn't been born who could resist that smile, and if you're not careful you'll have them all making fools of themselves."

"Oh, I think not," Jenny murmured. Her cheeks took on a pink glow.

"Has Peter asked you out yet?"

"No."

"Well, get to it, man." She dug at his shoulders with her fingertips. "Or else when the evening rush begins you'll find her swept from your side."

"Do you think I'd stay long enough to give those vultures a chance? And I'll thank you to let me do my own inviting." He turned back to Jenny. "Now that Artis has completely embarassed both of us, may I belatedly invite you out to dinner?"

"Tonight?"

"Yes, of course."

Jenny gave a quick little shake of her head. "No, I couldn't do that. This is our first night here, and I don't want to desert Cab."

"All right, another time then. May I have your number?"

She pressed her lips together in embarrassment, then looked at him from beneath the fringe of her bangs. "I'm afraid I haven't a notion what it is. I left in something of a hurry this afternoon."

Artis noticed the way the girl's eyes dropped with the final sentence, and she stored it away for future reference, wondering if it might be important.

Peter scribbled on a napkin, and then handed it to Jenny. "Then here is my number, and please do call. I would love to act as your tour guide and show you around the station."

"That would be lovely. Just let me get organized first." Jenny glanced at her watch. "Dear God, I had no idea it was so late. I've got to get back. Is there an AVC station near here?"

"Down one level and to your left," said Artis.

"May I escort you home?" Peter offered.

"Thank you, but that won't be necessary." The words were quick, almost nervous. "I don't think I can lose myself between here and the apartment. Thank you for the drink, and I will be in touch." She hurriedly shook hands with Peter, then turned to Artis. "It was very nice meeting you. I'll have to bring Cab here for a drink."

"I'll look forward to that." Artis touched Jenny's outstretched hand, then moved around behind Peter and rested her elbows on his shoulders. They watched as Jenny hurried through the curtain.

"Good Lord, doesn't her boss permit her to date?" Peter asked. "She acted as if she were terrified to show up with a man in tow."

Artis's fingers played idly through the waterfall of heavy chains that draped over her bosom. "Not *man*, Peter, *colonist*. I have a feeling that she didn't want her boss to know that she is already starting to make friends here."

"Well, how do you think I did? Will Lydia approve?"

"Very well, all things considered. I have a feeling that she will call you."

Peter pushed back from the table. "It's time for me to get home, too." He slipped an arm about Artis's plump waist, and kissed her on the cheek.

The woman leaned back against the support of his arm, and glanced up at him. Her lashes dropped languidly over her eyes, and she peered up from beneath them. "Sure you won't reconsider? I'm really great in the sack."

"I'm sure you are, Artis dear, but I fear I'm neither energetic nor athletic enough to keep up with you."

"That might be true, and perhaps you shouldn't waste your energy. You need to devote your attentions to Ms. McBride." She dug him in the side with an elbow.

Peter colored to his eyebrows, and shook his head. "Artis, I have a very bad feeling about all of this."

"As do I, my darling, but for reasons quite different from yours, I'm sure. Now, go home and try not to worry. Leave that to the old witches like Lydia and me."

"You're not including Tina in the coven?"

"She's too young."

"I see. Well, I hope I performed up to expectation."

"You were wonderful, and I'll tell Lydia so when I see her."

They stepped back into the main room, and Artis waved when he reached the door. Returning to the bar, she pulled out an inventory list and began checking off items.

She had toyed with the notion of trying to get close to the

judge herself, but rejected the idea. First, from Lydia's description he didn't seem her type; and second, she wasn't certain she could control her anger when she was with him. Being a member of the hearing board had been one of the pleasures of her life, for she tried to mother every human being who came within her orbit. Now she was denied this outlet and it rankled. Beyond that was what she viewed as an unforgivable curtailment of her freedom by the Earth authorities.

Staring down at the list, she realized she had marked off several bottles of champagne when she had been staring at gin. Angrily she jammed her inventory list behind several bottles of expensive bourbon. Uncapping one, she then poured herself a quick drink. Perhaps she was only picking up Lydia's anxiety, but she felt as if she were standing on the edge of a chasm, just waiting for the push to send her tumbling in. It was not a comfortable feeling.

Chapter Three _____

"That journalist called again," Jenny said as Cab stepped in the door of the apartment. She was curled up in a corner of the sofa with a comforter over her knees, a pot of tea steaming on the coffee table. Cab looked sharply at her. There was a hint of a strain around her green eyes, and she seemed subdued.

"What's all this?" He waved a hand at the tea and the comforter, then seated himself on the couch next to her. "You're usually a good deal more energetic this time of day."

She shrugged and reached for her mug. "I was thinking how it's the rainy season back home, and how I would be curled up in my window seat looking out at the ocean." She took a sip of tea. "I guess the unrelieved sameness of this place is starting to get to me. No wind, no weather, no storms."

"This is a switch. I've been the one who's been moaning for the past ten days. I thought you were fascinated with this place."

"I am, but can't I get homesick?" She set aside the mug, leaned back against the arm of the sofa, and gave him a glance from beneath her lashes. "Also, I'm bored."

"I'm doing what I can, Jenny," he said stiffly.

"Excuse me, but I don't agree." She sat up and clasped her hands around her knees. "We're not getting the word out to the people, and that's why I think you ought to talk with this journalist."

"Back to that, are we?"

"Yes."

"Jenny, I am not a media figure, I'm a judge. And I don't do interviews. I never have."

"Well you better do something or we'll find ourselves outbound for Mars without ever having heard a case on the first leg of the circuit."

He shot her an angry look. "I am aware of all this. And as for being bored you ought to be in my shoes. While you've been gadding about with that engineer, I've been staring at the four walls of this apartment."

"I have been sightseeing with Peter and to dinner with him twice. That does not, in my book, constitute *gadding*. Besides, if you would ever get out and mingle you might meet some people, too."

"I have nothing in common with these people."

"Oh, bullshit."

"Jenny!"

She chuckled at the shocked expression on his face. She knew how he hated profanity in women. "I'm sorry, Cab. Her amusement faded and she shook her head. "I guess that's just an indication of how testy we both are." She rested her chin in one hand and looked at him. "Cab, we've got to do something before we throw each other off the balcony. I know we've worked closely for three years, but we never had to *live* with each other before."

"Am I that hard to take?"

"No more than I am."

"All right." He stood up, slapping her lightly on the knee. "I'll do something to break the deadlock."

"What?"

"There are a group of professionals living in the System. It was really their place to hold a reception for us, but since they haven't, I'll hold one."

"It might work. They've been representing people before the hearing boards, so if they decide we're all right they may be able to encourage people to use our court."

"Exactly what I was thinking."

"I'll check with the ABA and see who's listed in the System, and I can check with Lydia about any nonmembers."

"Lydia," Cabot repeated. "So you're on a first-name basis with her?"

"Only marginally."

"Do you see her often?"

"Hardly at all; she's very busy. When I do see her she's very pleasant."

"She obviously likes you better than me."

"With good reason. You were insufferably rude and snotty to her that first day."

"She was rude to me, also, if you remember."

"Yes, but I expect better from you."

"That's not fair. Don't make me live up to too much. I might dissappoint you."

"I doubt it." She threw back the comforter and swung her legs off the couch. The bright, energetic sparkle was back in her eyes, and her earlier depression seemed to have vanished. "Can I invite someone out of the brotherhood?"

"Who did you have in mind?" he asked with a teasing smile, though inwardly he was aware of a niggling aggravation, knowing who she would name.

"Peter Traub," she said, and she suddenly looked very young and vulnerable.

He wanted to refuse, but could think of no good reason. He realized that during their years together he had never met one of her escorts. Maybe this was the reason—an instinctive sense on his part that led to this gut-deep jealousy. He reminded himself that he had no right to be jealous, having never made an overture toward her. And more to the point he didn't own her. Forcing a smile back to his lips, he nodded.

"Certainly, if you feel he won't be bored by all the lawyers."

"No, it's *me* who gets bored with lawyers."

"I know, and given your attitude I still don't understand why you joined the profession."

"Sometimes, Cab, I don't either." She looked at him with a serious expression. "I wanted to make a difference, and I thought maybe through law I could make that difference. That's why I came here with you, even though I, in essence, had to be demoted from full partner to mere law clerk. Out here I thought I might be able to finally put together what it is that the law is supposed to do, to represent."

He reached out, and took one of her hands, holding it lightly between his. "Then I hope my little reception works, and I'll be able to help you find those answers."

• • •

"This is terrible," Jenny muttered through stiff lips to Peter as they huddled in one corner of the apartment.

"I predicted it, didn't I?"

"Yes, but why did you have to be right?"

The tone was querulous and the response irrational, but Peter answered seriously. "Because I've lived out here for five years, and I know how my people react."

Jenny glanced about the empty room. The platters of hors d'oeuvres and bottles of champagne seemed to mock her, and she stared miserably at Cab's rigid back as he stood gazing out the window. The door chime sounded, and Jenny jumped like a nervous fawn. She and Peter exchanged startled glances, and she walked to the door.

The man who lounged in the hall was clearly not an attorney. A beer belly of truly magnificent proportions stretched the fabric of his shirt. His clothes looked as if he had slept in them, and his jowly face would have been better with a shave.

"Hi," he said, raising a nonchalant hand.

"Hi," Jenny echoed.

"Heard you were having a party. Thought I'd drop by. You don't mind do you?" he asked as he pushed into the room, Jenny giving like a wave before the mighty prow of his stomach. He glanced about the near-empty room, and nodded thoughtfully. "Hey, great party you're having."

Cab flushed at the undercurrent of sarcasm in the man's voice, and stepped forward. "Since you weren't invited, I don't see that you have any cause to complain."

"Yep, just like they said. Proud, real proud."

"Who are you?"

"Andy Throckmorton, at your service." He held out a hand, a card caught between two fingers.

Cabot accepted the card and avoided the handshake. He glanced from the card to the man before him. "You're that journalist."

"Ah, my fame precedes me."

"I told you repeatedly that I do not give interviews."

"Yeah, I know. That's why I decided to crash your party so I could report on what a big hit you were making in the System."

Peter sucked in his cheeks, and stared at the ceiling. Jenny leaned back against the front door and braced herself for the storm that was certain to break. There was a moment of silence, then Cab gave a short laugh and indicated the kitchen counter.

"What'll you drink?"

"Rum."

"Fine. Jenny, if you please." She shook her head and hurried into the kitchen to pour the drink. "Do you know this man?" Cab asked Peter.

"Personally?—no, but by reputation—certainly."

"Well, please enlighten me."

"I put out *The System Squeak.*"

"*Post,*" Peter corrected automatically.

"*Post, Squeak,* whatever. Hell, I put it out. I can call it anything I want. Besides, compared to the big boys groundside it is·a squeak." He looked up at Jenny, who had returned with his drink. "You're laughing," he accused.

"A little."

"Good. I like a lady with a sense of humor. Do you belong to this menagerie, or did they just call you in for the evening?"

"Sorry to disappoint you, but I'm overqualified for escort service. I'm Jennifer McBride, attorney and law clerk for the Fifteenth Circuit."

"Pleased to meet you," Throckmorton said, bringing her hand to his lips. It was an incongruous gesture, given his appearance and manner.

"So you're the editor of a local System paper?" Cab asked.

"Editor, writer, reporter, chief bottle washer. You name it, I do it. I also string for UPI. That's why I decided to interview you. I read all the groundside reports about how you were coming out here to bring truth, justice, and the American way to us poor benighted spacers. I thought it would be nice if the poor benighted spacers got a chance to read a story about you written by one of their own."

"So what do you want to know?"

"Cab, I thought you didn't give interviews?" Jenny asked.

"A man who's gone to all this trouble deserves to be rewarded." He cast an ironic eye over Throckmorton's disheveled form. "After all, he looks like he's been traveling steerage for weeks."

"Hey, it ain't easy being the only reporter in near-Earth orbit. I gotta keep moving."

"Where do you live, Mr. Throckmorton?" Jenny asked as she moved to the dining room table and poured out three glasses of champagne.

"Andy."

"Andy," she repeated.

"Ostensibly on the Moon. I've got a place at Serenity Base, but I'm never there. My lady keeps things running while I wander around, pretending to pick up news."

"Is your wife a journalist, too?"

"Nah, she's a chemist. But I'm supposed to be the one who asks the questions."

"All right, ask away," Cab said, accepting a glass from Jenny.

The fat man pulled out a tiny pocket recorder and placed it on the coffee table. There was a sharpness in his body language that had been missing only moments before, and his heavy-lidded brown eyes seemed suddenly very alert. Cab drew back warily into his corner of the couch.

"Okay, whip me out some background."

Huntington shrugged, and cocked his head to one side, considering what to say. "I was born in Boston, raised in a variety of places, primarily Boston and Washington. Moved to northern California about ten years ago, where I maintained a practice in San Francisco."

"Specializing in what?"

"Corporate work mostly, but I took any Constitutional cases that came my way."

"Why?"

"I'm good at it, and that's where the real precedent-setting cases are found."

"According to *Who's Who in American Law,* you're one of the foremost Constitutional lawyers in the country. That why you were choosen for the Fifteenth Circuit?"

"I'm certain it had a lot to do with it."

"As much as your close personal friendship with President deBaca?" Throckmorton's eyes pierced Huntington from beneath half-closed lids. Cabot's hand tightened on the stem of his glass. He forced himself to relax, aware that this man was no fool and would miss nothing.

"Naturally the President wanted someone he could work with. Someone who shared his goals and hopes for the System."

"And just what are those goals and hopes?"

"Maybe that question would be better addressed to the President."

"You're out here to represent the President's desires. Surely you know something of his plans."

"I am out here to represent American justice."

"Well, we certainly hope so," Andy replied somewhat dryly.

"I'm continually amazed at the distrust I seem to arouse in you people. I had no idea I was so formidable."

"You're not. It's what we dimly perceive lurking behind you that has us worried. You seem to be traveling with a dark and elusive penumbra."

Cab chuckled, and relaxed against the arm of the couch. He was beginning to enjoy sparring with the journalist. In spite of Throckmorton's seedy appearance, the man was quick and well educated.

"What is it you people fear?"

"The loss of our freedoms, our unique lifestyle."

"Maybe it has to give way as you draw back into the mainstream of American life."

Jenny and Peter exchanged glances. They were hearing a repeat of the discussion that always arose whenever they were together. They drew in closer, and settled on the floor in front of the coffee table.

"And maybe we're not ready to give up our frontier status and join your great status quo."

"I can't see that you have much choice. Technology continues to advance and it will pull you closer to Earth."

"But does technological advance have to be a means of repression?" He gestured at Cab with the tip of his pen. "If we are getting more civilized we ought to be able to tolerate diverse lifestyles. Conformity is not necessarily the mark of civilization."

"We're back to that negative perception you have of the Earth authorities. Why all this talk of repression and loss of freedom? I'm an American just like you, and I've lived in great comfort and happiness under this system for forty-two years."

"No." His hands slashed through the air, punctuating the word. "You're not just like me. That's what you haven't realized yet." Throckmorton paused to take a pull at his rum.

"You're a member of the elite, the ruling class. Of course you're comfortable with the existing order; it provides you benefits and security. You have a vested interest in maintaining the status quo. I don't."

"Come now, let's not deteriorate into a tired rehash of the social dialectic."

"Oh, I'm no Marxist. Far from it. But I do believe the old boy was right on one level. Economics is where it's at. It's the driving force behind most human decisions. That's why I remain skeptical when you say you are out here to serve the holy cause of justice. I think it more likely that you're out here to tie us closer to the governing authorities who are frightened by the incredible amount of economic clout we can wield."

Huntington studied the journalist over the rim of his glass. "You're an interesting man, Mr. Throckmorton, with very interesting ideas."

"Meaning I'm getting close to the mark?"

"I'm not going to get caught in that one."

"Then I will." Jenny set her glass to spinning on the crystal surface of the table, and watched the circle formed by the condensing moisture. "To some extent you're right, but not in the negative way I think you mean. The judiciary is forbidden to make laws, but occasionally it's necessary. The Supreme Court has the power, and the responsibility to legislate the tough issues that can't be handled in a democracy."

"Such as?" Peter asked.

"I was thinking of *Brown versus Board of Education*. A poll taken at the time of the decision showed that sixty percent of the American people supported desegregation, but there were too many powerful special interests to allow Congress to act. The blacks followed an alternative path to social reform through the courts, and it worked. The Supreme Court ruled against school segregation, and set in motion vast societal changes that might have taken years to come about otherwise."

"I'd say justice was done in that case," Peter said.

"Yes, but how much of the justice's decision was based on pure ethics"—she picked up her glass and moved it several inches to the right—"and how much on a very real fear of what would be the consequences"—the glass went back to its original position—"if the country didn't begin to chip away at the discrimination?"

Cab spoke up. "A judge always takes into account those kinds of social issues."

"Consider this," Andy said, raising a thick forefinger in a professorial gesture. "It was the very *institutions* of power that kept segregation in place. In the System a man can seek redress *directly* against any person or power that tries to deny him his basic freedom. Out here I can pursue any profession, at any time, in any place so long as I take the responsibility for my actions." He glanced from Cab to Jenny and back again. "Isn't that a saner way to manage things rather than relying upon the glacial movement of government?"

"Now, wait . . . wait." Cab set aside his glass and began to pace the living room.

"We're going to be here all night," Jenny said, pitching her voice below the level of the older men's conversation.

"I don't mind if you don't. And by the way, you're right; your judge is an impressive fellow." Peter quickly held up a restraining hand at the expression of pleasure that crossed her face. "Now don't misunderstand me. I still don't agree with your presence, but I'm beginning to at least understand your side of things."

"I'm glad. You don't know how hard it is when you think everyone is lined up against you."

"I'm sorry about your party."

She shrugged, and tossed back a long strand of hair. "That's okay. It's not the evening Cab and I had envisioned, but it's turned out very well," she concluded, her eyes following Cab's elegant figure as he prowled about the room with Throckmorton lumbering along beside him. "He needs to start making friends out here if he's ever going to serve the System."

"And what about you? How are you going to serve the System?"

She smiled and shook her head. "I'm just a minor cog in a very complex piece of machinery. I have no illusions about my impact on the cosmos."

"Don't be too sure of that, Jenny. You have the advantage of a very facile and open mind. You may have more to contribute than you think."

Three days later Jenny was waiting for Peter at suit storage when he came off shift.

"Well, this is a surprise," he said, handing his helmet to the engineer behind the counter, and beginning to peel out of the rest of the bulky suit.

"We got a nice article in the *Squeak,*" she said, holding out a sheet. "I ran a copy of it for you."

"So Justice Huntington won Throckmorton over to his side?"

"I wouldn't say that. Let's just say that Andy wasn't as brutal as he could have been. He indicated his fears about our presence, but he did give us a few positive scores."

"I'm glad. I hope it produces what you want."

"Well, we still haven't gotten any cases, but I'll hold a good thought."

"Since you're still one of the idle unemployed, would you like to do something?"

"I was hoping you'd ask."

"What? Not more sightseeing," he said with a laugh.

His hair hung sweat-damp and lank on his forehead. She reached up and smoothed the wet strands off his face. "Actually, I think I've seen everything there is to see."

"So what did you have in mind?"

She hesitated, then looked him in the eye. "I know it's a terrible time to ask you, especially since you've just come in from hours in free fall, but I was wondering if you would teach me how to handle myself in weightlessness."

"Why? Are you worried about falling out an airlock?" he teased, as he signed the log book.

"Being pushed out is a more likely occurrence," she retorted, "given your frontier forms of justice out here. But seriously, I want to go outside, and they tell me I can't until I know free-fall techniques."

"Consider me at your disposal, just as soon as I get a shower."

He led her away from the suit storage area, their magnetic boots clicking faintly on the metal floor of the hub, and left her at one of the free-fall exercise rooms, while he rushed through the showers at the swimming pool. When he returned he was dressed in shorts and carried a pair of soft gym shoes.

"I hope you have something more comfortable than those pants," he said as he opened the door to the room. "This tends to get hot and sticky very fast."

"I thought I might need something less confining, so I came prepared." She reached up and pulled off her silk top. Beneath it she wore a pale blue leotard. She tried to remove her pants, but they wouldn't slide over her magnetic boots. She frowned, then gave a laugh and pulled off the boots. "May as well plunge in," she said as she floated away from the floor.

"And when you try to take those pants off you're going to discover all the dangers of free fall," Peter replied, shedding his own boots.

She threw him an impish look, and began to wriggle out of the slacks. The inevitable happened. She suddenly found herself tumbling end over end in the center of the room. Peter's arms went around her body, and righted her. It was a strange sensation to be held lightly in a man's arms while floating serenely in air. She threw back her head and looked up into his face.

"I trust you won't think me too fresh, but can I help you out of those?"

"Thank you, I accept."

He slid his hands down her sides, snagging the pants at each cuff, and pulling them from her legs in a quick movement. Even that small amount of force sent her drifting off in a new direction, but he caught her hand, and kept her close.

Her hair floated in red-gold tendrils about her face and throat. He reached out and brushed them aside, his fingers sliding across the etched bones of her clavicle and sternum. Although she was uncertain, she was still having an easier time maintaining her position than most beginners in free fall.

"I'm impressed."

"By what?" she asked as she experimentally moved one leg.

"You have a great deal of natural balance."

"Well, it's nice to know that eighteen years of ballet didn't go utterly for naught."

"Eighteen years," he repeated. "Good God, you must have been a pro."

"By some standards I suppose I was."

"But you quit for a legal career. Why?"

She rested her hands on his shoulders. "It suddenly seemed terribly self-indulgent and self-absorbed. Also it's all body. I suppose I began to worry that my mind would be atrophied by the time I was thirty."

"Wasn't it hard to switch over?"

"No, not really. I had a very wise father. He allowed me to

do whatever I wanted, just so long as I put some of my energy and attention into school. Fortunately I didn't major in dance. I took other courses at the university so I was ready for law school."

"Do you still dance?"

"Of course. How do you think I keep this girlish figure? I just don't go at it with such single-minded intensity anymore."

He floated away from her, heading toward a wall plate set next to the door. "This room can be used for either handball or ballet," he said. "Just a touch of a switch and mirrors will slide in to replace the walls."

"No, don't," she said abruptly.

"Why? I thought you'd enjoy trying it."

"In free fall, anyone can do what only the great can do on Earth. I hate cheats, and I don't want to be one."

He reached out and steadied himself against the wall. "How like you," he said softly. "You know, my dear, you are really a most unique person."

"You're biased," she said lightly.

"No, I don't think so," he said, allowing himself to drift back to her. She held out her hands to him, and taking them, he raised her fingertips to his lips. She shivered a bit, and cast him a look from beneath the fringe of her dark lashes.

"With all the mirrors, this room must have some other interesting and perhaps less proper uses."

"Remember what I told you the first day; we don't recognize victimless crime."

"Do you want to postpone this lesson for a little while?"

"The principles are still the same," he said cupping her chin in one hand. "It's still a matter of action and reaction."

She smiled, and floated into his embrace.

Chapter Four

"Goddammit, Taylor. I don't need this kind of aggravation!"

The young Marine seated by the door to the Oval Office nearly broke a leg while struggling to get to his feet and salute before the President and his Secretary of State vanished inside.

Secretary of State Taylor Moffit, his long face made even more doleful by the worried frown that creased his forehead, tried again to thrust the report into deBaca's hands. The President ignored the computer disk, and swung over to the hidden bar set in a cabinet.

"But, Mr. President," Moffit began.

"Dammit, Taylor," deBaca said again. "I have neither the time nor the energy to address myself to every real or imagined slight I may have given to some Third World witch doctor who calls himself a political leader." He splashed scotch into a glass. "You deal with it. That's what I hired you for."

"This could be sensitive, Mr. President. We don't want this blowing up in our faces like that Argentine mess. Especially not in an election year."

The President made a rude noise. "Do you really think I'm worried about Richard Long?"

"Please, Mr. President, that's not the issue, and it would only take—" The Secretary broke off, interrupted by a rhythmic chiming from the wide desk in front of the French windows.

DeBaca froze, his glass partway to his lips, and rolled one

eye toward the desk. In another setting his expression would
have been comical, but in this place, this room, the gentle
chiming was the shrill of alarm, and the expression totally
justified.

The President jumped at the desk as Moffit came circling
in from the other side. Both men were desperate to see which
of the brace of telecoms was chiming, for both knew it had to
be trouble. Only an emergency call came straight to the President without the intervening filter of aides and secretaries.

The glass felt slick in deBaca's hand. He set the tumbler
on the table, and nervously wiped the palms of his hands on
his gray wool slacks. His eyes scanned the seven telecoms.

Oh, God, he wondered, *is this it?* This thought was followed
immediately with the inane little inward cry of: *Please, not
during my administration!*

But it was not the first com on the right. He was not about
to be called upon to exercise his powers as Commander and
Chief. He felt the breath return to his body. It still wasn't good,
however, for the com that was still monotonously blinking was
linked to his counterpart's office somewhere in the Kremlin.

He sank into his chair and flipped the accept button. The
beefy features of Yuri Tupolev flickered and stabilized on the
small screen.

"Good morning, Mr. President," he boomed in a bluff,
hearty voice. His lips stretched into a smile that seemed to
vanish into the pouchy flesh of his cheeks. DeBaca felt the last
tense constriction ease from his chest. If Yuri was jovial it
meant he had called to horse-trade, not to harangue.

"And to you, Mr. Premier. To what do I owe this unexpected
call?" deBaca asked, matching Tupolev's tone of jolly good
fellowship.

"A minor problem which I would like to solve before it
attains major proportions."

The President paused to light a cigarette, and exchanged a
quick glance with Moffit who stayed out of visual range of the
comnet. "Forgive my plain speaking, Mr. Premier, but any
problem of yours is likely to be a boon to me. So why should
I want to help?"

"Ah, but this *problem* rather closely concerns both of us."
The Russian's face hardened. "One of your large companies

has started buying ore from one of my lunar collectives. I would prefer not to send a platoon of Marines across the Moon to settle the problem. Such violations of UN treaty always cause howls of anguish from our smaller neighbors, and I would rather avoid the uproar." DeBaca shifted restlessly in his chair and Tupolev, realizing that his circuitous approach to the topic was losing his audience, hurried on.

"It occurs to me that we are in the unique position of being able to aid one another since you have put in place the machinery to deal with such a situation with a minimum of force."

DeBaca leaned back in his chair, the squeak of the springs was loud in the quiet room. "I take it you're referring to the new federal circuit?"

"Indeed yes, Mr. President."

The President rocked forward in his chair, his feet hitting the carpeted floor with a dull thud. "What's it to me if an American company buys ore from one of your bases?" Gripping the cigarette between his fourth and middle fingers he thrust it at the screen. Tupolev involuntarily pulled back from the glowing ash. "I've never been adverse to turning a little profit."

"Come, come, Mr. President." The Russian's face stretched in a porcine expression of good humor. "Let us stop fencing with one another. You share the same fears as the other space-capable nations. Why else did you introduce Justice Huntington into the System if not to reassert control? And why do you think our Ministry of Justice agreed to be bound by his decisions over major UN treaty problems? I know and understand your efforts, and totally approve of them. Further, I am perfectly content to use this method to gain control over *my* colonists."

"The technique is somewhat more subtle than you are wont to use," deBaca murmured dryly. Tupolev grinned, an expression that left deBaca wondering if the Russian would begin to vanish, leaving behind only a broad smile, like some sort of Slavic Cheshire cat.

The President took a long drag on his cigarette, then ground it out in a crystal ashtray. "Shall we just cut the crap and lay it on the line? What exactly is it that you want me to do?"

"We have all noticed the growing independence of the System colonists. Due to certain advantages that my political system has over yours, I have been able to maintain a greater degree of control than you. Now this miner Renko is openly flouting us. If he succeeds in disregarding the wishes of his government, others will follow, and we need these colonists," Tupolev said harshly. "Perhaps even more than you."

For an instant deBaca saw the terror and anxiety that beset a leader whose country was unable to produce even the essentials for its people. The moment passed quickly, however, and the smooth, urbane mask was back in place. Tupolev noisily sucked tea from a tall glass, then clearing his throat, continued.

"Again you may say, 'so this is all to the good for us,' but I know, Mr. President, that you wish to tighten the reins on your own colonists, corporations, and small miners as well, and here I bring you a perfect opportunity."

He drew a stubby finger down his nose, and tapped thoughtfully at his front teeth. "I do not wish the world to notice when I finally discipline the Garmoneya Collective, but I do wish the world, and my colonists, to notice when U.S. Steel stops buying their ore, and I wish to do this quite legally. What better than your Fifteenth Circuit to handle this problem?"

DeBaca rubbed the tips of his fingers over his lips, and considered. He and Cab had had one brief talk since the judge's arrival on EnerSun, and what Cabot had reported was not good. In the two weeks he had been aboard the station he had found no work, and had passed the time in frustrated research. Under the circumstances, forcing a case into a new court might not be such a bad idea. It might break the log jam that had developed, and encourage other people to use the court.

"It's possible we can do business, Mr. Premier, but I want you to understand that what ever *discipline* you have in mind, it won't involve this country."

"You need only look the other way, and I know your nation has had more than a little practice at that art." Tupolev grinned. It failed to draw an answering response from deBaca. To cover his faux pas he took a quick sip of tea, coughing slightly as it went down the wrong way. "The rest I will handle," he said catching his breath. "But we will discuss the details at a later date. One problem at a time, eh?"

"Fine." DeBaca's tone was curt. He was getting more than a little tired of Tupolev's heavy-handed humor at the United States' expense. "You'll start the formalities in motion?"

"You will hear from Petrov at the UN by this afternoon. The Oslo Space Utilization Treaty will be a nice vehicle for our protest."

"Fine, and I'll get things started on this end. Been good doing business with you, Mr. Premier."

"And with you, Mr. President," the Russian responded as his image faded from the screen.

DeBaca swung around in his chair and stared up at Moffit. The Secretary licked his lips, and sucked softly on the inside of his cheek.

"You disapprove?"

"Not disapprove precisely, sir. I'm just worried that this thing could get away from us." He took a few awkward steps toward the window.

DeBaca laced his fingers behind his head, and leaned back once more in the chair. "I need to send a message to the colonists, and this case should do that very nicely. Tupolev talks about the flouting of his authority, but I've got exactly the same situation with those arrogant bastards out there. If I don't get some cases into the Fifteenth Circuit, I'm going to look like an idiot. They're going to have to learn that we're out there to stay, and that we have the power to back what we do."

"But do we?" Moffit muttered under his breath.

"What's that?" the President asked as he reached for the intercom.

"Nothing, sir."

"Madge," he snapped into the speaker. "Get Reynolds at Justice over here right away." He cut the connection without waiting for a response.

"It's going to take some interesting bootstrapping to find a way from a UN protest to stopping U.S. Steel from buying Soviet ore," Moffit offered timidly to the back of deBaca's head.

"That's Reynolds's problem," he said, glancing at a paper, and then scribbling his signature across the foot of the page. "It's about time he and his people at Justice started playing their part. I didn't ram the Fifteenth Circuit through Congress just as an exercise in political gamesmanship."

"No, of course not, sir. Now about this African matter."

"Taylor!"

• • •

Evgeni reclined in an uncomfortable metal chair, his weight supported on his neck and tailbone, and watched the glowing screen where a new novel slowly unfolded. The book had arrived yesterday, along with a shipment of replacement suits, and he had rushed through his work in a fever of impatience, eager to slip in the disc and read.

Behind him on their narrow wall bunk, Irina and Analisa sat playing with a new doll. Each member of the collective had purchased some new and frivolous object in addition to the desperately needed equipment. And all of this possible because of a single sale to U.S. Steel! Evgeni smiled, savoring the pleasures of being a consumer.

He suddenly realized that several lines of script had flowed past him as he sat in a self-congratulatory haze. Reaching out with a finger he halted the marching text. As he rose and stretched, he gazed critically around the small living quarters. Its gray drabness had never bothered him before, but now with the promise of comfort, if not luxury, within reach, the room oppressed him.

He walked to the bunk and, leaning down, kissed the top of Irina's head. The wispy tickle of her fine hair against his lips was very sensual, and he felt a response in his groin. She seemed to feel an answering fire for she tipped back her head and planted a kiss on his lips.

"Bored so soon?" she teased when he finally released her mouth.

"No, I just couldn't sit still any longer."

"You need to learn to relax. There's no need now to be working all the time."

"I don't intend to work. I only wanted to pester my wife and daughter."

"Silly," Irina said, laying her narrow-fingered hand against his cheek. "I'm grateful to have you here pestering us rather than out on that plain."

Analisa listened with the halfhearted attention of a five-year-old with more interesting things to do while her parents exchanged endearments. Tiring of her parents' absorption in each other, she tugged at Irina's free hand and tried to shove a doll shoe into the one that Evgeni held.

Irina's attention slipped from her husband, and at that moment a page call whistled through the room. Evgeni crossed to the console and flipped on the receiver.

"Evgeni," came Gregori's voice, "you have a call from that Schultz person at U.S. Steel. He said it was urgent, and since he also acted as if it were private I thought I should route it to your room."

"Yes, good. If there is some problem we don't want Cheslav to hear of it."

Gregori grunted. "That little swine. He wants his share of the money and more, but he'll be the first to squeal his innocence if the authorities do come down on us." Evgeni acknowledged the truth of Gregori's statement, then settled back to wait for the call.

The screen flickered then stabilized, revealing the poster-hung wall of Harvey Shultz's office. Schultz stepped into range of the comnet, blocking off Evgeni's view of a Swiss alpine poster. The sales manager for U.S. Steel was a plump, middle-aged man, whose perpetually worried frown was offset by the kindness in his brown eyes.

It was this quality of interest and caring which had given Evgeni the nerve to continue with his mad scheme. If any other man had taken his first timid call to the U.S. Steel station he might have retreated in frightened confusion. As it was he had been routed to Harvey, and everything had worked out perfectly. Without needing embarrassing explanations, Harvey had understood the plight of the colony, and was very interested in the ore Evgeni had to offer.

In the early days of lunar exploration, the Soviets had bulled through their claims to some of the richest mineral deposits on the Moon, and as was usually the case in the dealings between the super powers, the United States had quietly acquiesced. Therefore, Harvey had a pretty good notion of the quality of ore the Garmoneya Collective could deliver.

After agreeing in principle to do business, they had kicked around the dangers inherent in the scheme, and Harvey soon agreed that the UN Nonmilitary Lunar Pact would stop any violent attempts to bring the collective back into line. Also, Harvey was a long-time station dweller, and he held the usual unvoiced contempt for the Earthside governments.

Evgeni was pleased to hear from Harvey for although they had never physically met he felt they were friends, but he found his pleasure fading to worry when he remembered that Gregori had said the call was urgent. Also the frown that perpetually creased the administrator's forehead had crept down into his eyes.

"Harvey, how are you?" Evgeni said in his heavily accented English.

"Very well, and you?"

"Fine."

"And the family?"

"They are all well. In fact they are here with me."

"Ah," Shultz murmured, then cleared his throat. "I'm glad I caught you in. We may have a problem."

"The ministry?" Evgeni broke in. His mouth felt dry.

"No, no. In fact, it's sort of funny. The trouble is coming from my government. The Justice Department has filed for an injunction in the Fifteenth Circuit."

The miner wiped a hand across his mouth, and struggled to follow the unfamiliar words. "I am afraid I don't understand, Harvey."

"It's like this. It seems that your people kicked up a dust in the UN a couple of days ago, and my government is, as usual, wetting in their pants. This led the legal arm of my government to ask for an order to keep us from buying ore from you."

There was a leaden weight in the pit of Evgeni's stomach. He forced down the bile that threatened to choke him, and kept his voice level. "And so you are calling to tell me that you can no longer—"

"Oh, no, no. Rest easy on that. Until this thing is thrashed out by the lawyers, it'll be business as usual. I just thought you should know what's going on. And I wouldn't worry too much. We've got a platoon of company lawyers whose only job is to handle this sort of thing. Chances are that after some hooting and hollering this whole thing will be settled in our favor. The Feds will be happy because they can tell the Russians that they tried, and you and I won't even know anything happened for all the difference it will make."

"I hope you are right, Harvey. Where is all this to take place?"

"On the EnerSun station."

"Harvey, will you please tell me when they will . . . how do you say it? . . . when they will hear this case? I cannot just sit here and wait."

"Sure, I'll be happy to tell you. But I warn you these things are really dull, and chances are it'll just be a waste of your time."

"It is my time to waste, Harvey, and beyond that it is not only my time, but my life that is at stake."

"Do you really think your government would go that far?"

"Yes, they really would. I know them, Harvey, all too well."

"Okay, Evgeni, I'll let you know when I learn anything. Well, I better let you go and get back to your family. I'll be in touch, and try not to worry."

"Right," Evgeni muttered at the now-empty screen. A pounding headache had settled into his temples, and he pressed the heels of his hands against his eyes. The featherlike touch of Irina's hands on his shoulders brought his head up.

"Perhaps we should stop now," she said quietly from behind him. "If we show enough contrition perhaps our punishment won't be too severe."

Puzzled by talk which she didn't understand, but sensitive to the fear and anxiety in her parents' voices, Analisa crept up to lean against Evgeni's knee. He stared down into her delicate face with it's high cheekbones and large brown eyes, while she stared questioningly up at him.

"No!" he said harshly. "We have come too far and risked too much to turn back."

"But if we defy them to the end, and then the decision goes against us—"

His hand chopped at the air, cutting off her words. "It will *not* go against us. This is an American court and American justice. We will have a fair hearing."

Her eyes held skepticism, but she nodded and said quietly, "God grant that you are right."

Chapter Five

"We've got a case," Jenny called over the lush, sensual texture of Brahms's first symphony. Huntington opened one eye and peered at her from where he lay on his bed. She waved the sheaf of printout. Cabot swung his stockinged feet off the plush beige comforter and sat up, holding out his hand for the papers.

Jenny moved across the bedroom, feeling as if she were being swept up and incorporated in the rich sound which swelled and ebbed around her. Cabot liked his music classical, and the volume symphony-hall shattering. He was old-fashioned about paper, too, seeming to view it with almost reverential awe. She knew better than to bring him a disc to run through the computer. He wanted the tactile sense of page and binding. His greatest wrench in leaving his home had been the loss of his extensive library. To him, books on a computer disc just weren't books.

Jenny watched impassively while Cabot scanned the motion. She had read the pleading as it had been chattering out of the printer in their apartment study, and there was something about it that struck her as indefinably wrong. She leaned against the wall, folded her arms across her chest, and waited for Cab's opinion of the document. After several minutes he looked up with a puzzled frown.

"Good, then it's not just me," Jenny commented.

"And what's your impression of all this?" Cabot half lifted the papers.

"If I had run into it in private practice I would have classified it as a spurious lawsuit."

"But we're not in private practice, and this *is* the Justice Department."

She stubbornly shook her head. "Sorry, Cab. There's something funny about this."

"You may be right," she said noncommittally, and padded across the room to where he had left his boots propped up against a chair.

"Where are you going?"

"Just to the front room, but I'm going to do a little digging. I feel at less of a disadvantage with my shoes on."

Jenny eyed the two-inch heels on the boots, but made no comment. Huntington caught her glance, and flushed. He rather defiantly pulled on the soft, brown ankle-high boots, and strode into the living room. The telecom rested on a small desk tucked in a corner near the front door.

After removing a card from his wallet, Huntington punched in the long code that was printed on it. The screen came to life, and Jenny caught a quick glimpse of a high-backed chair framed by French doors with a rose garden beyond before the screen was swallowed by the bulky form of the President. Wide-eyed, she stepped out of range of the comnet. She had known that Cab and deBaca were good friends, but she hadn't suspected that Cab had access to a private Presidential comline.

"Cab, how you doing?" deBaca asked, grinning into the screen.

"Bored."

"Don't worry, things are going to change." He looked smug.

"You sound quite confident about that."

"Believe me, something will be arriving."

"I think it may have done so already."

"Oh?"

"United States versus U.S. Steel Corporation, Inc."

The President leaned back and gave that slow, self-satisfied smirk that Huntington had learned to mistrust during their days at Harvard.

"What do you think? Looks good, doesn't it?"

"I think it looks a little thin." DeBaca's lips tightened in irritation at this jab.

"Maybe, but I'm not—" the President broke off abruptly. "Are you alone?"

"No."

"I need to talk with you privately, so if you would please send Ms. McFee—"

"McBride," Cabot testily corrected him.

"Oh, right, McBride. Anyway, if you'd just send her out of the room for a few minutes."

Huntington looked at Jenny, and indicated the door to her bedroom. He would not insult her further by sending her into the hall to cool her heels like some lackey, and he trusted her not to try to listen at the door. Jenny moved quickly from the room, but there was a rigid set to her slender shoulders.

"Okay, I'm alone."

"A man of few words," the President marveled after waiting in silence for several moments. "Aren't you the least bit curious about what I needed to say to you?"

"Yes, but I assume you're going to tell me at some point."

DeBaca gave up on the futile game of trying to force Huntington into the position of supplicant. "Actually, it's fortuitous that you called when you did. I had a note on my desk to ring you later."

Cabot shifted irritably in his seat. Today he was finding the slow unravelings of the President's motives more irksome than usual.

"So," deBaca said abruptly. "You don't like my little case."

"It smells like a day-old political rat."

"There is precedent for it."

"I assumed there had to be, but it's still a gobbler, and if I hear it, law schools will be using it for years to come as an example of excessive government interference."

"Try to think of it as another *Marbury* or *McCulloch*."

"Those were landmark constitutional decisions."

"And this one will be, too."

"Maybe."

"You know what they say, Cab. The winners get to write the histories and the laws. And in this case we're going to be the winners."

"Enough of this. What is it you want from me, Tomas?"

DeBaca leaned forward, and steepled his fingers in front of his face. "This is the perfect opportunity for us to begin reasserting the control which is so necessary if we are to continue advancing—"

"Oh, for Christ's sake! What am I? A whistle stop on your re-election campaign? Spare me the grandiose speeches. I'm a busy man."

The President's mouth took on a mulish set. "I thought you were bored."

"Not as bored as this is making me."

DeBaca frowned and irritably rearranged objects on his desk. At last he looked up into the screen. "I've got to win this one, Cab. I don't care what U.S. Steel comes in with. I've got to win." His expression softened, and he gave Huntington a pleading look. "Please, Cab, I'm counting on you for this one. This is what I put you out there for. And you gave me your word."

Huntington stared at the screen, and chewed on the bad taste that had suddenly formed in his mouth. He had expected this, known it was coming, but now that the moment had arrived he felt pushed, trapped, and, yes, somehow dirtied.

He had only been a judge for two weeks, and all of that time had been spent in idleness, ignored by the people he had come to serve. He had thought that he would welcome the opportunity to put these stiff-necked colonists in their place, but now he wasn't so sure. An illusion of impartiality would have been nice, and now deBaca was removing even that from him. On Earth, seated in the Oval Office, it had been easy to agree to Thomas's schemes; but here, in space, and invested with the powers and duties of a jurist, he was finding it hard to summon the certainty he had felt that day in the White House.

The President remained silent, and Cabot inwardly cursed Tomas for his forbearance. If deBaca had started to push, he would have had a reason to resist. As it was he was left trapped in his word, and without provocation or a compelling reason he would not willingly break the promise he had given to this old friend. Cabot gave a defeated sigh, and the President's face creased into a satisfied smile.

"Good. I knew I could count on you, Cab." He gave a jolly laugh. "For a minute I was beginning to think they put something in the water up there that turns everyone into a rebel."

"Meaning I'm a tame dog?" Cabot asked ominously.

"No, no, of course not. You're a patriot, Cab. Always have been."

Huntington felt a stab of pain at the hinge of his jaw, and he consciously relaxed his gritted teeth which had clamped together at the President's soothing and effusive tone.

"Right," he said at last. "Okay, Tomas, you'll have your decision."

"Stop looking so grim, Cab. It won't be that painful. Judges have been making law for five hundred years, and it's usually been for the people's own good."

Huntington tried to imagine telling the independent and self-assured Lydia Kim Nu that he was forcing her to do something for her own good. The image presented was ludicrous. He squeezed the bridge of his nose, trying to banish an incipient headache. He suddenly realized that Tomas was saying good-bye. He forced his attention back to the screen. They exchanged a few quick banalities, and the com went dead.

"May I come back now?" Jenny asked from the door. Her tone was very formal, her expression severe, and Cab wondered if he had made the right decision in acquiescing to deBaca's demand. True, he and Tomas had been close in the old days, but Jenny was here now, and her loyalty was something which he shouldn't throw aside lightly.

He nodded, watching the graceful sway of her hips and the proud, confident set of her shoulders as she crossed the room. It was a strange thought to have at this particular time, but he suddenly realized that this woman, this very beautiful woman, was sleeping only twenty-five feet from him. The possibilities presented by the situation were numerous, and he wondered that he had never before considered them.

"Do the colonists think we're sleeping together?" he abruptly asked.

"Cab!" Jenny muttered, flushing a deep pink.

"My word," Cab said, leaning back in his chair. "I didn't think you could be embarrassed."

"You just took me off guard, that's all. And no, I don't know what the colonists say about us. I don't go around asking them what they think my sex life is like. Besides, I spend a lot of time with—" She cut off.

"With Peter Traub. Yes, I know. You're always going off to some party or softball game."

"You sound sulky."

"Maybe because I feel a little left out. Why didn't you

include me, Jenny? We've always been a team up till now."

"I didn't think you were interested." She stopped and tilted her chin up as if considering how much more to say.

"Go on."

For a few moments she plucked at the beaded embroidery on the wide cuff of her shirt. Then, throwing back her hair, she said, "We're so disliked up here, and most of the distrust centers on you. I wanted to get to know the people without that handicap, so I put some distance between us." It was delivered in a level, matter-of-fact tone that effectively removed any insult.

"Thank you. Good, refreshing honesty," Cab murmured, thinking back on his tortuous conversation with deBaca. "And if I asked you to include me?"

"I'd do it provided you kept an open mind and tried to learn something about life out here."

"You're very harsh."

"What else can I be when it's apparent that you came here with your mind already made up, and when you have secret conversations with the President about a case we're about to hear."

"Aren't you going to ask me about that conversation?"

"No. If it's private, it's private, and we're talking about your attitude toward and isolation from the colonists. Don't try to change the subject."

"All right. I'll concede that I've been remiss in my duties. Now will you take me around? Let me meet people?"

"I'd like that, and I think you're going to be surprised with what you find."

The quiet, humorous smile that he kept hidden much of the time tugged at his mouth. "I hope not. I might have to alter my carefully constructed preconceptions."

"It'll do you good. Especially now that you're about to start adjudicating for these people. You need to understand their circumstances so you can make decisions that are best suited to their needs."

"And if I don't?"

"Don't what?"

"Don't make decisions best suited to their needs?"

"But you wouldn't do that, Cab," Jenny said, giving him

an odd look. She missed his wince for she had turned and was walking into her room.

"Why do I have the feeling that this party is going to be a disaster?" Lydia asked no one in particular as she walked into the kitchen of her apartment. A long skirt, shot through with metallic threads of green, red, blue, gold, silver, and maroon, shimmered as she walked, and there was a faint chiming from the tiny bells that were sewn into the hem.

"Not a chance," Muhammid replied from where he was vigorously shaking a cocktail mixer. "I'm making the drinks, and they're guaranteed to remove all constraints and inhibitions within thirty minutes."

"Somehow that doesn't comfort me. This thing is going to look like an armed summit anyway, and if tongues should be loosened, and people forget their manners they're likely to tear my apartment to pieces."

"I told you we should have had it at my place," Artis said from the counter, where she was arranging canapés on an inlaid tray. "I'm used to brawls, and most of the furniture in my bar is of the nonbreakable variety."

"We could not entertain all this brass from Earthside in a bar, no matter how popular or famous it might be."

"You worry too much. These are government white men. They don't know how to start a real fight," Muhammid stated.

"Prigs," Artis said succinctly, licking a bit of cream cheese from one finger.

"Undoubtably, but for better or worse they're here, and the company told me to make them welcome." Lydia gathered up the filled tray, then headed back into the living room with the hors d'oeuvres. "This is going to look like the regional conference of the ABA," she muttered as the door fell shut behind her.

The room was starting to hum with low-pitched conversation and the chink of ice against glass. The only people who had arrived were station dwellers, Lydia noticed as she took a quick circuit of the room. She spotted Andy Throckmorton sprawled in a chair and looking as if he had already made deep inroads on the liquor cabinet.

"You're not going to pick up much gossip if you're too pie-eyed to understand it," she said, placing a hand on his shoulder, and leaning in to whisper in his ear.

"Oh, hello, Lydia. I'm not here for gossip."

"Oh, so you just came by to lap up my free booze, is that it?" she asked with a laugh.

"You wrong me, madam. I would never take advantage of your hospitality. Now, your beautiful person is another matter. I'd take advantage of that any chance I got."

"Sorry, you're going to have to stand in line. Joe has first place."

Andy snapped his fingers with disappointment. "Dammit, he has all the luck. Well, where are all these high-powered legal minds? I wanted to find out a bit more about this case for my readers."

"Your guess is as good as mine. Maybe they're being fashionably late."

Or maybe they just don't intend to show up at all, she thought sourly as she drifted over to Peter Traub.

"Are we likely to have any of the brass arrive?" she asked him quietly.

"Jenny said she and the judge would be here. For the rest I cannot speak."

There was a chiming from the door page, and Lydia moved to answer the summons. Jenny and Cabot stood in the hall. Jenny looked stunning in a strapless green gown that matched her eyes, and whispered softly about her feet as she stepped into the apartment. Huntington looked no less elegant in a high-necked black jacket and matching slacks. The severity of the color was old-fashioned, but it suited him well, and he made the other men in the room seem suddenly gaudy.

"Judge," Lydia said, extending her hand. "I'm glad you could make it. We haven't seen much of you the past month," she couldn't resist adding.

He ignored her jab. "Thank you for the invitation. Has John Malcomb arrived?"

"Since I don't know who he is I really couldn't say."

"He's chief counsel for the Justice Department."

"Then I can guarantee he's not here. You two are the first out—" She caught herself, and amended the word. "Visitors who've arrived."

"How do you classify the attorneys for U.S. Steel? Outsiders, too?" Huntington asked as he lifted a glass from the tray being carried by one of the waiters on loan from The White Owl.

"No. They'll definitely be spacers if they win the case," Lydia said with a smile.

"There's been very little publicity about this case, but everyone aboard this station seems to be very well informed about its circumstances and details."

"Word travels fast out here. And since this is something that concerns all of us we're naturally interested."

Artis arrived at Lydia's elbow, an exotic figure in a shimmering gold kaftan and an elaborate headdress of turbaned material, bangles, and feathers. Her bracelets jangled as she extended her hand to Huntington.

"Introduce us, Lydia. This is the man who took my favorite job, and this is the first time I've ever laid eyes on him."

"Justice Cabot Huntington, this is Artis Barnes." The chime sounded again, and Lydia excused herself.

"I take it you were on the hearing board, too?"

"Yes, and I was very attached to my role as mentor, mother, and auntie to the various people who came before us."

A smile tugged at the corners of Cab's mouth. "Well, I'm sorry I had to deprive you of your counseling, but it really was necessary to get a coherent legal system out here."

"And I'm not coherent? How ungallant, sir!" Artis exclaimed, pressing a hand to her bosom. Her eyes sparkled, and she seemed amused with her own dramatics.

"Forgive me," Cab said with a slight bow. "No insult was intended. But might I suggest that you could better serve the brood you appear to be mothering by becoming a psychologist."

"I thought about that," Artis said thoughtfully, tapping at the side of her nose with a pudgy forefinger. "But it would have taken too much time away from my business."

"Which is?"

"I run a saloon where I dispense exotic libations and provide a relaxing atmosphere in which persons of all sexes and interests can discover one another."

Jenny cast a nervous look at Cabot, wondering how he was going to respond to his first dose of Artis. There was a momentary pause, then Huntington threw back his head and burst out laughing.

Artis gave him an affectionate pat on the arm with her fan,

throwing Jenny a reassuring smile. "I knew from looking at you that you were a man of sense who wouldn't be offended by a little plain speaking."

"No, no, far from it," he said, still chuckling. "I was just trying to picture Chief Justice Donaldson's face if I ever told him that justice was being dispensed in the System by a madam."

"Please, Justice Huntington," Artis said in failing accents, "say, rather, a simple business woman who provides a haven for lonely people." The effect was unfortunately ruined by the mischief in her eyes.

"Cab," a new voice called across the crowded room. "Good God, man, it's been two years if it's been a day. How the hell are you?"

Huntington turned and smiled with delight as the tall, angular form of his old friend, and raquetball partner, John Malcomb, came loping toward him. He knew the assignment of John Malcomb to argue the case for the government had been yet another attempt by deBaca to stack the deck, but he found it hard to mind for the man was a fine lawyer and a good friend. Malcomb was followed by a serious round-faced young man whom he introduced as his assistant, Richard Weinrod. Cabot politely shook hands with the younger man, then turned eagerly back to his friend.

Artis slipped her arm through Jenny's, and they moved away. "I think the old-boy network is in full swing, and women would be definitely *de trop*," she said in an undertone to the younger woman.

"You're right, but I can't help but resent it."

"There's Peter. Go and visit with him, and let his quite proper admiration of you soothe your ruffled feathers."

Jenny squeezed Artis's arm. "Sounds like a good idea. Talk to you later."

"Damn, it's good to see you," Cabot said. "How has life been at Justice?"

"Hectic, and if the President hadn't put on the screws I wouldn't have taken this case. Traveling up here, arguing, and traveling back takes more time than I've got."

"Not so loud," Huntington said, raising a cautionary hand. "It might be better if we kept deBaca out of this conversation."

Malcomb followed Cabot's glance at the milling colonists, and gave a quick nod. "I see your point. So tell me about your beautiful mother. I swear I'd marry her if she'd have me, twenty-three-year age difference or not."

Cabot laughed, and motioned to one of Artis's discreet waiters to bring a drink for Malcomb. "Still ambassador to Great Britain, and still puttering around that forty-two-room house, pretending it's 1880."

"Wonderful woman."

Peter motioned toward the two men who occupied the center of the living room and asked, "Isn't that a bit chummy for the judge on a case and one of the opposing lawyers?"

Jenny stared down into her glass and twirled it, watching the ice cubes form a whirlpool in the amber liquid. "It's hard for lawyers and judges not to get to know each other. After all, we come out of the same schools, belong to the same clubs, and meet in the same courts. John is an old friend of Cab's. I really don't think there's anything wrong in their catching up with each other."

"Funny," Peter said, staring at the door. "But I don't think the two people who just came in would agree with that assessment of the situation."

Jenny looked quickly to the door. Standing just over the threshold was an ancient Japanese-American gentleman. His seamed face was the pale yellow color of autumn leaves, and his black hair was streaked with silver. He was leaning on the arm of a small, wiry Hispanic woman whose dark eyes seemed to smolder as she regarded Huntington and Malcomb still engrossed in conversation. Her eyebrows formed a single black line across her forehead, and when she frowned, as she was doing now, the aspect was one of great ferociousness.

"Do you know who those people are?" Peter asked.

"The woman's new to me, but that's Kenneth Omi Furakawa. He's one of the top corporate lawyers in the country. I didn't know he was under retainer to U.S. Steel."

"Maybe they brought him in to offset the overwhelming firepower and advantage from the Justice Department."

"What do you mean by that?" Jenny asked, turning to face him directly, her drink splashing over her hand with the force of the motion.

"Why don't we just wait and see how the case develops, and then I won't have to make you angry tonight by expressing an opinion you don't want to hear."

"You think Cab is in collusion with Justice. Is that it?"

"Let's just say I'm considering the possiblity."

"There is no such possibility." Her face seemed to close down, her green eyes becoming hard and flat. "Also, under the circumstances I think it would be a good idea if we don't talk anymore tonight. I don't really want to fight with you, and frankly you're pushing me to it."

"Okay, Jenny, but I fear you're being naive." As she fixed him with a piercing gaze, then jerked away and started toward Cab, Peter reached out and closed his hand around the soft skin of her upper arm, holding her in place. "Although I do hope for all our sakes that you're right. I'm just a suspicious son of a bitch," he added quietly.

As an attempt to pacify her, it was a failure. "I'll see you in a few days, Peter," she said coldly. "I'm going to be very busy working with Cab on this case." Shrugging free of his restraining hand, she moved swiftly to Cab's side.

"Was that a tiff I just perceived?" Tina asked, joining Peter in his corner.

"'Fraid so, boss. I may have come on a bit too strong with Jenny, but I must admit it's a tad unsettling to see the judge and the men in the black hats in such close and friendly conversation shortly before a major case is to be heard. I'm not sure I could have kept my mouth shut, and it will do no harm if I did plant a few seeds of doubt. It might just make my fair Jenny watch her boss a bit more closely."

At the door Furakawa and his assistant exchanged pleasantries with Lydia, then moved to join the knot of lawyers in the center of the room. The System dwellers seemed to be hugging the walls, as if they were trying to remain inconspicuous while still being within eavesdropping distance of the strangers. Andy was less polite. He pushed forward until he was hovering over Jenny's left shoulder.

"Ken," Huntington said pleasantly to the Japanese-American, holding out his hand. "I'm surprised to find you up here. It isn't exactly an easy trip." He regarded the elderly man, whose fragile bones seemed to be etched beneath the wrinkled skin.

"This is likely to be a precedent-setting case, and I like

precedent-setting cases," Furakawa said softly.

"Actually this case is a load of bullshit."

Huntington stiffened. "I beg your pardon?" he said in his iciest Back Bay voice.

"My assistant, Ms. Angela Martinez," Furakawa said smoothly, indicating the glowering woman. Cabot reluctantly extended his hand.

"This case is a blatant piece of harassment," Martinez continued, ignoring Cabot's outstretched hand. Her boss maintained a Buddha-like smile. "And everyone knows it. It's been filed purely to make trouble for the colonists. Since when have we ever been concerned about someone ripping off the Russians?"

"Why so vehement, Ms. Martinez?" Cabot asked coldly. "It's good to zealously represent your client's interests, but the court expects some degree of objectivity."

"Ms. Martinez was born in the System, Cabot," Furakawa explained in his faint, fluting voice. "She quite naturally views this case as an assault against her people."

"Then perhaps she shouldn't be on this case since she is so emotionally and personally involved."

"And one could also perhaps argue that you should excuse yourself from this case, given your long and deep friendship with not only Mr. Malcomb but the President, as well."

It was a cunningly thrown barb, sharp and well placed, and Cabot's cheeks reddened with anger and embarrassment. "Nonsense! It's ridiculous to pull someone off another bench just to hear this case. It's not that important."

"Its lack of importance must, of course, explain the presence of Mr. Malcomb, one of the top attorneys in the Justice Department, and with all humbleness, my own presence. But of course, you would know best." Furakawa took Angela's arm and they moved away.

"Whew," Malcomb muttered, running his fingertips lightly along his hairline. "This is shaping up to be more of a fight than any of us expected. I'm beginning to wish the President could have picked somebody else. I hate to go up against a pro like Ken with a case as—"

"Tough as this one," Cabot hurriedly interrupted him, noting Andy Trockmorton's bird dog–like interest in the conversation. Jenny gave him a hard look which he ignored.

The door to the apartment slid open, and a powerfully built man of medium height strode into the room.

"Joseph," Lydia called joyfully, for she hadn't really expected to see the head of the Reichart empire. He usually shunned any contact with Earthside government representatives. She moved swiftly into his arms, and gave him a kiss on the cheek.

"I'm glad you're here," she whispered.

"Couldn't leave you to face the lions alone."

With the entrance of Joe Reichart, Malcomb went absolutely rigid. His hand tightened on his cocktail glass, and his face stiffened into an expression of outrage. He drew in several heavy breaths as if trying to calm himself, but he was unable to hold back the words.

"Goddamm it!"

"Good God, John, what's the problem? You look on the verge of apoplexy," Cab said in an undertone. He was embarrassed by his friend's outburst and his furious expression. "Calm down," he added after a furtive glance around the overcrowded room.

"When I find out who invited that son of a bitch to this party I'll . . ."

"I did," Lydia said, stepping forward to confront him. "And you'll do what?"

Malcomb hesitated, thrown off stride by the manager's imposing presence. "I just finished trying a very acrimonious and difficult case against Mr. Reichart and his company."

"Which he lost," Joe said helpfully with the strange, cynical smile that almost always curved his lips firmly in place.

"Joseph has been battling you bureaucrats in lawsuits for years. I can't be expected to keep track of every case and the lawyers for each side so I don't offend your sensibilities by bringing you together in the same room. Besides, this is my home, and I'll bloody well invite whom I please," Lydia concluded with some asperity.

"Well said, my dear," Reichart murmured.

"I thought this party was to welcome us to your station. Inviting the man who has been a thorn in the side of the federal government for the past thirty years is hardly showing a conciliatory attitude toward the government."

"First, I gave this party because I was ordered to by the

President of EnerSun. Your presence on my station is hardly a source of pleasure to me, and not something for which I would throw a party. Secondly, I didn't know I was expected to show a *conciliatory* attitude toward the government," Lydia said in a dangerously low voice which carried easily in the sudden hush that had fallen over the room.

Malcomb turned an odd shade of dusky red, and took a quick gulp of his drink. Jenny plucked nervously at the pearl choker that clasped her throat. The eyes of the colonists, many of whom she had begun to regard as friends, seemed hostile and alien to her. She edged closer to Cab.

"It is late, and I admit that a shuttle trip is tiring for an old man like myself," Furakawa said softly from where he sat on one of the couches. "I think my assistant and I will retire."

"That sounds like a good idea, sir," Weinrod said earnestly. He had been hovering on the periphery of Cabot and Malcomb's conversation all evening. He now revealed his unease by tugging nervously at his superior's sleeve.

"Yes," Malcomb said with a toothy smile to Lydia. "I think we'll turn in, too. It's been a great party, but we don't want to be the guests who didn't know when to leave." He gave Lydia's hand a quick shake but didn't meet her eyes. She gave him an amused look, and forbore to point out that the government lawyers had in fact just arrived.

Huntington sat his glass on a table. "Perhaps it would be better if we broke this up now." He glanced from Angela's hostile face to Malcomb, who sifted nervously from foot to foot. "That way we'll avoid any more wild accusations or unpleasant confrontations."

Angela gave him a level look. "At least not in your courtroom. I wouldn't be so complacent about the rest of the System."

Huntington ignored her, and started for the door. Jenny started to follow only to be caught by Peter. He took her by the elbow and pulled her aside.

"The real party's going to start now," he said quietly. "Why don't you stay?"

She looked seriously up into his face. "Because I don't belong. I'm a stranger, the enemy. You all really hate us. Tonight, for the first time, I realized that."

"Not hate, Jenny, never that."

"Distrust, then, but it could become hate very easily. Look at Angela."

Peter remained silent for several moments, then nodded. "Yes, that's true. I won't deny it. But whether that distrust turns to hate is going to depend on what happens in that courtroom."

"It will be all right, and I stand with Cab."

He released her arm, and raised his hands in a gesture of resignation. "Okay. You stick with your judge. But we'll all be watching, and whether you want to admit it or not, you'll be watching, too."

Jenny tossed fretfully beneath a tangle of bedclothes. At last she sat up and pummeled at a recalcitrant pillow as if the physical assault would still the endless circular speculations that had banished all hope of sleep.

She tossed back the covers and padded barefoot to the wide window with its vista of trees and the empty river bed. The trees were indistinct shadows in the darkness, and the channel of the river could only be guessed at. Wearily she leaned her head against the cool glass, and contemplated the coming day.

At nine tomorrow the hearing for injunctive relief brought by the United States government against U.S. Steel would begin, and there was no doubt that Furakawa would open with a 12(b)(6) motion to dismiss for failure to state a claim upon which relief could be granted.

There was also no doubt that the case should be dismissed. Jenny had read and reread the pleadings in the days since their arrival, and had poured over case law, searching for precedents. There were a few. Unfortunately all of them were very flimsy.

"So Cab will dismiss the case," she said aloud, needing to hear the words.

And if he doesn't?

The unspoken question hung in her mind; that tormenting question that had kept her awake for most of the night. If he didn't dismiss did it prove the collusion between Cab and Justice that Peter suspected? Or would it only be Cab hearing the case to the end so he could write a scathing decision that would forever discourage this kind of unwarranted government interference?

There were no answers to the questions, and finally Jenny

distastefully and reluctantly looked at the final option. What if Cab held for the government against U.S. Steel?

Such a decision would be wrong, and if it came what would she do? Resign? Accept it as part of that very large gray area where most attorneys spend their lives? Stay with him and try to convert him? But convert him to what? She didn't even know what she believed anymore.

Her temples were throbbing with pain, and Jenny realized that the rim had lightened and she could now distinguish the leaves on the outflung branches of the trees. The great secondary mirrors that created night and day in the station were tipping, allowing the sunlight to flow once more into the station.

The new day that she so feared and dreaded had unquestionably begun.

Chapter Six

Through the door of his chambers, Huntington could hear the scrape of chairs, Malcomb's hacking smoker's cough, and the low murmur of spectators come to watch the Fifteenth Circuit in action at last. Cabot stood behind his desk frowning at nothing. Then, realizing that time was passing, he reluctantly gathered up the pleadings for the case, and wished again that he had the nerve to close the proceedings to the public.

He had, of course, rejected the idea. Primarily because he knew a closed hearing would infuriate Tomas, who wanted the case to be a warning to System colonists. He had also rejected the notion because he knew it would be an act of cowardice on his part. He didn't want the residents of the System to see him indulging in creative lawmaking; nor did he want them to see to what lengths his devil's bargain with Tomas would drive him—but he had no choice.

He dropped the papers back onto his desk, and sank into a chair. The chronometer inset in the desk top seemed to reproach him, the glowing numbers glaring balefully up at him. He was already ten minutes late calling the court into session, and yet here he sat shivering in his office.

He knew Furakawa would move to dismiss, and he knew he was going to deny that motion. He even knew how, and it was all good law. He had found it himself because he hadn't been able to face Jenny with the request.

I should have had more guts, he thought. *I should have*

looked her in the eye, and told her I was going to deny the motion and, moreover, grant the injunction. So get out there, Jennifer, and find me the law to support my judgment. I may be an asshole, but, by God, I'll have a decision that squeaks with legal precedent.

But he hadn't said that, he hadn't had the courage, and now God alone knew how she would react. Muttering an oath, he swept up the papers, and stepped to the connecting door between his chambers and the courtroom. It whispered open, and the eyes of the spectators fixed on him. To his oversensitive imagination it felt like a physical blow. Fixing his eyes grimly on the bench, he strode quickly to it, his black gown swishing about his ankles.

"All rise," Jenny called, doubling as she was as both clerk and bailiff.

There was a herdlike scuffling as the lawyers and observers rose to their feet. Huntington dropped into his high-backed chair and gave a nod. The crowd returned to their seats, and silence fell over the room. Cab kept his eyes on the pile of papers before him while Jenny read the name of the case and parties currently before the court. His skin seemed to prickle from the scrutiny of some fifty pairs of eyes, and he felt absurdly small seated in the big chair, like some child involved in a game of dress up.

And aren't you? he thought bitterly. *You're dressed for the part, but it takes more than a rusty black gown to turn a person into a judge. Damn Tomas!* he added for the hundredth useless time.

Jenny had completed her reading, and an expectant hush fell over the assembled people as they waited for him to begin. Cabot shifted to the edge of his chair, and looked down at Malcomb.

"Mr. Malcomb, are you ready to present your prayer for injunctive relief?"

"I am, your honor."

"Then please begin."

"Your honor." Furakawa's dry old voice whispered like dead leaves through the room.

"Yes, Mr. Furakawa?"

"My colleague and I would like to present a motion before Mr. Malcomb begins his learned presentation. It will delay matters only a little, and may very well result in the expediting of this matter."

Cabot tapped a pen on the bench and inwardly cursed the urbane old Japanese-American. He had hoped to forestall any motions to dismiss, but the old fox wasn't going to miss an opportunity to put Cabot on the pin. He took a quick sip of water, and nodded abruptly.

"Very good, Mr. Furakawa. Please make your motion."

Furakawa gestured to Angela Martinez, and she stepped to the bench with a folder. Huntington accepted the motion, and the attorney then handed the second copy to opposing counsel. Furakawa removed his glasses, which were a total affectation, and thoughtfully polished them with a handkerchief.

"As you perceive, my associate has handed you a copy of a 12(b)(6) Motion to Dismiss for failure to state a claim upon which relief may be granted. I do not think it necessary to take the court's time with a long perusal of this document or the arguments in its favor. The case law supporting our motion is easily summarized, and overwhelmingly demonstrates the spuriousness of the government's case."

Malcomb shifted irritably in his chair at Furakawa's denouncement, and Weinrod leaned over to whisper urgently in his superior's ear. Malcomb cut him off with a sharp shake of his head and a chopping gesture with his left hand.

"Your honor," Furakawa continued, "this case represents an unwarranted invasion of the private sector by the federal government, with its only support being a decades-old UN Treaty of questionable validity or application. In the case of *Martin versus Grenfell*, the court held that—"

"Objection," Malcomb said, rising to his feet.

"Sustained," Huntington said without asking Malcomb to elucidate. "Counselor," Cabot said very softly, leaning in over the bench. "It appears to this court that the case is not as clearcut as you would have us believe since you have launched into a discussion of relevant case law. In fact, it appears to this court that you are attempting to argue your case under the guise of a 12(b)(6) motion. Further, despite your arguments to the contrary, the United States government is not acting beyond its authority, and there is ample precedent for this position. I refer you to *Youngstown Sheet and Tube Co.*, which although denying the seizure of the steel plants did in fact indicate that there is such a thing as the "national interest," and that actions may be taken pursuant to it, and *Illinois versus City of Milwaukee* which holds that there is a federal common law. These two cases taken in conjunction establish to my satisfaction that there are issues present which should be litigated."

Furakawa politely inclined his head, but a cynical and knowing smile curved his lips. "May I congratulate your honor on an excellent piece of bootstrapping, but I anticipated that my motion would be something of an exercise in futility."

"Have you anything of *substance* to add, counselor?" His voice had risen, and he struggled to regain his calm.

"No, your honor, I have nothing to add that would be acceptable to you."

"Motion denied."

He slammed down the gavel, and then forced himself to look at Jenny. What he saw in her eyes made him die a little inside. Unable to halt the gesture, he reached out toward her. She jerked her head as if avoiding the invisible touch, and rising, stalked from the courtroom. There was a murmur from the gallery, and Cabot saw Andy Throckmorton leap up and rush out after her. He banged the gavel several more times to restore order, and to relieve his own chaotic feelings. He found himself worrying about what Jenny might say to the journalist. Then he realized that was a pretty inane thought when he had probably ruined for all time whatever it was that they shared.

You can lose their love, you can even lose their friendship, but God help you if you lose their respect, he thought bleakly.

He squeezed his eyes shut, fighting the oncoming headache. With a gesture, he indicated for Malcomb to begin. The Justice Department lawyer rose to his feet in a smooth motion that perfectly reflected an urbane elegance coupled with a deep sincerity and belief in his cause. It was a consummate performance, and Huntington had to admire it. He concentrated desperately on Malcomb's presentation, hoping it would drive from his mind the look on Jenny's face as she had walked from the courtroom.

It was a well-rehearsed speech, but Huntington winced several times over the cases that Malcomb cited as support for the government's position. Their applicability was tenuous at best, but fortunately John had the good sense to skate lightly over them and focus on the necessity of maintaining peaceful world relations, the brotherhood of man, and the dignity of nations. It was an impassioned display, and not one shred of it would stand up under close legal scrutiny.

Furakawa's gnomelike face held an almost beautific expression of smug satisfaction, and Cabot had the desperate feeling that a trap was closing inexorably around him. There was a blinding pain behind his eyes, and he again cursed Tomas for putting him in this impossible situation.

Malcomb concluded and returned to his seat. There was an impatient buzz from the gallery. Furakawa had begun to gather his notes, but Cabot was not prepared to continue with the proceedings just yet. He checked his watch, and noted with relief that it was eleven-fifteen. It was perhaps a bit early to break for lunch, but he doubted anyone would find it odd if he postponed the hearing of U.S. Steel's argument until the afternoon.

"Mr. Furakawa, it is rather late in the morning, and I'm reluctant to have you start only to be interrupted for lunch. Therefore I am recessing this hearing until one o'clock this afternoon. Is that satisfactory?"

"Perfectly, your honor. It is a great comfort to know that you wish to give my presentation such close attention."

"Mr. Malcomb?" Huntington asked, his eyes sliding away from Furakawa's face.

"That's fine, sir."

"Court is recessed until one o'clock this afternoon." He banged down the gavel, then hurried from the courtroom into the safety of his chambers.

After stripping off his robe, he flung it onto a chair, where it hit the back and slithered with a satiny hiss to the floor. He ran his hands agitatedly through his hair, dislodging his wild forelock so it fell across his damp forehead. Sinking down onto the couch, he waited for the court to clear before going in search of his own meal. Not that he was hungry, but he felt he should eat if he were going to make it through the afternoon.

At last he rose and stepped back into the courtroom. There was still one person sitting in the visitors' box, and Huntington realized with a prickle of the hair on the back of his neck that he had been deeply aware of the man all morning, but hadn't really seen him until now. He was dressed in faded gray coveralls which seemed to reflect the gray weariness in his face.

There was a frown of concentration between his thick brows, and he was unwrapping a sandwich with painstaking care. His hands were blunt, rough, and powerful, the hands of a laborer. But it was the pair of eyes that captured and held Cabot, and he realized that those eyes had been riveted on him all morning.

Huntington paused behind the railing that separated the spectators from the lawyers. The man looked up, and his eyes widened at the sight of Cabot, an expression of respect flickering across his face. He rose awkwardly to his feet, and ducked his head several times as if attempting to bow, but uncertain how to execute the maneuver.

He suddenly froze as if realizing how awkward and ludicrous he appeared, and for several moments he and Huntington stood in rapt contemplation of each other. It was Huntington who broke and looked away first, shaken by the desperate plea, the childlike hope and trust shining in the man's eyes. Cabot hunched his shoulders as if against a blow, and rushed from the courtroom.

The room was filled to capacity. People, unable to find a seat in the gallery, stood along the walls or squatted on the floor. From his vantage point on the bench, Huntington could see Lydia Kim Nu standing by the door to the courtroom with Andy next to her. There was still no sign of Jenny. He had returned to their apartment for lunch, hoping to find her there, but the rooms had reproached him with their silent emptiness. His stomach had rebelled at the thought of food, so he had spent the past hour and a half walking tensely through the rim.

And now it was time to begin again. In an hour, perhaps a little more, he would be rendering the decision expected of him by Tomas and, yes, by Malcomb. He knew it would be an unlovely thing: a decision cobbled together out of shaky legal precedent and questionable constitutional validity, but a decision that he firmly believed to be necessary for the democratic well-being of the System as well as the Earth.

He nodded to Furakawa, indicating he could begin his presentation. Furakawa tossed his glasses onto the table and gathered up his notes. There was something in the set of his shoulders and the lines about his mouth as he moved to the podium that made it plain that the old lawyer knew full well the futility of his effort.

Cabot glanced at the gallery, and was arrested by the expression on the face of his lonely watcher. Seen against the backdrop of the well-dressed people of the EnerSun station, it finally struck Cabot who the man must be—Evgeni Feodorovitch Renko. The man could only be the Russian miner who had started this entire mess.

Cabot felt a surge of resentment against the man, as if he could blame him for placing him in this untenable position. He knew it was irrational and unworthy of him, but he welcomed the emotion because it would make it easier to do what had to be done.

An hour passed. Huntington had to admire the way Furakawa demolished the government's case, but it made no difference—could make no difference—in the outcome. Furakawa completed his argument and sat down. There was a spasm of nervous movement through the assembled people, like the shudder of some great beast when it realizes that danger is approaching. It was over quickly, and a deathly silence fell over the room.

Cabot squeezed his eyes shut, praying for strength and calm. In a few minutes it would be all over, and his infamy would be apparent to everyone.

He didn't give a damn about Evgeni Feodorovitch Renko or the U.S. Steel conglomerate. It was his pride that rebelled against this public humiliation and denigration of his name. He groped back, seeking the certainty he had felt that day in the President's office. DeBaca was right, the colonists were out of control, and wasn't this a painless way to take back that control? Far better to sacrifice one small mining colony than risk a confrontation between Earth and System.

He felt reassured and comforted by his conclusions. Opening his eyes, he found everyone regarding him with puzzlement, and he realized with embarrassment that he must have been sitting like a stone effigy for several minutes while he battled through his crisis of conscience. He arranged his hands on top of the pile of papers, and began to speak.

"During the past few hours we have heard arguments by learned counsel for both parties. Mr. Furakawa has argued most persuasively that the Oslo Space Utilization Treaty of 2049 does not address the present situation where a single small operator is selling goods or services, but rather goes to the basic question of the fair usage of the resources of the solar system. I feel that the learned counsel has given too narrow a reading to this treaty, and has also failed to consider the penumbras implicit in the wording of the treaty.

"Mr. Furakawa also argues that the United States government's injunction against U.S. Steel constitutes an unwarranted interference with free trade since this situation cannot be held to fall under the commerce power of Congress. He further argues that this is nothing more than political gamesmanship between the United States and the Soviet Union, and is therefore out of place in this courtroom.

"Although we concede that this case does not fall within the traditional boundaries of the commerce power, we feel that Mr. Furakawa has failed to consider the case of Dresser Industries in 1982, where it was held by a federal court that the federal government could penalize a U.S.-based company for the sale of goods by its foreign subsidiary to the Soviet Union in the face of a trade ban imposed by the President. This would also be 'political gamesmanship' under Mr. Furakawa's definition, yet it was held to be a proper exercise of federal power by the courts of our land.

"This is a difficult case because we are sensitive to the hopes and aspirations of the miners of the Garmoneya Collective. However, their wishes must be weighed against the importance, even necessity, of maintaining a peaceful and harmonious international climate. If countries allow their citizens to undercut one another in this new frontier, order will soon be replaced with chaos.

"Therefore, after due consideration of all these factors, I am compelled to hold in favor of the Justice Department's request enjoining U.S. Steel from further purchases from the Garmoneya Collective. It is so ordered." He brought down the gavel.

There was an explosion of sound as everyone broke into frantic conversation. Kim Nu gave Huntington a level look, shook her head as if greatly disappointed, and then walked out of the courtroom. John Malcomb shook hands with Furakawa, then stepped to the bench.

"Well, Cab, I guess that's it. We'll probably have to fight the next round at the Supreme Court. I'm sure Ken won't give up on this."

Cabot nodded absently, not really hearing what his friend was saying because Andy was leaning over the gallery rail, calling to him.

"Well, I guess we now know what the President's goals and aspirations are for the System. . . . " He paused, and stared sardonically at Malcomb and Cabot. "Although I admit being fucked over by a politico is, I'm sure, not what any of us had in mind."

"How dare you!" Malcomb began.

"Don't worry about it, Mr. Malcomb. It may not be what we had in *mind*, but it sure as hell is what we *expected*."

"Don't pay any attention to him, Cab," John said, reaching up to touch Huntington on the arm.

But Cabot wasn't aware of him for his eyes were on the miner Renko. The man sat numbly while the other spectators pushed past him. His hands were balled tightly in his lap as if he feared he would lose control if he released them. Slowly he raised his head and stared at Huntington.

Cabot felt as if the air had been driven from his lungs. The look from Renko was worse than Jenny's abandonment and Andy's contempt. For the man who faced him was a man without hope, and the terror in his eyes was the terror of a man who has heard the gallows trap fall.

Chapter Seven ‗‗‗‗‗‗‗

"My thanks, Mr. President," Yuri Tupolev said.

"My pleasure, Mr. Premier." DeBaca reached over and took a sip of coffee. The early morning sunlight filtered in through the windows, reflecting off the crystal chandelier that hung in the sitting room, and glinting on the CRT screen where deBaca had been reading the *Post*. The front page contained a picture of Richard Long looking glum in the midst of a snow-covered corn field in Iowa with the caption, LONG CONTINUES TO FALL FURTHER BEHIND. DeBaca smiled with pleasure at the headline, then returned his attention to Tupolev. "But let's not forget that's one you owe me."

"Ah, but the favor is not completely paid. There is still the small matter of discipline."

"I don't think this is the time to be considering such a move. After all, we still have an appeal to the Supreme Court to deal with."

"But, Mr. President, if you allow me to administer the discipline we will not have a problem. It will, as your lawyers say, make the issue moot."

"No Supreme Court hearing?"

"No Supreme Court hearing."

"What is it you need, Tupolev?"

"Simply what I said before, Mr. President. A blind eye."

"I think that can be arranged," deBaca said, tightening the sash on his bathrobe.

• • •

"So it is over," Evgeni quietly concluded. He picked up a mug and took a quick gulp of tea. It scalded the roof of his mouth, but he almost welcomed the pain for it brought tears to his eyes, and for an instant dimmed the faces of the people who stared at him like slaughter-bound oxen.

It was very late by the collective's day/night cycle. Analisa nodded in Irina's arms, and Nessa's seven-month-old son gave an anguished squall. She shifted him to her shoulder, and absently patted his back. Evgeni had forced the parents to bring their children to this meeting for he wanted everyone together when they made the decision that had to be made.

The silence continued, and Evgeni allowed his eyes to rove about the shabby common room where he had shared so many meals, dances, and parties with the other people of the collective. The gray metal walls, battered tables and chairs, and harsh light from the ceiling panels had always filled Evgeni with depression, but tonight it all seemed terribly precious, warm, and safe.

"What's going to happen to us, Evgeni?" Gregori finally asked, his usual rumbling growl reduced to a murmur by his fear.

"They'll come after us. I'm not certain what they will do, but they have to punish us, make an example of us."

An agitated murmur ran through the room, then died away. Cheslav Sukolsky suddenly bolted from the knot of unmarried men who were huddled together in one corner. He advanced stiff-legged to Evgeni, who stood behind a table at the front of the room. His eyes darted furtively about, and his hands clenched and unclenched at his sides.

"And who got us into this, I ask you?" he shrilled, spittle flying from his mouth with the violence of his feelings.

"No need to be dramatic, Cheslav," Evgeni said wearily. "I know I am responsible, but now we must make plans for our survival."

"I have an excellent one," Cheslav said, turning his back on Evgeni and facing the assembled miners. "Let us turn *him* over to the authorities. We'll say it was his idea, and that he forced us. Then they will leave us alone."

"If you believe that you're an even bigger fool than I thought you were," Evgeni said scornfully. He circled quickly around the table, and stepped in front of Sukolsky. "There will be no forgiveness. Our only hope is to flee."

"What are you suggesting?" Sergei asked, releasing his wife Anna's hand.

"I've talked with Irina. She and I are going to take Analisa, and head for the Afrik Combine. The Afrikers are independent and not overly impressed with either the Americans or our government. They will give us sanctuary."

"And how will you travel?" Gregori asked.

"On foot. It is only some fifty kilometers to the Afriker dome, and it will draw less attention than vehicles."

"So you are proposing that we all suit up and stroll across the lunar landscape with our wives and children in tow," Boris said scornfully.

"Yes."

"Well, I for one think you are crazy. My boys are only babies. Besides, I think you are the one who is being overly dramatic. What is the worst that can happen? That they send us back to Earth." Boris looked about the room, nodding at the murmurs of agreement. His wife Natalia clutched at her twin boys, who knuckled their eyes and looked sleepy.

"And I think you are being naive," Evgeni said, filled with a growing desperation at their refusal to face facts. "You know how the commissars work. If spanking a baby is good, spanking it with an ax is even better. We've got to get out of here!" His voice rose for he could see from the blank, hard stares that he wasn't reaching them. The safety, comfort, and familiarity of their home, and their fear of the airless waste outside was turning them from him. Coupled with this was the human capacity for hope. They simply refused to accept that things could be as bad as he described them. Evgeni's shoulders sagged and he stepped back to the table, slumping onto the stained plastic surface.

Cheslav glared at him with angry boar's eyes. "I say we should turn him in as a show of good faith," he snarled.

"No," Gregori said slowly. "No, we will let him do as he wishes. Evgeni and Irina have been our comrades, working and suffering beside us. I will not betray them. If they wish to leave, let them." There were again murmurs of assent, and Cheslav hurried back to join the other single men. There was the whisper of low-voiced conversation.

Evgeni gazed at the familiar faces which had suddenly become strange and alien. They stared at him with flat, hostile eyes, urging him to take his family and his troublesome ideas and go. In that instant Garmoneya seemed suddenly far more attractive and comfortable than he had ever believed possible. Maybe Boris was right and the punishment would be mild. He couldn't leave and face the dangers of the lunar waste and an uncertain welcome at the end of the journey.

His doubts must have been reflected on his face for Irina suddenly stood, settled Analisa on her hip, and marched to the front of the room. She placed Analisa's warm, chubby form in his arms, and looked at him from beneath level brows.

"I want a life, Evgeni," she said gravely, her doe's eyes pleading with him. "You must give me that life."

He buried his face against Analisa's neck, breathing in the rich child scent of her. A shudder ran through his body as he made the last emotional break with the past. Slowly he rose, Analisa cradled in his arms. Irina took his arm and led them toward the door.

"Now! Don't let them go! We can use them!" Evgeni heard Cheslav yell. A heavy weight slammed against his back, and he staggered and dropped Analisa, who gave a wail of terror as she hit the floor.

The little girl's cry, combined with his own desperation, gave him uncanny strength. Reaching over his shoulders he seized the clinging hands, ripped them loose, and sent the miner Pavel flying over his head. It would have been an almost impossible move for him on Earth.

Pavel smashed into the wall of the commons room, and sat spraddle-legged on the floor, groggily shaking his head. Sergei was circling to block the door, but Evgeni didn't have time to deal with him for Vladimir was advancing on him, his great arms making slow circles in the air in front of him. Evgeni eyed the distance, and ducked under Vladimir's outstretched arms, plunging for Cheslav. The cringing, rat-faced man was the leader of the attack, and Evgeni hoped that by taking him out the others would subside.

Irina hauled Analisa up by one hand, and headed for the door. Her usual expression of timidity had been replaced with a militant set of her pointed chin. Sergei made a rush to cut off the woman and child. Rather than fleeing for the door as

Sergei had expected, Irina dropped Analisa's hand and seized a metal chair from a nearby table. Sergei tried to halt his forward rush, but it was too late. He continued to charge forward as Irina thrust the legs of the chair between his legs. He cart-wheeled to the floor, and Irina finished the matter by clouting him firmly with the heavy chair.

Realizing Evgeni's intent, Cheslav had begun to backpedal, trying to get out of range. Vladimir turned and went after Evgeni's unprotected back. With a bull-like roar he crouched and rushed forward to tackle the smaller man. There was a moment of bone-jarring impact, then the floor seemed to rise up and smack Evgeni on the chin. His teeth snapped shut on his tongue, and he tasted the sharp coppery flavor of blood. The pain rose into his head, half blinding and stupefying him. Through a haze he saw Cheslav's booted foot pulling back for the kick that would subdue him. His eyes squeezed shut against the coming blow. It never fell. Instead he heard the smack of a fist connecting like the bite of an ax in wood.

He opened his eyes to see Cheslav sprawled against an overturned chair, blood pouring from his broken nose. Gregori, still massaging his knuckles, was just turning to face Vladimir, who still sat on Evgeni. Vladimir rose, and charged at the burly miner. It was like a clash of buffalo for both were large, barrel-chested men with forearms like knotted branches. Evgeni pushed himself to his knees, wincing at the pain in his ribs.

"Go!" Gregori bellowed. "We will hold them. Go! Go!"

Evgeni staggered to his feet and stumbled for the door. Irina was already partway down the hall, heading for the suit storage room. Analisa pelted breathlessly behind.

They spun around a corner and darted through a sliding door into suit storage. Evgeni feverishly searched through the suits, pulling down two that had had their air, water, and food pellets replenished. They were two of the suits they had bought from the Japanese, and they were wonders of engineering next to the suits that had been supplied from Omsk. Unfortunately Omsk had also not seen fit to supply children's suits, and after the collective had begun to sell to U.S. Steel such a purchase seemed a luxury that could be delayed a few more months. Evgeni was now regretting that decision.

He helped Irina into a small suit, and then tightened the straps to take it in still more. Irina was a small and slender

woman, and the suit still bagged about her. He had selected
one of the largest suits for himself. He began to climb into the
bulky pants when he had a thought.

"Damn! I need some way to strap Analisa to my back."

"I will get something." Irina vanished through the door, and
Evgeni continued dressing. Moments later she was back with
several sheets. Using his teeth, Evgeni tore them into long
strips, and he and Irina arranged Analisa comfortably on his
back. They gave her a sip of water and one of the painkillers
from the suit's MedPac to make her drowsy. Eventually he was
dressed, although he looked like some nightmarish hunch-
backed alien.

They stumped to the air lock and cycled it open. There was
no sound of pursuit, so Evgeni presumed that Gregori and Boris
had held the other men, or they had abandoned their plan to
use him as a bargaining chip. He still believed they were fools
for staying, but in another way he hoped he was wrong—for
their sakes at any rate.

The barrel plain stretched before them. Evgeni made a quick
turn, watching his helmet compass to get his bearings. The
Afriker dome lay in the Montes Apennine northeast of the
collective. They would have to skirt the right outcropping,
the last piece of the Montes Caucasus which hugged the domes,
but at least they wouldn't have to labor over the mountains
themselves. For the moment Evgeni felt fine, charged with a
nervous excitement, but he knew it wouldn't last, and he also
knew that sooner or later Analisa was going to become a bur-
den.

But for now none of that mattered. They were free, and
they were not going to wait passively for their masters to come
and mete out their punishment. Evgeni looked at Irina, then
jerked his head in the direction of the distant Afriker dome.
She nodded, and he settled into a long, ground-eating lope.
None of the women had had very much experience outside of
the domes, but Irina was young and agile, and she soon caught
the rhythm of running under low gravity.

As he bounded along, Evgeni contemplated the possibility
of settling in the asteroids and starting his own mine. It was
an attractive picture, and he allowed the daydream to help him
along.

•   •   •

The Soviet patrol boat slipped wraithlike across the radar screen. The young airman, his round freckled face reflecting the boredom of a man nearing the end of his watch, stared with dull hostility at the intruding graphic. It was nothing new or unusual, Soviet boats often teasingly entered American space in a childish game of "I dare you," but the airman cursed its presence because it meant he had to stare more intently at the glowing screen. He waited patiently for the boat to veer off and return to the Lenin Base, but it kept coming.

Perplexed, the airman risked a glance over his shoulder at his superior who lounged behind a desk. "Lieutenant Williams, I've got a Soviet bogey, only this bird isn't going home. It's continuing across our airspace."

The lieutenant tipped his chair back onto all four legs, lifted his feet off his desk, and crossed to the radar station. An empty coffee mug swung negligently from one finger. He rested one hand on the back of the young airman's chair, and watched the graphic of the Soviet patrol boat continue its steady flight across the screen. Shaking back his sleeve, he checked his watch.

"No problem, McGraw. Resume your watch."

"But, sir, shouldn't we inform—"

"Relax, it's all been cleared."

Uneasy, but unwilling to question any further, the young man returned his attention to the screen. The boat continued its slow progress, then suddenly a small piece separated itself from the body of the boat and arced away.

"Jesus Christ! Lieutenant! Confirm missile fire from Soviet patrol craft!" The young man's voice soared out of its normal baritone range. He reached out and frenziedly began punching coordinates into the computer at the left of the radar screen. "Projected target area is—"

A heavy hand fell on his shoulder. "Leave it, Airman."

He swung around in his chair to face the lieutenant. "But, sir, this is a violation of the treaty. And shouldn't we figure out where that thing is going to hit?"

"Drop it, McGraw. The word came down from upstairs. Don't mess with this boat."

"But, sir," he argued. His eyes rolled back to the screen. He was frightened by the lieutenant's unconcern, and terrified of that deadly line homing in on some unknown target.

"Forget it, Airman." It was a command.

"Yes, sir." Queasy with fear, yet mesmerized by that advancing line, McGraw watched as the missile found its mark.

Other eyes saw the missile find its target. Irina and Evgeni had reached the edge of the outcropping which hugged the collective. Another few steps would take them past its rocky point, which would block forever their view of the domes which had been their home for the past seven years. There was no need for words. They both stopped and looked back, pausing for one final farewell to the life and people they had known.

Out west, and some twenty-five hundred feet up, sunlight glinted off aluminum paneling. Frowning, Evgeni flipped down the magnifying faceplate, and concentrated on that brief flash of light. It came into focus, a snub-nosed, wide-bodied craft that skimmed along some twenty kilometers from the collective. Patrol boat, Evgeni identified, and he watched, waiting for it to land and disgorge the troops he had been expecting.

Instead it seemed to belch, shuddering briefly from the force of the missile launch. The propellant rockets in the tail of the missile ignited with a hellish orange glow, and the patrol boat turned in a tight arc and raced back south, not even waiting to see the missile do its work. Evgeni grabbed Irina, and jerked her behind a jumble of rocks. They dropped to the ground, and he pulled her face tight against his chest. They huddled together, eyes squeezed shut, and sensed rather than heard the deep-throated rumble as the nuclear warhead detonated on the rocky surface of the moon. The ground heaved slightly beneath them, and it was over.

Evgeni rose cautiously from behind the boulders, and looked back at the collective. His gaze was obscured by a rapidly falling cloud of dust, but he could just make out the ragged edges of a new manmade crater, which had joined the ancient pockmarks of the moon.

Evgeni became aware of an ache in his fingers where he desperately gripped Irina's shoulders, and her dry sobs filled his ears. He released her, and took two quick steps back toward the collective.

"Murderers!" he screamed, shaking his fist after the dwindling boat. "Filthy murderers!" His voice broke on the last word, and he felt tears burning behind his eyes, forming an aching lump in his throat. Analisa stirred restlessly on his back, murmuring in her sleep. Irina's hand gripped his shoulder.

"Come," she said firmly. "We must go."

"But our friends," he said weakly, indicating the still-roiling dust storm.

"Are dead. And if we are to survive we must not think of going back. Now come." She turned and strode resolutely away, vanishing around the point of the outcropping. Evgeni wavered, took one final look at what had been his home, and followed.

The hours passed. Evgeni found that with both he and Analisa using the air, the supply dwindled far faster than he had anticipated. They stopped, and Irina dropped a fresh cannister into his Evac unit. Her oxygen was holding up much better than his so they still had two extra cannisters. He hoped it would be enough. He sucked on the water nipple, allowing himself one swallow. He wished there were some way he could give the child a drink, but it was impossible.

His radio babbled and chattered with the endless conversations that crisscrossed the Moon. While they traveled, he had been constantly scanning the frequencies, checking for signs of pursuit. None had come, and he realized that the authorities believed that everyone had died in the destruction of the collective. As he started to chin off the radio, since it was no longer necessary, a news bulletin penetrated the tired haze that seemed to have wrapped itself about his brain.

"Soviet Lunar control has today reported the tragic destruction . . ."

"Irina listen. Band five," Evgeni ordered.

". . . Garmoneya Mining Collective in a freak meteor hit. There were no survivors, and this tragedy once more points out how fragile and vulnerable—"

Evgeni cut the connection, and anger and hate rose through his body like a burning wave. His exhaustion lifted, and he raged back and forth, dust rising in small puffs from beneath his booted feet.

"Liars!" he shouted.

"What else did you expect?" Irina asked quietly. "For them to admit to their crime?"

"But their crime will be discovered for there *are* survivors! We will tell the world of their perfidy."

"And what of the American perfidy?"

Her words brought him up short, and he halted his agitated

pacing. He stared at the empty blackness of her faceplate, and considered the horrible truth in what she had said. The Americans had to have known of the Soviet attack. In fact the attack could not have come without their knowledge and tacit approval. His rage died leaving a cold, gut-knotting anger.

"They will pay," he said simply, and they set off once more across the Mare Serenitatis.

They continued their march, and Evgeni, stumbling in weariness, decided that he had been a madman. It had all seemed so simple—a walk to the Afrik Combine—in the warmth and safety of the domes. Now the reality was becoming a nightmare, and a potentially deadly one.

Analisa had begun to whimper with thirst and the pain of her uncomfortable position, but after a while even those small cries died away. She was now an inert mass, dragging Evgeni to the ground. They had stopped to replace the tanks, and now both he and Irina were breathing off only one cannister. Irina had toiled on in stoic silence, but her breaths were beginning to sound more like gasping sobs as she struggled on behind him. She staggered and sank toward the ground.

Evgeni awkwardly spun and caught her around the waist, holding her erect. Desperately he scanned the horizen, searching for some sign of the Afriker dome, but the jagged mountains blocked his view. Nothing but glare and shadows met his straining eyes.

He shifted Irina in his grasp and began to plod ahead, encouraging her with hoarsely whispered endearments. She moved forward like a zombie. They mounted another hill, and looked down into a valley filled with smooth white domes. Small ground cars darted through the domes like crazed insects scurrying through a field of exotic mushrooms.

There was the taste of copper in Evgeni's parched mouth, and his lungs labored, sucking at the nearly dry air tank. His left arm shivered with strain, and Irina almost slipped from his desperate hold.

There, he thought. I've seen it, but it's too far to walk so we'll just rest here. At least we saw it.

He sank down to the ground, cradling Irina's head in his lap. There was a sudden flare of resentment as he squinted down at the station.

If you die on this hill, who will avenge Gregori and Nessa, and Boris and Natalia, and all the rest?

Someone will do it.

Who? There is no one left but you.

This inner, demanding conscience, which he hadn't even known he possessed, had somehow attained human proportions and seemed to be seated next to him on the hard stony ground, goading him on.

All right, all right, he thought wearily.

He chinned on the radio to emergency broadcast, and began to call for help. Several of the scurrying ground cars jerked to abrupt halts, and Evgeni began to giggle for he could almost picture quiveringly alert antennae as the insects searched for the intruders. A gray fog was obscuring his vision, and he could no longer hear his own voice. He slipped away into a warm, dark world of peace and rest.

Chapter Eight _____

It seemed to take hours to climb up through the curtains of darkness that had held him bound in confines of his own mind. If it had been a place of rest and comfort he might have tried to stay there, but it had been a frightening, kaleidoscopic world where the faces of his comrades came rushing out of the blackness to scream soundlessly at him, and where brilliant, colorful explosions ate at the surface of the moon, sending blossoms of dust spiraling into the lunar night. As it was, he was just as pleased to leave.

Slowly Evgeni became aware of his surroundings. He was lying on his side in a very comfortable bunk, covered with a soft blanket. Above him he could hear the whisper of a ventilation system pumping air through a building. But which building? The last thing he recalled was looking down on the Afriker domes.

He carefully opened his eyes, almost fearful of what he would see. An older man was seated in a chair, quietly watching him. Evgeni sat up abruptly, the blanket slipping down to his waist. A wave of dizziness sent black dots dancing behind his eyes, and his head seemed to be trying to float off his shoulders. He realized he was nude beneath the cover, and he settled quickly back down, pulling the blanket up to his chin.

The man gave a low laugh. "Not to worry. You were in pretty tough shape when they brought you in here. Getting you nightclothes seemed a minor issue when compared to treating you for oxygen deprivation."

"Who are you? And where is my wife? My daughter?"

"They're either having a meal or at the playground. Amazing, isn't it, how quickly our better halves recover from stress or trauma."

Evgeni stared hostilely at the man. He had no idea why he was here or what he wanted or why he was nattering on about the nature of women. The man smiled, deepening the creases in his bronzed face.

"You're probably wondering why they sent some senile old man in to pester you. If it's any comfort to you, I may be old, but I'm not senile—at least not yet. And to answer your first question, I'm Joseph Reichart."

The name was not unknown to Evgeni. Even in the workers' paradise, Reichart's name had become synonymous with independence and resistance in the System.

"Mr. Reichart, forgive my rudeness." He cautiously sat up in the bed, propping himself against the back wall. "I am not myself."

"I would be very surprised if you were. Whatever possessed you to set off across the lunar landscape?" The question was casually asked, but Reichart watched Evgeni closely.

The miner stared down at the top of the blanket and nervously pleated the material between his fingers. "I do not understand why you are interested. I am nothing, only a Soviet miner."

"You talked a lot when you were first brought in. Some of the things you said were very interesting so von Lutz called me. I did a little digging and discovered that you were the miner who led that short-lived revolt at the Garmoneya Collective. Now I hear the collective has been destroyed by a meteor, and the Russians are claiming there are no survivors. This seems an interesting contradiction since here you are, and you are manifestly a survivor."

"We were lucky," Evgeni mumbled. Now that he was safely at the Afriker dome, his need for vengeance had subsided. He had tested the power of the governments once before and with disastrous results. Why should he try it again? He was one small man with the two mightiest nations on Earth ranged against him. If they thought he was dead, so much the better. It would be safer that way.

"Or you were smart," Reichart said. Evgeni darted his eyes at the older man, then looked quickly back down at the blanket. "Like I said, you talked a lot when you were first brought in." Reichart fished about in a pocket of his coat.

"What is it you want me to say?"

"I want you to tell me what happened out there."

"Why?"

"What they did was barbaric."

"Since you already know about it why do you need me?"

"I need you to prove it."

"They think I am dead. It is better if I remain so."

"What do you want, Evgeni?" Reichart asked as he pulled out a pipe and tobacco pouch, then methodically began to fill the pipe.

"I . . . I don't know what you mean."

"For your family, the future."

"Peace," he said quietly, dropping his head to stare down at his folded hands.

"Sorry, I can't promise you that. Why don't you be a little more specific."

Evgeni looked bitterly at the American. "All right, I'll tell you what I want! I want a home beyond the reach of the commissars and the hypocritical Americans. A place where I can work and earn a living for my child. A place where I can be free and keep what is mine. Now see if you can promise me that, Mr. Reichart!"

"I can't promise you'll work—only you can do that—but I can offer you the opportunity. I have large holdings in the asteroids. If you want a chance to mine out there, I can give it to you." He paused to light a match and puff the pipe into life. "But it's a quid pro quo world, or ought to be , so if I do this for you I'll want something in return."

"And that is?"

"Your help. I intend to nail the men who authorized this atrocity."

"Why? Why should you care?"

Reichart smiled slightly, but it was a grim expression that never reached his eyes. "Aside from the fact I hate barbarism,

I've been waiting for a chance like this for the past twenty years."

"What for?"

"I need something to prove to the people of the System that the Earth authorities are not their friends, and that it's time we started dealing with them as equals rather than supplicants."

"What would I have to do?"

"Make a statement. Demand justice. I'll handle the rest."

"I have seen an example of your *justice*. I'm not certain I wish to try it again."

"Your presence will make it impossible for Cabot Huntington to rig this decision. The world will be watching. He'll have to rule with fairness and impartiality."

"And what if my *presence* is removed? The kind of men who would nuke helpless people would not hesitate to kill me."

"You'll be on my station. No one can reach you there. The people who live on my station are trustworthy, and I can see to it that no one else is allowed to dock." He gave an ironic smile. "That's one of the advantages to being a truly private citizen."

"You would give me my own mine?"

"I'll get you to the asteroids, I'll help you stake a claim, and I'll set you up with enough equipment to get you started. After that you're on your own."

Evgeni stared at the far wall. He had stuck his head up out of the pack once, drawn the attention of the great and powerful, and the result had been the deaths of his friends and companions. He didn't see how he could risk it again. At least he now enjoyed total anonymity. No one would hunt a dead man.

On the other hand a dead man had very little future. He had no assets aside from the clothes on his back, and the suit which had carried him across the moon to safety. As a day laborer in the South African base, he would be hard pressed to give Analisa the opportunities he craved for her. It would be harsh and brutal in the asteroids, but the rewards to be gained were high, and here sat a man with the power to give him his dream. All he needed was the courage to once more rise above the common denominator, and be counted as an individual. And if Reichart could indeed protect him, where was the risk?

He was still frightened, terribly frightened, by what this

man was asking of him, but he realized he could not refuse. His own personal desires aside, Reichart was offering him the chance to avenge his friends and companions. His cowardice could not be allowed to stand in the way of that.

He looked at Reichart. "I will do what you wish."

"Excellent. I'll send your family in to you, and we'll leave as soon as you're ready. The sooner we're on my station, the happier I'll be."

"Not as glad as I will be," Evgeni said, a spark of humor beginning to show as his spirits lifted.

"I'm sure." Reichart rose from the chair and crossed to the door. "I'll send someone in an hour or so. I'm sure you and your wife have a few things to discuss, and I need to talk to von Lutz."

"Yes, sir."

He stared at the closed door for several moments, then threw back the cover and bounded from the bunk. He regretted the precipitous move almost instantly for the wave of dizziness once more assailed him, but even the physical discomfort could not dampen the sense of excitement which gripped him. A few minutes ago he had been a frightened, cowardly, and hopeless man. Now, thanks to Joseph Reichart, his nerve had returned, and he had a future worth contemplating.

"Mr. President," Michael Dobson, Chief of White House Operations, called as he stuck his head in the door of the Oval Office. He was a slender, efficient-looking man with pale gray eyes, and pale blond hair cut drill sergeant short.

"Yes, what is it?" deBaca's brows drew together in irritation. He hated to be interrupted during meetings. The President sprawled in his chair while the other occupants of the Oval Office sat in a respectful semicircle in front of his desk.

The other people in the room looked up in surprise at Dobson's uncharacteristic intrusion. They were Attorney General David Reynolds, Dana Edwards of Health and Human Services, Taylor Moffit from State, and several White House staffers. It was a cold and blustery late September day, and the light filtering in through the French windows was a dull slate-gray.

Dobson stepped farther into the room. "I just got a rather strange and cryptic call from Joe Reichart."

"That asshole specializes in being cryptic. What the hell does he want?"

Dobson frowned. "He didn't seem to want anything, sir. He just said, 'if I were you I'd have the President turn on the television. There's going to be a statement that I think he'll find interesting.'"

"That's it?"

"Yes, sir."

DeBaca exchanged glances with his aides. "Anybody know what this is all about?" Heads shook, and the President sighed. "Okay, let's see what that rabble-rouser is up to now."

He pulled out a drawer, revealing a complex control panel, and flipped several switches. With a quiet hum, a five-foot screen slid out of the ceiling and clicked to a halt at eye level for the person occupying the desk. The staffers adjusted their chairs, and Dobson moved unobtrusively to one wall where he could watch.

The screen came on, showing Joe Reichart seated at a long table. The wall behind the table was a dull, gun-metal gray, but several fine southwestern paintings broke the monotony. Reichart lifted his head and stared seriously into the camera.

"My friends, never before in a career filled with flamboyant gestures have I, as a private citizen, called for a news conference. The networks have been kind enough to grant me this time, and I thank them." Joe shifted slightly in his chair, and leaned in on the camera.

"Only an event of the gravest importance could have driven me to such an action, and indeed an act of horrifying barbarism has occurred. I have called for this news conference so that the truth concerning this event may be revealed and the men who perpetrated it are punished.

"Three days ago there was a newscast concerning the tragic destruction of a small Soviet lunar mining collective by a meteor hit."

A rhythmic *tick*, *tick*, *tick* filled the office as deBaca began to flip a pen over and over between his fingers, allowing it to tap the desk on each turn. Moffit glanced over his shoulder at the President, and was shocked by the white, frozen expression on the man's round face.

"It was more of a tragedy than anyone knew, for there was

no meteor shower. The people of the Garmoneya Mining Collective were brutally murdered, and there is a survivor to prove it. I now turn the remainder of this news conference over to Evgeni Feodorovitch Renko."

There was an inarticulate sound from the desk, and deBaca fell back in his chair. Dobson quickly filled a glass of water, and rushed to the President. Edwards and Reynolds also moved swiftly to the desk, Edwards to loosen deBaca's tie, and Reynolds to phone the White House doctor. The three staffers muttered in bewilderment, and Taylor Moffit stared fixedly at the screen. He tasted bile, and struggled to force away the rising sickness.

Evgeni Renko glanced nervously off to his left as if seeking support. He nodded jerkily, then faced the cameras.

"The liars on Earth have said that my friends died because of a meteor shower, but that is not true." Evgeni paused, his fingers twisting through one another. He drew in a deep breath. "They died because they dared to challenge the authority of their masters groundside. The United States and the Soviet Union, not content with taking our livelihood from us, also took our lives. I survived only because I suspected such treachery, and I was fleeing with my family to the Afrik Combine. We were only kilometers from the collective when I saw the patrol boat. I also saw the missile which killed my friends and companions." For the first time since the broadcast had begun, Evgeni looked directly into the cameras. His voice lost its timorous, breathy quality, and gained in strength and power.

"It was a Soviet finger on the button that destroyed my friends, but they could never have done this act in stealth and secrecy if they had not had help from the Americans.

"I have requested and received sanctuary from Mr. Reichart, and now I call upon the United Nations and the peoples of the world to punish this terrible act."

He unfolded a small piece of paper which had been concealed in the palm of his hand. "I therefore demand that an international hearing be held before the federal court of the Fifteenth Circuit of the United States to act upon this violation of United Nations Treaty 1423 prohibiting the use of nuclear weapons on the Moon."

Reichart stepped smoothly back into camera range. "That

concludes this broadcast," he said simply, and the screen went dark.

Dobson leaned forward and switched off the television. A deathly hush, like the kind that fill funeral homes and mortuaries gripped the Oval Office. Suddenly a crystal tumbler smashed against the left wall. Everyone jumped and looked at deBaca, who had risen and was staring at the empty screen, an expression of fury twisting his face.

"Goddamn him!" he said in a low voice. "He's been trying to ruin me for twenty years, but I'll be damned if he's going to succeed this time either."

"Surely, Mr. President," Edwards from HEW began, "an investigation will reveal that we had nothing—"

"Oh, don't be an asshole, Dana." The woman blanched. DeBaca jerked an arm at the other people. "Out, all of you get out of here." The three staffers and Edwards scurried out of the door, and Dobson, Moffit, and Reynolds began to follow. "Not you three. I need you."

Taylor Moffit continued toward the door. "No, Tomas," he said quietly as he took the door handle. "You may need me, but I don't think I can work for you any longer."

"So, you're ratting out on me."

"I warned you three weeks ago that this could blow up in our faces. Well, it has, and I have no desire to stay around and help you sift through the debris. You'll have my resignation within the hour." The door closed softly behind him.

"So what the hell are you staring at?"

Reynolds quickly averted his eyes.

"Are you going to resign, too?"

The Attorney General made an inarticulate sound, then shook his head in a quick negative.

"Good," deBaca said, thrusting a finger at him. "Now get back over to Justice and get started on this mess."

"We're going to have to take part in this hearing?"

"Of course we're going to have to take part!" the President shouted. "What are you, some kind of idiot?"

"But if it's a Soviet matter," Reynolds said feebly.

"You stupid fucker!" DeBaca swung around to gaze out at the rose garden.

Dobson took Reynolds by the elbow, and propelled him

firmly toward the door. "I think what the President is suggesting is that you take a good look at a lunar atlas," he concluded smoothly as he urged the Attorney General over the threshold. He then shut the door, leaned against it, folded his arms across his chest and stared at the President.

"We're in shit, Mike."

"Up to our eyebrows."

"We'll have to take part in that hearing. Within fifteen minutes every news service in the world will have discovered that that Soviet boat had to fly across an American military installation to reach that collective."

"Is there anyway to trace it back to you?"

"No, the orders went out in a very vague form. At the worst it will only look like some kind of foul-up in communication. I'll sacrifice anyone, right up to the Secretary of Defense, to keep this away from the White House."

"Hope it works," Dobson said as he crossed to the hidden bar, and then poured himself a drink. "'Cause otherwise we can just kiss the election good-bye."

"You don't sound very hopeful."

"I'm not paid to be. I'm paid to stamp out brush fires, not ignore them."

"Can you stamp this one out?"

"It would be easier if that Russian weren't holed up on Reichart's station."

"Do you see a way to get him out?"

"Two or three, but we'll need Defense."

"Then get Tolucci over here, and do it. Meantime, go out and give Goldstein something to appease the press."

"And after that?"

The President turned slowly back from the window. "Do you have much faith in prayer?"

"No, not much."

"Neither do I, so let's see about putting our faith in Cab."

The telecom chimed, and Cabot flung himself off the couch, answering it before the first signal had faded. "Hello, hello! Jenny?"

"Sorry to disappoint you," came Lydia's voice as her image settled on the screen. "I think you better turn on the television. There's going to be an announcement that you need to hear."

He swallowed his disappointment, and slipped the impassive mask back into place. "An announcement of what?"

"Just turn it on."

"Must be something rather important if it caused you to call me. Our communication has been somewhat limited up until now."

"I don't have time to discuss our relationship right now. Just turn on the set." She broke the connection.

Cabot walked slowly back to the sofa, and stretched out on the cushions. Lifting the remote, he switched on the wall screen. Ten minutes later he stood in the bathroom rinsing the taste of vomit from his mouth. He leaned forward over the basin, and studied his face in the mirror. It didn't look that much different from the face that had looked out at him that morning. The same narrow features, high cheek bones, and upswept brows reflected back at him from the glass. But there was a difference. There was a shadow of horror and guilt in the smokey gray eyes.

Killer, he thought, staring down at his hands where they gripped the edge of the stainless-steel basin. *What kind of society allows a criminal to sit in judgment on the innocent? No, no use to blame society. This guilt rests on me. Yes, and on Tomas and Malcomb, and all the rest of us great men. Here's an academic puzzle for you, Cabot, my man. You like theory so much. What judge not only rigged a case, but by his decision condemned twelve people to death?*

He began to laugh, a high, brittle sound that broke into a harsh sob. Horrified and embarrassed by his lack of control he bit down hard on his lower lip.

Tears are for more common individuals, Cabot. People in our position haven't the time to behave in such a self-indulgent fashion. Please remember it.

His mother's voice echoed in memory, and suddenly he was seven with a broken tooth and a bloody face, hiding in the bathroom of the West County Hunt Club after taking a spill from his pony. He buried his face in his hands, and wished that all pain could be that transitory and easily cured.

He slowly straightened and walked stiffly into the kitchen. There he filled a bucket with ice, took a tumbler and a bottle of Scotch out of the cabinet, and returned to the front room. Depositing the load on a table, he methodically arranged the table and a chair in front of the wide picture window with its view of the empty river bed.

He marked the passage of time by the fall of the level of liquor in the bottle. Sort of a reverse hourglass, he thought foolishly as the telecom chimed again.

It had begun to signal over three hours ago, and it had continued without letup almost every ten minutes. At first it had irritated Cabot, but now he was past such petty annoyances. It provided only a discordant counterpoint to his tormented thoughts. The chiming stopped, and he carefully poured another drink, waiting for it to resume. It didn't. Silence filled the apartment, heavy, impenetrable, frightening.

He tossed back the drink, shuddering a bit as it went down. "So quiet," he whispered, as if "quiet" were a living creature that would leap out and rend him if it suspected his presence.

It had been quiet for days. Ever since Jenny had walked out of the courtroom and never returned. Quiet, empty, sterile. He stood and clutched at the back of the chair for support. Cautiously, teetering a bit, he moved to her bedroom. It was quiet and empty, too. Very empty, for her belongings were gone.

Cabot returned to his chair, and sat staring out the window. The sunlight began to retreat as the secondary collecting mirrors began their slow tilt into nightfall.

"No sunsets," he said aloud, thinking of the fires that had lit the sky over the Pacific Ocean, and the view he had had from his home in Carmel. "No sunsets," he repeated, and the statement struck him as extraordinarily melancholy. He sniffled a bit, and fished for a handkerchief.

He sat for several more minutes, then nodded, rose, and headed for the door. The telecom started ringing as he reached it. He ignored it and, closing the door behind him, made his way to the AVC stop.

Fifteen minutes later he stood in front of Peter Traub's door. Stepping forward, he leaned on the bell. The buildings of EnerSun were well insulated and he couldn't hear if anything was happening, so he continued to hold down the bell. The door slid open, and Peter stood framed in the opening, clinching a bathrobe about his waist.

"Yes? Oh." He glanced over his right shoulder back into the apartment.

"Is Jenny here? I've come to talk to her."

"No, she's not here," Peter said, stepping back and thumbing the door switch. The panel began to slide closed.

"What is it, Peter? Who's there?" Cabot heard her voice calling from somewhere in the apartment.

"Jenny!" he yelled, and lurched forward as the door settled in its groove. "Jenny!" He continued to shout her name, and accompanied the shouts by pounding on the metal surface of the door. The door opened, and Jenny stood there, arms folded across her chest, her face cold.

"You're drunk!"

"And you're not dressed." Cab stared stupidly at the shadowed vistas of neck and breast revealed by the inadequately buttoned man's shirt, and at the length of bare legs thrusting from beneath the flapping tail.

Jenny flushed and bit her lip in vexation. "What do want?" she asked, infusing the words with steel.

"You went away."

"It's brilliant of you to notice. Yes, I did."

"And you didn't come back."

"That's right."

"Why did you do that?"

She flung her hands into the air, and paced away into the apartment. Cabot followed. Peter was no where to be seen. "Well, why do you think?" she demanded flinging herself onto a couch.

"Don't make me answer that," he said in a muffled voice, and turned away.

"Is that how you're going to handle it? Ignore it? Pretend it didn't happen? That you didn't hand down a decision that led to the deaths of twelve people?"

"I didn't do it! They might have killed them anyway! It's not my fault!"

"Strange to think I worked with you for five years, and knew so little about you." Jenny said, rising slowly to her feet. "I suppose it's often that way, though. We never see the flaws in a person that we love until we're forced to it." She stood silently for several moments, not looking at him. "Better call your friend Malcomb at Justice, and have him send you a new clerk. I'm finished."

"Jenny!"

It was more a cry of agony than a speaking of her name,

and it cut through her resolve. The decision, so carefully arrived at in the dark hours of sleepless nights, failed before the misery and despair in his voice, and she knew she could not leave him.

"Jenny," he said again, and held out his arms to her. She moved into his embrace, feeling odd at this sudden shift in their relationship.

During their years in practice they had scrupulously avoided any hint of personal involvement. At most, Cabot might have touched her shoulder as they researched together in the library, or taken her elbow as a gesture of courtesy when entering a room. Now, as his arms closed about her, a thrill, consisting of equal parts of excitement and dread, ran through her body.

She stood awkwardly in the circle of his arms, not knowing what to do with herself. His head dropped to rest on her shoulder, and she felt tears dampening the material of her shirt as he wept soundlessly. She was shocked and frightened by this breakdown of a man whose control and self-possession were legendary. Hesitantly she reached up and stroked his hair.

"Jenny, I'm . . . I'm going to be sick," he suddenly gasped.

"In here," she said, seizing him by the shoulders and propelling him to the bathroom. He kicked the door shut behind him, and she moved quickly into the bedroom to change.

"You're going back," Peter said, and it wasn't a question.

"Yes," she said, pulling clothes out of the closet and unbuttoning the shirt. "I have to." She dressed quickly and retrieved her suitcase. Peter silently handed her her clothing, watching while she packed.

"You're not arguing with me," she said at last.

"You know your own mind. I won't insult you by arguing with you. May I say though," he said, removing a handful of underwear from her hands and pulling her into his arms. "That I enjoyed every moment."

Her body molded to his now-familiar form, and she rubbed her cheek against his chest. "You act as if it's over. Just because I'm going back to work with Cab doesn't have to change things."

"We'll see," he said softly, and kissed the top of her head.

She pulled back and looked up at him. "What's going to happen now?"

"You're asking me?" he said with a smile. "I would say things are very much in yours and Huntington's hands. You're the representatives of law and order in the System now, remember?"

"Don't joke, Peter. Look what happened the last time the circuit handed down a decision." She slammed down the top of her case and sealed it. "We're frauds, and everyone knows it now."

"Then you'd better develop some credibility, and quickly, because there's no one else to prevent a major break between Earth and the System."

"And just what would that entail?"

"Better we not find out," he said, and his face was grim.

"Feeling better?" Jenny asked as Cab came dragging into the kitchen. His eyes were bloodshot, and a day's growth of beard shadowed his cheeks. He watched her drop sliced strawberries onto a bowl of cereal, and gave a delicate shudder.

He chewed experimentally on the taste in his mouth, grimacing. "I'll live, but I'm still not sure if I want to." He pulled out a stool and sank down at the breakfast counter.

"Do you want something to eat?"

"No," he said quickly. "Just some coffee."

"You know where it is," she said, pouring milk over the cereal, then seating herself at the counter.

"I think our relationship has just taken a fundamental shift," Cab said as he prepared the coffeemaker.

"Why? Because I won't make coffee for you?"

"You always used to."

"That's true, but I also used to work for you."

"You don't work for me now?"

"No."

"Then what are you doing here?"

She dropped her spoon into the soggy mass in the bowl, sighed, and shook her head. "Damned if I know."

"Jenny, you can't walk out on me now. I need you for this hearing."

"Why? You seem to be perfectly capable of rigging decisions on your own. You don't need my help."

He slammed the measuring scoop onto the counter, and turned to look at her. "That was uncalled for!"

"Don't growl at me, I'm not impressed! And if it wasn't rigging perhaps you would care to tell me *what* it was? There was no support for what you did. Peter was right, you were in collusion with Justice, and I was too stupid to see it!"

"Don't I have a side in this, or are you so certain of my guilt that you won't even listen?"

"You're going to have to make it pretty damn good, Cabot." She dumped her bowl into the disposal/washer unit. "Because I've received five calls from the White House and six from the Justice Department before I finally turned off the telecom. I haven't noticed Evgeni Renko clogging the comnet to get in touch with you. Your friends in government must be pretty damn anxious to lock down your support."

"And they're not going to get it," Huntington said quietly. He quickly lifted a hand to forestall any comment on her part. "Don't mistake me. This doesn't mean I'm embracing the colonists' brand of revolution. It just means I'm not willing to play Tomas's game any longer. The men who are responsible for this atrocity will be punished," he smiled crookedly. "Myself included. Now, have I still got a law clerk?"

She stared at him for a long moment, then nodded. "Yes, Cab, you do." He held out his hand to her, and she stepped to him closing her hands around his. "So what do we do now?" she asked after several moments.

"This is going to have to be handled very carefully. I can't just call up deBaca and tell him to fuck off. We're going to have to keep the people groundside guessing, and for that we need Joe Reichart."

"How so?" Jenny asked with a frown.

"You have no idea of the level of anxiety groundside. If Tomas thinks he's totally lost his ace he may react violently, and whatever form his reaction takes it won't be pleasant for the colonists. Reichart is orchestrating this thing, and since I'm now going to be playing in the orchestra rather than acting like a dissonant tone on the outskirts of the music, we better get our acts together."

"He won't accept an overture"—she winced at her inadvertent pun—"from you. Lydia and Reichart are very close. I think you should talk to her first."

"You're probably right." He ruefully shook his head. "I guess my self-imposed punishment is going to start a little sooner than anticipated."

"What do you mean?"

"Eating crow in front of Lydia Kim Nu was one of the ways I was going to try and atone for what happened."

Jenny smiled. "It won't taste any better the longer it sits. Go get dressed, and I'll call Lydia and set up an appointment."

"I never thought I'd be welcoming you to my office," Lydia said, leaning across her scrupulously neat desk, and extending her hand.

"And I never thought I'd be working with you, Ms. Kim Nu," Cabot responded, shaking the proffered hand. The office was spartan, with simplistic chrome and plastic furnishings. Only two touches relieved the work-oriented, no-nonsense atmosphere: On one corner of the desk sat a tremblingly delicate flower arrangement in an etched crystal vase, and hanging near Kim Nu's large chair was a wind chime consisting of seven crystal spheres, each hanging in its own silver ring. Occasionally a current of air from the ventilation system set the chime in motion, and a breathless, tinkling music resulted.

"I suppose that's the issue, isn't it," Lydia said, resuming her seat and motioning Cab into a nearby chair. "How much we want our truce, however temporary or permanent it may be, known outside of this circle."

"By this circle I presume you mean Mr. Reichart."

"Among others," Lydia said without volunteering more.

Huntington stared thoughtfully at the blue-green Earth just swinging into view on the view screen behind the manager's desk. "Tomas C. deBaca is not a man you cross with impunity. He responds to a direct challenge like a bull to a red flag."

"Meaning you don't want to be the target of his attack."

"I didn't say that. I just think we ought to carefully consider our moves before we make them. I've told Jenny, and I'll tell you: I'm no rebel. The fact that I'm in this office doesn't mean that I approve of your attempts to separate yourselves from Earth control."

"Then why are you here?"

His expression hardened. "Because I don't like being used."

"You were perfectly willing to serve the government's interests when you came up here."

"No one had died then."

"So oppression is okay, but you draw the line at murder?" Huntington's eyes flinched away from hers. "If that's how you feel it must be characterized. I don't view it as oppression, but rather the proper exercise of governmental power."

"All right," Lydia said with a quick gesture as if brushing away a troublesome insect. "We won't argue semantics. I'll let time and experience educate you for me. Meanwhile, what do we do now?"

"I can present a certain level of stiffness and outrage to Tomas, he'll expect that from me, but I think it best if he not realize the depth of my revulsion. As long as he thinks I'm still on his team I can render a decision on this UN hearing without interference."

"Then we better give him another target to hold his attention while you do your work. Joe will probably be best for that. He loves to enrage people. Waving a red flag at the President of the United States will amuse him."

"Then he's got a damn strange sense of humor," Cabot muttered, thinking of the power residing at 1600 Pennsylvania Avenue, which could be exercised at the press of a button.

Lydia seemed to sense his doubts. She smiled. "You're worrying. Don't. The authorities would never directly confront Joe. They haven't got the nerve."

"I hope you're right." He pushed out of his chair. "Well, I've been incommunicado long enough. It's time I answered those frantic calls from Justice and the White House, and I'll set things in motion for the hearing."

"And then?"

He paused at the door and looked back. "And then certain people are going to have their noses rubbed in that mess they made on the Moon," he said, his eyes narrowing with anger.

"Yourself included?"

"Don't worry, Ms. Kim Nu. You'll have your satisfaction."

Chapter Nine _____

The last slanting rays of sunlight filtered through the gold and rust leaves of the beech tree outside the study window, and struck fire from the facets of the crystal decanter on the desk top. The open window also brought the spicy, comforting scent of burning leaves. Ever since they had repealed the Clean Air Act, deeming it unnecessary as electric and air cars replaced gas-powered vehicles and the last heavy industry moved off-world, cities and towns had once again been filled with the heralding smell of fall. Taylor Moffit liked it. It reminded him of his childhood in Montana, for his father had never been one to follow regulations which struck him as silly or made the work on the ranch harder.

He turned a snifter in his fingers, watching the way amber liquid swirled languidly around the sides of the glass. A day had passed since his stormy exit from the Oval Office, and the letter of resignation still lay unsigned on his desk. He knew what he ought to do, but it was hard to give up a lifetime of power.

And beyond his own selfish motives there were political considerations attached to his resignation. If he jumped ship it would be a clear message to the press and the people that he knew or believed deBaca to be guilty of the charges that had been leveled against him, and it very well might throw the election to Richard Long. Whatever he might think of deBaca, he didn't want to see his party suffer. He also knew that if the

Democrats suffered a major defeat, and believed him to have contributed to it, he would never serve in public office again.

So I'm a self-centered son of a bitch, who doesn't want to rock the boat, for fear that my little dinghy might get swamped in the ensuing wash, he thought, and took a sip of brandy.

He replayed the scene in the Oval Office, felt again the bile rise in his throat and the pounding behind his eyes as he realized the evil that had been done because of the President's and Tupolev's little *accommodation*. He looked down once more at the letter, and wrestled with himself.

Would his resignation really solve anything or was it just a futile gesture whose only accomplishment would be to ruin his career? *After all, life is a series of compromises,* he argued inwardly. *I wasn't responsible for what happened on the Moon. I didn't even know about it.*

"I never compromise." And for a moment the memory evoked by those words was so strong that Taylor almost could feel the heat of the stones burning through his shirt as he lay belly down on Black Rock Mesa, gazing out across the high deserts of New Mexico.

"Everyone compromises," he had argued that day with Joe Reichart.

"I don't. I always do what I think is right, and the devil take other people."

"And if you turn out to be wrong?" Taylor had asked, rolling onto his back, and looking up at his classmate, whose head was outlined against the deep blue of the New Mexico sky.

"Then I correct it, if I can, and go on. But I never look back, and I never act solely to accommodate other people."

"You're not going to be a very popular person."

"I can live with that," Reichart had said with a grin.

Nearly forty years had passed since that conversation, and he still isn't compromising, Taylor thought. He set aside his glass, and rose from the chair behind his desk. Clasping his hands behind his back, he paced to the window. The sun was down now, and gray twilight came creeping through the streets of Georgetown. If he squinted he could just discern several stars peeking through the branches and leaves of the beech tree, but they were shadowy and indistinct, muted by the powerful street lights that marched the length of the east coast. He thought back on the night skies of Montana, and wondered where in all that majesty rested the Reichart station.

Joe had wanted wealth and the freedom that great wealth bought, while Taylor had wanted power and politics. Both had achieved their goals, but at what cost? Taylor had a feeling that his had been the higher price.

You're purer than I am, Joe, he thought, and swinging back to face the room, he leaned against the casement and stared at the telecom on the desk.

It took him awhile to get through. The station had not only shut down all traffic, but was screening all incoming calls as well. Finally in desperation he told the hostile communications officer, "Look, tell him it's Taylor Moffit, that I'm living among lunatics, and I need some expert advice. If he says no I'll understand, but I'm sure he'll speak with me."

Within moments Reichart's amused countenance filled the screen. "Dear God, Taylor, what are you trying to do? Scuttle your career?"

"It was going down yesterday, but I wanted to do something worthwhile before I sank without a trace."

"So you called me?"

"Yes. What do you need, Joe? You're fighting a big one here, and you're going to need all the help you can get."

"You've never offered it before."

"Your battles with the government to circumvent federal regulations or avoid anti-trust suits didn't hit me where I live. You know money's never interested me."

"Yeah, I know." Reichart paused and lit his pipe. "But why should I trust you? All of this could be a sham."

"And so what if it is? You're safely out of reach, all deBaca can do is howl about how you're tampering in sensitive matters of national interest, and you're doing that all ready."

Reichart grinned with delight around his pipe. "True. Okay, I'll trust you on this one, for old times' sake." He leaned forward intently, and jabbed at the screen with the stem of his pipe. "I've got to find hard evidence, memos and such, to hang this squarely on deBaca."

"You've got me. I was there when he and Tupolev talked."

"That's nice, but that won't cut it. We need a trail from the lunar base right back to the White House, and we'll have to move fast to find it before they get organized and remove any trace."

"So what do you want me to do?"

"You're still the Secretary of State, and you know how to use a computer. Get into the Pentagon and find me that trail."

Taylor swallowed several times, and tried to calm the jumping in his stomach. He reminded himself that he had been on his way out anyway, and as for the party? Well, hell, party loyalty seemed pretty weak when weighed against his own integrity. Might as well go out with a bang instead of a whimper, he thought, but it still didn't banish the fear.

"Sounds pretty cloak and dagger," he said at last. "I wonder if I'm the man for you on this job?"

"I seem to recall a friend of mine who helped me break into the law school computer and read the property exam while it was being written," Reichart said reminiscently as he tapped the ashes out of his pipe.

"Dear God, I'd forgotten about that," Taylor said with a bark of laughter. "Joe, we're bad men."

"No, we're not, just creative." His eyes hardened, holding the Secretary with the force of his will. "Can you do it for me, Taylor? We haven't got much time."

"I'll try."

"No, trying gets you trying. If that's the best you can do I'll find someone else."

"Okay, okay, Jesus, you haven't changed," Taylor muttered. "All right. Assuming they haven't gotten there before me, I'll get you what you need."

"Thanks. You know, you're going to come out of this a hero."

"Only if you win."

"The guys in the white hats always win. You know that."

"Not in my world."

"Then you're living in the wrong world," Reichart said as his image faded from the screen.

"You realize that I'm powerless as far as producing any concrete results are concerned," Cabot said as he scooped more lamb couscous onto his plate. It was a welcome change from the standard station fare of rabbit and chicken. Expensive, but welcome.

"What do you mean?" Tina asked, her wineglass partway to her lips.

They were gathered in a private dining room at The White Owl: Muhammid reclining in a nest of pillows like a burly, black caesar; Lydia cool and impassive and seated next to Joe Reichart; Reichart himself looking knowing; Trevor Martin seated next to Artis and keeping a wary eye on the exotic figure of the plump saloon keeper; Artis was resplendent in a black and silver gown with a dusting of silver sequins in her hair and eyebrows, her gaudiness only served to highlight Flo's nervous and washed-out appearance; Jenny was gazing thoughtfully at the elderly teacher.

"Have you ever heard of the case of *Worcester versus Georgia*?"

"Of course I haven't," Tina grumbled. "I'm an engineer not a lawyer."

"In 1827 the Cherokee Indians, in an effort to keep the state of Georgia from taking their lands, adopted a constitution, and declared their independence as the Cherokee Nation. The Georgia legislature countered by extending its laws over them and directed the seizure of their territory." Cabot paused for a sip of the heavy red wine. "The Indians were no fools, however. They hired a prominent lawyer and appealed to the Supreme Court. There were two related cases actually. In *Cherokee Nation versus Georgia 1831*, Chief Justice John Marshall gave the majority opinion that the Indians were 'domestic dependent nations' and had a right to the land they occupied until they voluntarily ceded it to the United States. Then in *Worcester* the court held that the Cherokee Nation was a definite political community with territory over which the laws of Georgia had no force and into which Georgians could not enter without permission."

"What happened?" Tina asked.

"Most of the Cherokees are today found in Oklahoma. Give you an idea?" Jenny said quietly.

"But why? The highest court in the country had reached its decision. Why were the Indians moved?" Trevor broke in, a puzzled frown between his eyes.

"Because the Supreme Court had no real power. Only the President, with the armed services at his command, could have given the decision the teeth it needed. And President Jackson summed up his own feelings as well as the inate powerlessness of the judiciary when he said, 'John Marshall has made his decision; now let him enforce it.'"

"Then how does anything ever change?" Trevor asked.

"First, because over the years the Supreme Court has gained in prestige, which gives it a large amount of intangible power. Second, in most cases the decision of the court represents an attitude or position which most of society is willing to accept as good or even necessary. A president is unwilling to fly in the face of that kind of societal opinion."

"Sometimes it ain't necessarily a 'large' segment of society that's willin' to see the changes come. Sometimes it's because they're scared of a smaller segment of that society—like us uppity niggers—and willin' to make concessions to keep us from their throats," Muhammid purred, stretching among his pillows like a large, dangerous cat.

"A good point," Cab said. "But it pinpoints the problem we're faced with. I have neither the power nor the prestige of the Supreme Court, nor have I an army at my disposal to enforce whatever decision I render against Messieurs deBaca and Tupolev. When the Fifteenth Circuit acts on a matter of UN treaty we, in essence, become a branch of the International Court of Justice, and like all courts of international law we have only three ways to see our decisions enforced."

"And those are?" Trevor asked.

"We can hope that the pressure of their peers will cause a government to act in a proper manner, we can hope that other nations of the world will try a boycott to force compliance with the ruling, or there is the final option—war. And I must say, although the authorities groundside are worried about you, they're not frightened enough to grant you the kind of concessions that Muhammid was talking about because they don't expect you to go into open warfare with them."

"Then maybe we ought to miscalculate the trajectory on a couple of million tons of processed ore, and dump in on New Jersey instead of the Atlantic," Tina said, showing her teeth in an expression that had little to do with humor.

"My God, what are you saying!" Flo cried. "These are our own people you're talking about."

"Yeah, you're right, Flo. Better make it Washington. That way we'll be sure of only getting the fools and assholes," Tina said with a laugh. The older woman didn't look mollified. Instead she clasped her hands tightly before her on the table, and refused to look at the rest of her companions.

"Frankly, I'm with Flo," Cabot said firmly. "If you're going to try stunts like that just let me know beforehand so I can immigrate to Mars or better yet Pluto. DeBaca will swat you like flies, and you're sitting ducks up here for ground-launched missiles."

"Worried about your ass, Judge?" Muhammid asked.

"You're damn right I am! I sure as hell don't want to be a martyr to your cause, whatever the hell that happens to be, and I'm quite sure that a large number of the people on these stations don't want to either."

"But you don't know that, anymore than you know what defensive measures can be taken by the stations," Reichart said. "But we're wandering far from the subject. With any luck at all, that kind of open warfare won't become necessary. Our more immediate concern is the hearing, and nailing deBaca and Tupolev."

"That's not going to be easy. I know Tomas. If there is anything linking him to the Russian action, he'll have it removed before any discovery efforts can unearth it."

"True, if I waited for formal discovery, but I cheat."

"What do you mean?"

"I've got someone on the inside already trying to find any links from the White House to the Pentagon to the base. If they're there we will get them."

"That will certainly make my job easier, but that brings us right back to the original point—any decision I reach is going to be an exercise in futility. DeBaca and Tupolev aren't going to stand by meekly and let me slap their wrists in public."

"I agree."

"Then what's the point in all this. I know why I'm doing it, but what are your reasons, Mr. Reichart?"

"Similar to yours I'd expect." He took a bite of lamb and chewed slowly. "First, principle, but that's the least of the reasons. More important for our goals is the publicity. So you see," he said, shifting to face Cab, "I don't care if you can deliver me deBaca's head on a platter or not. I just want the people, theirs and ours, to see what kind of men sit in governance over them."

"So that they'll perhaps decide to remove these people from their positions?"

"Perhaps."

"As I've told Lydia, I cannot condone revolution."

"That's fine. I'm perfectly content with what you're doing."

Cabot eyed Reichart suspiciously, for there was something almost too bland, too agreeable about the tycoon's easy acceptance of Cabot's position. "All right, so long as we understand one another."

"So what happens now?" Artis asked, leaning across the table to fill wineglasses.

"In terms of the universe, this dinner party, or what?" Lydia asked, cocking an eyebrow at her.

"In terms of this hearing! What else would I be concerned about right now?" Artis said in exasperation.

"I've set a tentative date for the hearing three weeks from Monday," Cabot said. "And I've appointed a lawyer to represent Mr. Renko."

"Oh, who?" Reichart asked.

"I think you'll approve the choice. It's Kenneth Furakawa."

"You're right, I am pleased," Joe said. "But I'm surprised, as well. Ken really put you on a pin in that last hearing. I didn't think you'd be too keen on him right now."

"Maybe I'm trying to demonstrate that I'm not the unmitigated asshole that you all think I am," Cab said with a slow look around the table. "Ken is highly knowledgeable in the area of international law. He is also known to be sympathetic to the System, and his inclusion will put everyone on notice that this is not going to be a kangaroo court."

"I love it when he talks like a lawyer," Artis whispered to Trevor, and dug him in the ribs with an elbow.

"Thank you," Cab said, lifting his glass to her, and nodding his head. "Now I'm going to see if you'll like me any better when I act like one, too."

Lydia also raised her glass and regarded Cabot over the rim. "You've gone a long way toward proving yourself to me, Judge. Any man who can admit he's made a mistake and try to correct it is worth a second chance."

There were murmurs of assent from the rest of the table, and the party broke up a short time later. Jenny and Cabot walked side by side past darkened stores toward the AVC.

Several times he seemed about to speak, but he always stopped himself. Jenny spotted the softly glowing globe that marked the stop, and started across to it. Cab kept walking.

"Here's the stop," she said.

He turned back. "Why don't we walk for a while. It's—" he began, then caught himself, looking embarrassed.

"A nice night?" Jenny finished for him.

"Stupid wasn't it? It's always a nice night up here."

"Takes time to get used to all of this," she said, moving to join him.

He made no reply, and they continued walking. Jenny dug her hands into her skirt pockets, then glanced quickly over at him. The diffuse light from windows and an occasional street lamp played over his face, highlighting the sharp angle of his cheekbone, the line of the jaw, the hollow of the eye sockets once more partly obscured by that unruly lock of hair. She was trying to decide if it was a Byronic or Napoleonic face when he spoke.

"Will you give me a second chance, too?"

He took her off guard, and she slowed to a stop, staring after him. "That's a stupid question," she said after a long pause. "I've moved back, I'm working with you again. What more do you want?"

He shrugged, not looking back. "Maybe just to hear you say it."

"Okay, consider it said."

He turned and walked back to her. "No, say it." They stood eye to eye in the silent darkness. No breath of wind or faint insect sound offered a distraction from the intensity of his gaze. The unnatural quiet of the station held her locked in a moment more intimate than any she had ever before experienced. She stared into Cab's eyes, noticing, as if for the first time, the circle of smoky gray outlining the paler gray of the iris. She wondered how she could have spent five years in close contact with this man, and have never before perceived him as a man.

Suddenly off in the distance a dog barked. She grasped at that reminder of familiarity, of a life left behind, and retreated from this new, unexpected, and possibly dangerous ground. With her face averted, she fumbled in her handbag and mumbled, "I'll give you a second chance, Cab."

"Thank you, Jenny."

It was a long, silent walk back to the apartment. Cab unlocked the door and stepped aside, allowing Jenny to precede him into the living room. She touched the wall panel, bringing up the lights in the room. Cab walked into the study and froze just past the threshold. A thin sheaf of papers lay in the receiver box of the computer.

Crossing to the desk, he cautiously lifted the sheets and looked at the front page. It was a familiar document. He had handled a lot of them in seventeen years of practice. He had seen substantially fewer in his brief time as a judge. He drew his finger across the heading, marveling at how much excitement those few words could arouse in him.

> *Thomas Wayne Howard, Plaintiff.*
> *versus*
> *Jacqueline Moria Lindsey, Defendant.*

"Cab?" Jenny called from the door. "What have you got there?"

He held the papers out to her without answering. Taking the pages from his hand she read through the complaint.

"Congratulations," she said with a smile. "Looks like the System has decided to give you that second chance, too."

Chapter Ten

"Cab," Jenny whispered.

"Yes, what is it? I *am* hearing a case," he muttered out of the corner of his mouth as she leaned in over him where he sat at the bench. The attorney for the plaintiff looked puzzled, and seemed to lose his train of thought as he watched the exchange at the bench. Cabot gave him a smile, and indicated for him to continue.

"You've got a call."

"You interrupted me for that?"

"It's not just any call, it's John Malcomb, and he is insisting that he talk with you. I told him you were hearing a case, but he remained adament."

"Dammit! Excuse me, Mr. Fowler, I'm afraid I have received a call that requires an immediate response. Could we take a five-minute recess, please?"

"Of course, your honor," the man said politely, and his counterpart at the defense table also nodded her assent.

"Malcomb, what on earth can he want?" Cab asked as he and Jenny hurried into his chambers.

"Your guess is as good as mine."

"Hello, John, what can I do for you?" Huntington said as he slid into the chair behind the desk.

"Hi, Cab, I wanted to talk to you about this Renko affair."

"That's not something I am permitted to do, and you know it, John."

"Look, Cab," Malcomb said, holding up a placating hand when he saw Cabot's face take on that cold and remote expression. "I know you're angry. Why, hell, you have every right to be, but don't let it blind you to what Reichart is trying to do."

"If you've called to discuss personalities, I'm really not interested," Cabot said, reaching for the disconnect button.

"No, wait! Now just hang on, Cab. I called because you're making a very basic legal mistake, and I don't want to see you crucified for it."

"I'm touched. And just what is this *basic* mistake?"

"Renko has no standing to bring this case. He has suffered no personal harm in this case. *He* wasn't killed at that collective, and he lost no relatives in that attack. Therefore there is no justiciable controversy. He's just an interested party. Now if one of the relatives of the slain people were to come forward that would be a different matter, but you don't see them rushing forward to bring this case."

"With good reason! They'd bloody well end up in a work camp in Siberia if they so much as opened their yaps. Sorry, John, I'm unmoved by your argument, and couldn't you come up with something better than a *standing* issue for God's sake?"

"It's a valid issue," Malcomb said stiffly.

"You're right, I agree it is, but I'm not going to use it to deny Mr. Renko his day in court. This case is too important, and it touches on too many basic human rights to be avoided by a cheap trick like this. Legal technicalities have been used too often to deny justice to the people. It's not going to happen this time."

Malcomb wet his lips. "Cab, you're making a big mistake. I'm offering you an easy way out of this thing so take it for Christ's sake, or otherwise I can't say what might happen."

"So deBaca's angry, is he?" Cab said with a hard glitter in his eyes.

"You don't know how angry. Come on, Cab, use your brains, don't throw everything away on a minor thing like this."

"Minor! You call this minor? Twelve people died as a result of this minor affair! Maybe it's not much when compared with Afghanistan, or Central America, or South Africa, but it's enough for *me!* You can tell deBaca to fuck himself!" He jammed down the disconnect button.

"I thought you weren't going to tip your hand to deBaca until you absolutely had to," Jenny remarked from where she leaned against the door.

"I wasn't." He looked sheepish. "I guess I lost my temper."

"I can't blame you. God, how smarmy they all are! Well, you better get back out there," she said, jerking her thumb over her shoulder. "This is your first real case, and you wouldn't want to make them feel unimportant."

"Ken Furakawa is on line, now," Jenny said as Cab reentered his chambers.

"My God, it's like Grand Central Station around here. I wonder what his problem is? Well, at least I timed this recess right," he said as he stripped out of his robe, and crossed to the desk.

"You may wish you were still in court when you hear why he's called," Jenny replied, moving to sit on the corner of the desk.

Cab gave her a questioning glance as he took the call off hold. The shimmering rainbow pattern of a held call evaporated, and Furakawa's seamed face gazed out of the screen.

"Greetings, Cabot. I hope I find you in good health?"

"I'm fine, thank you. And you?"

"Very well in body, but the spirit is doing less well."

"You only get cryptic and Oriental when something's gone wrong."

Furakawa smiled, a secret little expression that narrowed his eyes and gave him the appearance of a delighted Siamese cat. "You know me too well and, yes, there is a problem, and it is not a good situation. It will be very uncomfortable for you."

"I'm getting accustomed to the heat," Cabot remarked dryly, thinking back on his earlier conversation with Malcomb.

"This will, I'm afraid, turn up the temperature. I am going to ask you to find the President in contempt." The breath went out of Cab in a quick puff. "I told you you weren't going to like it," Furakawa said in response to Cabot's expression.

"Contempt?" Cab finally managed to repeat.

"I'm afraid so. I have sent interrogatories. They have been ignored or returned. I requested a deposition. It has been as rudely refused. I cannot represent my client if I am not permitted to engage in adequate discovery."

"I take it you're having the same success with the Soviets?"

"Yes, but there is little we can do in that circumstance. I don't expect Yuri Tupolev to understand the concept of a rule of law. I do expect if from the President of the United States."

Cab leaned forward, one hand gripping the arm of his chair, and tightened his jaw. "You put through the paperwork. I'll handle the rest. I do want to thank you for warning me before this hit."

"Your job is not an easy one. I didn't want to make it any harder than it already is."

"It's good of you to feel that way after that stunt I pulled on the U.S. Steel case."

"We have discussed it, and for my part I consider it forgotten."

"You're a good man. As to our current situation, I don't think we've seen anything yet. This one can only get worse before it gets better."

"I understand. Very well, then, you will formally hear from me by tomorrow."

"That'll be fine." Cab broke the connection and leaned back in his chair, hands laced behind his head.

"You won't be able to avoid deBaca on this," Jenny said.

"I know."

She paused, looking down at her hands. "Cab, how much worse is worse?"

"If I knew that I'd set myself up as an oracle." He grunted, and ran a hand through his hair. "It's certainly bound to pay better, and engender more respect than this job. I'm beginning to feel like the ultimate political football."

"Just wait until you talk to deBaca. You may feel like a deflated football then."

"Thanks for the encouragement," he said, grabbing her by the hand, and pulling her closer to his chair.

"I always try to help," she responded lightly, brushing her hand down his cheek.

"How could he do it? How could he do it?" deBaca repeated as he flung himself about the confines of the Oval Office. Michael Dobson watched impassively from where he sprawled in an armchair, while David Reynolds nervously wrung his hands and kept sidling toward the drapes over the French windows. Dobson idly wondered if the lawyer was going to wrap himself up in the heavy blue fabric and try to hide.

"I did try to warn you, sir," Reynolds murmured, pulling out a handkerchief and patting at the film of sweat on his upper lip. "Remember, Malcomb and I have been in contact with Justice Huntington, and I can tell you now, and I'm sure John would concur, that he is in no mood to be reasonable."

"*You've* been in contact with him, but *I* can't get him on the line and I put the son of a bitch up there." His index finger thrust at the ceiling. "Just what the hell does he think he's playing at, holding me in contempt."

It was obviously a rhetorical question, and no one tried to answer. Dobson unfolded himself from the chair and moved lithely to the desk. He was a big man, but he moved with the controlled grace of a dancer. He dropped the morning edition of the Times into the reader, and swung the screen toward deBaca.

PRESIDENT AND PREMIER FOUND IN CONTEMPT, the banner headline shouted, and below it at the bottom of the page was a color picture of Evgeni with his family, relaxing aboard the Reichart station.

"This can't continue. You're losing ground in the polls, and we're too damn close to the election to have this thing dragging on. Long is making political hay out of it all."

"Well what the hell do you suggest I do?"

"You put Huntington up there. He's supposed to be your man. Get him on the line and find out what went wrong."

"I know what went wrong," deBaca growled, dropping heavily into the chair behind his desk. "He has a cramp in his conscience. I've known Cab since he was an undergraduate at Harvard. He's always been incredibly prickly when he thought his honor has been impugned."

"So how did you handle him then?"

DeBaca glanced up at Dobson and drew back his lips in a mirthless smile. "Smoothed his ruffled feathers by promising not to do it again."

"Then do that now, but for God's sake do something. We've got to get this tied up, and out of the minds of the people before November."

"He's refused all my other calls. Why should this time be any different?"

"It may not, but if we have to, we'll pull him in here or you'll meet him on the orbiting Air Force platform."

DeBaca ran a hand over his face and sighed. "Okay. You two clear out. Cab and I don't need an audience."

Reynolds bolted gratefully for the door. Dobson followed more slowly.

The call went through immediately. This time there was no irritating, endless chiming with no one answering on the other end. Nor was he smoothly and politely brushed off by that damned redheaded assistant. This time Cab himself answered.

"Glad you decided to break the silence," deBaca grunted.

"I figured we'd need to talk after my holding was announced."

"You could have talked to me first, spared me all of this embarrassment in the press."

"I didn't feel it was my job to remind you of your duties and obligations."

"And just what the hell is that supposed to mean?"

"You're a lawyer, Tomas. Your refusal to take part in discovery obstructs and defeats the administration of justice by this court."

"For Christ's sake! I'm the President of the United States!"

Huntington's expression hardened, his eyes like chips of gray ice. "All the more reason for you to follow the lawful decrees laid upon you by a court of this land. If you expect the colonists to obey our laws, then surely their government has the first obligation to obey those same laws."

"You're a dreamer, Cab."

"If I am then it's certainly preferable to the *reality* I was living in a few days ago."

"What's happened to you, Cab? You knew what we were trying to accomplish when I sent you out there, and you concurred. So what's changed?"

Huntington looked thoughtful, and tugged at a sideburn. "You've never been on the bench, Tomas. It's an awesome responsibility. It's as if that black robe carries the entire weight of history. All those decisions, all those men striving for eight hundred years to create a coherent system of justice. It can't just be shed in the interest of some short-term gain."

"You think I can't understand? What the hell do you think I'm sitting in the middle of?" DeBaca waved an agitated hand, indicating the room around him. "You think you're the only one who can understand the imperatives of history? Well, you try sitting in this seat, buddy, and see how it feels."

"Then live up to your heritage. Great nations like great men must keep their word, Tomas."

"You're not back in law school, so stop quoting Justice Holmes to me." They sat in silence for several moments, then deBaca ran his hand over his face and sighed. "Okay, Cab, what'll it take to get you to lift that contempt ruling?"

"Your cooperation. It's not that arduous, nor is it without precedent. Back in the 1970's, I believe, no fewer than three Presidents were deposed in the White House."

"At least one of them had done something wrong," deBaca muttered, looking hurt. He watched to see how Cab would respond. There was no change in the expression on the narrow aristocratic face on the screen. If anything, it became more aloof and neutral. "Then you think I'm involved in this mess?" deBaca shouted.

"I don't know, Tomas. I wasn't there, and you won't submit to discovery."

"Then I'm damning myself with my own silence?"

"I think so, and I'm sure I'm not alone."

"No, you're not." The President smiled, a contrite little-boy smile that held the full measure of his charm. "Okay, you win, Cab. I'll answer the interrogatories and I'll let Furakawa hold his deposition."

"Thank you, Mr. President," Huntington said with a slight inclination of his head.

"There is one more matter I'd like to discuss with you."

"Yes?" Cab inquired, raising one eyebrow.

"You're upset about the way my actions have 'obstructed' the adminnistration of justice, but what about Reichart's actions?"

"What do you mean?"

"His actions are a disgrace. He's making sure this Renko fellow is plastered across every newspaper in the world and featured on every newscast. If it's wrong for me to exercise my executive privilege then surely it's wrong for a private citizen to, in essence, have this case tried in the press."

"I have no control over what's printed or reported. What are you asking?"

"Take the Russian away from Reichart. Bring him to the EnerSun station where you can keep him from the press. Then this thing can have a chance to quiet down."

"First, I don't think that's necessary, and second, I don't have that power. Evgeni Renko is a private citizen living on a private station. I have no authority to seize him."

"But I do, and I'll back you up."

"No!"

"But damnit, Cab. The man's going to have to appear before the court sometime."

"And when that time comes I have every confidence that he will appear, but in the meantime I will not forcibly remove him from his sanctuary."

"You're starting to make me angry, Cabot," deBaca muttered. "You're saying that Renko needs sanctuary, and I also have the strong sensation that you're implying that he needs to be protected from *me*. I don't like that, and I don't like the way you're demanding concessions, but giving nothing in return. I put you there, and I can bloody well take you away."

"If you feel you have the grounds to remove me from the bench, then by all means do so. But I tell you now, I will not be bought and I certainly won't be intimidated."

"You're lining up with these colonists."

"No, I'm not! I'm acting as conscience and principle dictate. I can't be less than what I am. Don't ask it of me, Tomas. For the sake of our years of friendship, please . . . don't push me!"

"This thing is bigger than both of us, Cab. I can't promise you won't get squeezed," deBaca said, and his black eyes were hard and flat.

Huntington stiffened and drew himself up. "Just remember that your hand is in the vise as well, Tomas."

"And *you* remember that I'm the one with the power to turn the screws."

Huntington seemed to struggle for a moment as if he were about to say more. Instead he reached out and broke the connection, leaving deBaca staring at an empty screen.

The President found himself quivering with tension and fury. Never in all the years had he felt such anger and bitterness against an old friend. He brought his palm down on the intercom with a resounding *thwack*.

"Yes, sir?"

"Send in Dobson."

The White House Chief of Staff stepped quickly through the door, and scanned the President's face. "I take it it didn't go as planned."

"Self-righteous bastard!" He swung the reader around, and stared grimly at the screen. "Well, I won't put up with this anymore. I want Renko out of Reichart's hands. You've got everything worked out?"

"Yes, sir."

"Then get him!"

"We've been monitoring them for two hours now, sir. There's no doubt, they're headed here."

Joe Reichart rested his hand on the panel in Station Control, and watched the two small images blipping doggedly across the radar screen.

"Try warning them off."

"I have, sir. No response."

"Well, try again."

"Yes, sir." The technician leaned forward and switched on the radio. "Reichart Station to approaching shuttles, this station is closed to outside traffic. Please pull off." They waited tensely. There was no reply and the shuttles kept coming.

"Any idea where they're from?" Reichart asked.

"No sir, they came up on our blind spot."

"We're going to have to move those SDS satellites," Reichart muttered almost to himself. Straightening abruptly, he crossed the equipment-filled room to Lysette Manjou, Chief of Operations for the station. "Are they close enough for us to take a look?"

"Easily," she said shortly. Turning away, she flipped a switch, and the shielding slid back from one of the viewing ports. The stars glittered diamond-hard against the black of space, and outlined against them were two snub-nosed crafts. A floating chunk of asteroid tumbled past the port, momentarily obscuring their view of the shuttles.

"Nothing to indicate who sent them," Reichart said.

"We do have ways to deal with unwanted visitors," Lysette reminded him.

"I know, but I question if this is the time to display our firepower. There will be a hell of a brouhaha groundside if they find out that we uppity bastards have had the audacity to arm ourselves."

"So we let them dock?"

"We may have no choice. But let's find out who they are."

Reichart crossed quickly to the control panel for the large orbiting telescope, which was a fixture of the station. Seating himself at the computer, he punched in commands and coordinates, shortening the range and bringing the lens to bear on the incoming ships.

The lead ship began its swing in for docking, and there on its side, brought into clear focus by the powerful lens, was an American flag. Farther back near the tail was a serial number and the Air Force insignia.

"Son of a bitch!" Joe yelled, exploding out of his chair. "Where's Evgeni?"

"How should I now?" Lysette said.

"Well find him."

"What about those shuttles?"

"I'm not going to open fire on the U.S. Air Force, for Christ's sake! Now get on the horn and get the station alerted. Anyone who finds Evgeni should try to meet me at my private shuttle. I'll get Irina and Analisa."

"Why them?" Lysette called after his retreating back.

"Because if they get their hands on them," he called over his shoulder as he pelted for the elevator, "Evgeni will cave in and say anything they want him to. Better we lose none of them, but I'd rather risk Evgeni than his family," he concluded as the doors to the elevator slid shut behind him.

Chapter Eleven

Reichart shot out of the elevator on the housing level, and paused to find his bearings and to kick free from the cumbersome magnetic overboots. The emergency broadcast system carried Lysette's voice through the torus as she calmly informed residents of the boarding and requested that the Renkos report to the shuttle launch bays in the hub. An AVC pulled in and disgorged a knot of five people who split off in different directions. Joe recognized Janina Faraday who flew for Reichart Industries, and he gave a shout. She glanced over one broad shoulder, and waited as he ran to meet her.

"Where are you headed?" he asked.

"Day care center to get my kids."

"Can Ralph handle it?"

"Why? You need me for something else?"

"I've got to find the Renkos and get them off the station."

"And you need a pilot."

"That's right."

"Count me in. It's like a goddamn police state when troopies can march into our backyard," she grumbled, falling into step beside him.

They passed more residents, all who waved or nodded to Joe, but didn't try to engage him in conversation. It was obvious he was in a hurry. Joe noted the overall lack of panic in the rim, and gave a nod of satisfaction. He had expected no less, but it was still gratifying to see the efficient way his people dealt with the crisis.

He had to admit that he had an advantage over any ground-side mayor. His people were competent and highly trained professionals who were used to dealing with events. Also the lack of population density helped. In the crowded, teeming streets of New York or Delhi or Rome, panic could quickly spread, infecting people, and turning them from individuals into a mindless behemoth. Here, with eight thousand people scattered thinly through more than a million meters of surface area, and a number of those eight thousand in their work pods outside the station proper, it was easier to keep control.

He had managed to exit from an elevator/tension spoke quite near the Renkos quarters. He sighted the terraced apartment that climbed up the curved walls of the torus, and began jogging down the winding walkway. Lifting his watch radio up to his lips, he called the control room.

"Situation?" he asked.

"The docking is almost complete," Lysette's voice came back.

"We're running out of time."

"No shit."

"Stall them. Close the spokes and jam the elevators."

"Aye, aye, sir, but eventually they're going to get through to the control room, and get things running again."

"I understand, and I don't want any martyrs. Just buy me some time."

"Will do. Hey!" Her voice crackled from the radio. "If I shut down the elevators how are you going to reach a shuttle?"

Reichart smiled. "I built this station, remember? I'll get there." He snapped off the radio and turned to Janina. "Wait here. Maybe we'll get lucky and they'll be at home." Janina nodded, and Joe bounded up the stairs to the third apartment. His urgent hammering brought no response, and he cursed under his breath. He tried to think *where* in all of the shops, offices, homes, and farms Irina and Analisa could have gotten to.

Precious moments were ticking away while he stood dithering outside the apartment. He glanced down to where Janina stolidly bounced up and down on the balls of her feet, head pulled down between her heavy shoulders, and he tried to decide what to do. He paced across the terraced balcony, frantically upsetting a pot of geraniums as he passed by. The green ceramic pot shattered, sending dirt and flower petals tumbling across the patio. The sight of the scarlet blossoms jogged something in his mind, and he remembered Irina's almost pathetic enjoyment of the greenery which filled the Reichart station.

"The park!" he muttered aloud, and took the steps two at a time in his haste to reach the ground level. Despite her bulk Janina stayed right behind him.

It wasn't far to the park, and he found them even before he reached it. Irina was running, tendrils of pale blond hair snaking about her face, her gait awkward and lopsided as she struggled to balance Analisa in one arm and a satchel of toys in the other. Her face was flushed with fear and exertion, and her eyes were dark wells of terror. Joe doubted she even saw him when he waved. She came abreast of him, and he reached out and gripped her by the shoulders. She gave a sharp cry of terror and recoiled back.

"Easy, easy," he said soothingly as he had to many a frightened horse back on the New Mexico ranch. "You're all right."

"The announcement! They said soldiers are coming?"

"Yes, that's right," he said as he turned her, propelling her back into motion.

"My government?"

"No, mine." There was a wealth of irony in the tone.

"But why?" she began, then stopped as the answer came to her. "Evgeni!"

"Yes, I'm afraid so. Irina, where is he?" Reichart asked as he lifted Analisa off her mother's hip and settled the little girl in the crook of his arm. Janina silently took the satchel.

"In the hub. He has been studying with Dr. Philstrom, learning better mining techniques so he would be ready for the asteroids. . . ." Her voice trailed away at the expression on his face. "What is it? What is wrong?"

"The hub's been closed, and it's probably crawling with soldiers by now. There's no way we can get to him. Our only hope is to keep you and Analisa out of their hands. Come on." He took her by the hand and headed off at a brisk pace only to be jerked back as she balked like a recalcitrant foal.

"No, I will not go! I must be with Evgeni! I will not leave him!"

For one brief moment he longed to just cold cock her, and carry her like a sack of grain to his shuttle. He resisted because he understood the sense of fear and loss which gripped her. He was asking her to abandon her husband. She deserved at least an explanation.

He set Analisa on the ground where she clung to his leg like a small burr, and took Irina by the shoulders. "There is no way he can avoid being caught. That's bad enough, but think how much worse if he has you and the child to worry about, too. These are evil men we're dealing with, and they won't hesitate to use you as a way to reach Evgeni. You've gone through so much already, don't let it go for nothing by becoming a means for blackmail."

"They will use us to make Evgeni retract what he has said, no?"

"Yes."

Her jaw tightened, and her brows drew together in a straight line over her eyes. "No. I lost friends that day. I will not lose honor, as well. There must be someone left to speak the truth. I will go with you."

"Good." He breathed with relief. "And now we've got to hurry. They'll tear this place apart looking for you, and we've got to be safely away before they do."

"Where will we go?" she asked, panting a bit as she trotted to keep up with his long-legged strides.

"Outbound to Mars or the asteroids. We can catch a ship at the deep space launching platform. If we can get there, we'll be safe."

"You are coming with us?"

"It would seem the most prudent route. If I stick around I may find myself in some military blockade or federal prison, depending upon what kind of trumped-up charge deBaca can invent."

"But if the hub is closed how will we reach a shuttle?"

"I had this station built with a bolt hole. Guess I always suspected I might have to use it."

"And this lady?" She glanced back at Janina, who plodded silently along behind them.

"Joe's a great guy," the woman said matter-of-factly, "but piloting a shuttle isn't one of his skills. Fortunately he ran across me, and I'm going to fly you out of here."

"That is very brave of you."

"Brave, hell! I'm just pissed. They may as well learn now that they can't push us around," she concluded, militantly thrusting out her square jaw.

"They will not be happy when they find we are gone," Irina said timidly to Reichart.

"No, but at least we won't be around to experience their displeasure." He stared ahead, trying to ascertain how far to the next spoke. He momentarily considered taking a transport, but rejected the idea. Better to have mobility when the troops arrived.

"I only hope in their anger they do not hurt Evgeni," Irina added softly. Joe looked down at the top of her head and tried to think of something comforting to say. Unfortunately nothing suggested itself.

"Now remember your orders," Captain White said from where he balanced at the shuttle hatch. "Move fast, secure all elevators and shuttles, and keep *cool*. You've seen the pictures, you know who we're looking for, so find them and keep it to a minimum of fuss. We sure as hell don't want any incidents."

"Yeah, right," Sergeant Pruden muttered to his seat mate. "That's why we're forcibly boarding a civilian space station, and grabbing people who've never done anything to us."

"What was that?" the officer snapped out.

"Nothing, sir. Just running over things with Douglas."

White eyed the twenty-nine men on the transport shuttle. There was some coughing and some shuffling of magnetized boots on the metal flooring, but no one ventured a comment. He heard a hollow clang as the shuttle locked firmly to the docking bay.

"Right, then," White said with a jerk of his head. "This is it."

The double row of men rose, swaying from their seats, and slung their shotguns over their shoulders, checked sidearms, and fell into line behind their officer. There were a series of bumps and clanks as the outer door cycled open, then the interior of the hub lay before them. They moved out in a foot-sliding jog. Two bays down the other shuttle was disgorging its contingent of men. Throat mikes clicked and chattered as the officers sent small groups of men running in all directions.

Fifteen minutes later the hub was secured, and Evgeni Renko stood shivering between two large Emergency Response Force airmen. With him was a stoop-shouldered white-haired man who had the beginnings of a large bruise over one eye. White checked the photograph against the man who stood before him. It was a match.

"You're Evgeni Renko?" He stumbled a bit over the first name.

"Da."

"Where's your wife and kid?" The man's face took on a sullen, almost bovine expression, and he stared pointedly past White's left shoulder. "It's only a matter of time till we find them so why don't you just spare us all a lot of grief."

"Grief!" the old man suddenly spat out. "You talk of grief you . . . you hoodlums. You Gestapo!"

"Who the hell is he?" White asked one of the enlisted men. He could feel himself beginning to burn beneath the collar at the old man's tone and expression of contempt.

The airman shrugged. "Don't know. He was with Renko, and he started kicking and beatin' on us when we came in. That's how he got the bruise. He practically ran himself into my fist."

"You'll pay for this. Mr. Reichart will not stand still for this kind of blatant piracy and kidnapping!"

"Mr. Reichart isn't going to have much choice since he'll be joining us," White said with equanimity.

A young lieutenant trotted up. "Sir, the elevators to the rim have all been shut down, and the doors to the control center are locked."

White sighed. "Okay, let's see if we can convince them to be reasonable without having to burn down the doors. Put Mr. Renko aboard the shuttle," he called over his shoulder to the privates.

"What about the old guy?"

"Lock him in a closet, stick him in a shuttle, I don't care, just so long as you keep him out of the way."

One of the men put a hand on Evgeni's shoulder and pushed him toward the shuttle. He twisted back to face the captain. "Where are you taking me? I have a right to know." His voice was ragged with fear and tension.

"No place near as bad as it would have been if your people

had caught you first. You're going to be placed in protective custody aboard the EnerSun station."

The takeover proceeded. A strikingly beautiful woman opened the doors to the control room just as they were preparing to unlimber the torchs. Moments later the elevators were running, and the squads began to pour into the rim. White and Delany, his counterpart from the other shuttle, left fifteen men to hold the hub, and joined the rest of their troops in the search for Reichart, and the woman and child.

Deep within one of the spokes Joe, Irina, and Janina climbed laboriously for the hub. Joe had used his coat to strap Analisa to his back. He needed both hands free to climb the long and narrow ladder from the rim to the hub. The spokes were filled with conduits carrying power cables, life support, elevators, and a multitude of other technical equipment. This spoke, however, held an empty conduit set with metal rungs. Twenty-five years ago Joe had felt like a paranoid when he had instructed his engineers to include this bolt hole. Now he was grateful for his foresight. Behind him he could hear the women panting with exertion, and his own heart was laboring with effort. But the climb became easier as they moved from the one gee rim to the almost weightless environment of the hub.

Although the decreasing gravity was a boon now, Joe was already worrying about the situation when they reached the hub. None of the trio were equipped with magnetic boots, and he was quite certain that Irina couldn't handle herself in near weightlessness. There were sure to be guards in the hub, and they would have to be removed quickly and quietly if his little band of refugees were to escape.

He reached the platform at the top of the spoke and, clinging to the access hatch, made room for Janina and Irina. They all huddled about the hatch, bouncing gently at the end of hand holds.

"Okay. This spoke bottoms out right next to my private docking bay. The shuttle is there, but there's sure to be a guard or guards nearby." The two women stared intently at him. Irina's face was tight with fear while Janina's broad, fat-cheeked face had the look of a furious baby. "Irina, have you ever worked in total weightlessness?"

"No."

"Then here's what we'll do. We'll strap Analisa to your

back, and then tether you to Janina. While I handle the guards you'll head for the shuttle. It's not going to be easy," he said to the pilot. "Having the extra drag is going to throw off your sense of control and trajectory."

"I can handle it. I'm not built like a longshoreman for nothing," Janina grunted.

"All right, then. We go."

It took awhile to transfer Analisa to her mother, and then get both of them hooked to Janina. All three of the adults were wringing with sweat by the time it was accomplished, and several times Irina had had to cover Analisa's mouth and nose to keep the child from crying out. Joe rested his head against the hatch and waited for his breathing to quiet before he risked a look. At last he opened the hidden hatch about an inch, and took a cautious look into the hub level. The shuttle bay stood beckoningly open about ten meters to his left, and lounging in front of it stood two Response Force guards. Their rifles were slung over their shoulders, and they passed a cigarette back and forth between them as they discussed the prospects for the Super Bowl.

Joe sucked in several quick breaths, gripped the edges of the opening, and with a powerful thrust of his arms and shoulders launched himself into the room. The men's eyes widened in shock as he flew through the air toward them, and one reached back for his rifle. Before he could unlimber the weapon Joe was on him, his feet hitting hard and true in the center of the soldier's chest. He went down in a welter of flaying arms and legs, and he struck his companion a glancing blow with his right arm.

The resistance of boot to body sent Joe caroming off in the opposite direction, but he tucked and executed a quick flip that put him closer to the wall of the hub. Out of the corner of his eye he could see Janina—like an ungainly gooney bird struggling to get into the air—plunge and glide toward the door of the shuttle with Irina and Analisa bobbing behind. The wall came up to meet him, and with a quick touch of his foot he sent himself flying back toward the soldiers.

The first man was still down, but his companion had kept his feet, and now had his shotgun out. From other parts of the docking level Joe could hear shouts, and he knew he was running out of time. The rifle was coming up, and the double barrels looked like cannon mouths. Joe gave a sharp twist, and set himself tumbling to the left. There was a roar as one barrel let loose, and Joe felt the wind from the pellets flick across the top of his head. He instinctively hunched, pulling his head down between his shoulders like a turtle retreating into his shell, but he still managed to adjust direction sending him once more toward the soldier.

He feinted with his right hand, and when the man arched his body to avoid the blow, he followed up with a powerful kick to the man's midriff. This time his aim was off, however, and his boot scuffed across the side of the man's ribs rather than connecting solidly in the center of his torso. It was obviously painful, but not incapacitating, and Joe decided he had been a hero long enough.

He looked toward the shuttle. Janina was floundering, but she had almost made the docking hatch. He flipped again, and this time used the ceiling to give himself a new burst of speed and direction. The hatch loomed before him. Janina gripped the edge of the docking bay and, untethering Irina, shoved her into the shuttle. The shotgun roared again, and Janina gave a grunting cough of pain. A red pattern blossomed across her left shoulder, and a few droplets of blood floated like dainty red bubbles into Joe's face. Desperately he wrapped his arms around Janina's broad back, and they floated/fell into the shuttle.

"Can you fly?" he called as he cycled shut the hatch.

"Hell, yes." She gritted as she experimentally shrugged her shoulder. "I only took the outside edge of the pellets."

"Yeah, I know. The main body of the blast went between my head and your shoulder. Not a very comforting experience, I must say."

"Get strapped in," the burly pilot called as she kicked herself to the flight deck. "I'm going to take this baby out of here like an eagle with sore feet."

Joe hauled Irina and Analisa to flight seats and got them strapped down. He settled into his own seat just as a rush of power shivered through the shuttle. His mouth tasted of acid, and his muscles were beginning to ache from the stress and reaction. He rested his forehead against the port, and watched as they pulled away from the station, his station, in a long looping arc.

Next to him Analisa was whimpering with fear. Irina was murmuring to the child, but her voice kept breaking, and the obvious distress in her mother's voice added to the girl's hysteria. Her cries began to increase in volume, spiraling higher and higher like a rising air-raid siren.

Joe looked back at the station. Already it was beginning to appear no larger than the rim of a balance wheel in a lady's watch, set against the stars that filled the dark infinity of space. He felt a momentary rush of sadness and regret, then slowly he began to grin. Sure he was leaving his home, his life, his livelihood, but what other man at sixty-two had this kind of opportunity. He had been sparring with the Earth powers from behind lawyers and accountants for years, and it was beginning to pall. Whatever happened now it had been a hell of a moment.

Box office, he thought as he leaned back in his seat, and contemplated his mad attack on the two young Emergency Force men. *That's what it was, total box office*.

"I'm supposed to have done *what?*" Cab enunciated with unnatural calm.

"I thought you'd be surprised," Andy Throckmorton mumbled around the cigarette that hung loosely from his lips. He leaned forward and lifted the ceramic lighter off the coffee table. Jenny perched tensely on the back of the sofa, her hands knotted in her lap.

Huntington raised a hand to his forehead and closed his eyes. He was still trying to make sense of what he had just heard. "Run this by me one more time. I'm still not certain I'm getting the whole picture."

"Oh, you're getting the picture all right. It's just that the mind is unwilling to accept the full magnitude of the story."

"Spare me the histrionics, Andy. Just give me the—"

"The facts, ma'am," the journalist interrupted, then sighed and waved a hand at Cabot's blank look. "Forget it. You're clearly not an old television junkie."

"Andy," Huntington said warningly.

"Okay, okay," he settled his bulk more comfortably on the couch, and rested his hands on his knees. "Just picked it up off the wire that a contingent of Emergency Response troops have landed on the Reichart station and seized Evgeni Renko.

He is currently being brought under armed escort to the EnerSun station where he will be kept in protective custody until the conclusion of the UN hearing." His voice took on a singsong quality as he repeated verbatim the story he had heard. "This action has been taken at the express command of Federal Judge Cabot Huntington, who feels that the circuslike atmosphere created by Renko's presence on the Reichart station is undermining the judicial process." Throckmorton took a deep breath and cocked an eye at Huntington. "I think that pretty much covers the high points."

Cabot flung himself out of the armchair and began to pace the confines of the living room. "How could they? I *never* issued any such order. In fact I specifically told Tomas that I would take no action to remove Renko. Dammit, I won't put up with this. We'll get this thing settled once and for all," he said over his shoulder as he headed for the telecom.

"And just what are you going to do? Call up the networks and the newspapers and tell them that it wasn't you who issued that comminique, but rather your great good friend Tomas C. deBaca or his minions once more taking the law into their own hands?" Cabot stopped, and turned slowly back to face the portly journalist. "Face it, Cabot. They've got you by the short hairs. If you try to deny this now . . ."

"I'll look like an idiot," he concluded quietly.

"So what do we do?" Jenny interjected. "We've got two shuttle loads of flyboys on their way to the station with Renko in tow."

"The troops are Lydia's problem," Throckmorton said with a dismissive wave of a hand. "More to the point is what deBaca thinks he can gain by having Renko under your supervision?"

Cab drifted back to the sofa and rested his hand on Jenny's shoulder. "I don't know," he said slowly. "He knows I'll never back him on this. If he wanted Renko silenced, why not just take him back to Earth?"

"There's an awful lot of support being generated groundside for Renko. He could become a real political thorn in the side if he were detained at Fort Bragg or wherever," Jenny mused. "On the other hand it would be a lot easier to keep things quiet on a ten-thousand-person station. Particularly if the Emergency Response Forces remain."

"No news in, and no news out," Andy mused.

"The whole situation is ridiculous. Tomas must have lost his mind to behave in this insane way."

"He's a politician who's watching his power crumble in his hands. Of course he's behaving like a maniac. Logic is not anyone's strong suit when they feel threatened," Andy said.

"That doesn't comfort me." Cab ran a hand through his hair. "I've had a hard enough time dealing with Tomas the past few days. How can I possibly reach him now?"

"You can't," Andy said bluntly. "You're just going to have to do whatever it is you feel you must do."

"But what the hell is that supposed to be?"

"Don't ask me. You're the one who's ostensibly in control around here."

"The operative word in that sentence is *ostensibly*."

"So what are we going to do?" Jenny asked. "Pack up Renko and send him back to the Reichart station?"

"Us and who else? As you pointed out, there are two boat loads of Air Force troops on their way to this station, and I can assure you they aren't going to be taking their orders from *me*." Cabot sucked in a deep breath and exhaled slowly. "I suppose all we can do is keep Renko safe until this matter is resolved."

"That may be tougher than you think," Andy muttered.

"Not if we have the station behind us," Cabot replied. He began to once more wander about the room, seeming to be talking more to himself than to his two companions. "Tomas will leave the troops. I certainly would if I were in his place. So that means we'll have to keep them isolated and off balance."

Throckmorton gave a snort of laughter. "What happened to the cool, calculating attorney I interviewed only a few weeks ago. Hell, Cabot, you're starting to sound like a real fire-breathing radical."

"Please," Huntington said, looking pained. "There's nothing radical about abhoring the use of military power. Why, as Americans it's almost programmed into our genes. Now, enough talk. I'm off to see Lydia. Care to come along?"

"No, thanks," Andy said, heaving his bulk off the couch. "I'm gonna hightail it off this station before the Gestapo arrives and keeps an honest journalist like me from reporting the news."

"I sort of wish you could stick around," Jenny said as she walked him to the door. "It makes us feel less outnumbered if friends are with us."

"That's sweet, pretty lady," he said, tapping her cheek with one pudgy forefinger. "But you may be glad you've got someone on the outside before this thing is over."

"Dear God, listen to us. We're already into a siege mentality," Cab said.

"Nothing unusual about that. Especially since we can all hear the draw bridge being pulled up behind us." He opened the door, and gave them one long, serious look over his shoulder. "You two take care. I'd hate for anything to happen to you."

"So would we," Cab replied curtly.

"You mean to tell me I have to sit by idly while my station is boarded and occupied by troops?" Lydia shouted at the telecom screen where Alex Sullivan, President of EnerSun, Inc., sat tensely in his groundside office.

"You have to understand our position. We've got the SEC—"

"Don't talk to me about the SEC! I've got ten thousand people up here whose civil liberties are about to be violated. Your contract problems with the government don't concern me."

"Well they damn well ought to! You're up there because of EnerSun, and EnerSun is where it is because of federal support. We agreed to house the Fifteenth Circuit, and we will continue to provide whatever the feds want."

"Even if it means direct circumvention of our constitutional rights? This is a direct violation of *Van Clive versus Odell.*"

"No, it's not. In that case the troops occupied the van Clive station over the objections and against the will of the inhabitants."

"And that's not happening this time," she muttered under her breath.

"What was that?"

"Nothing."

"Anyway, as I was saying, this is a completely different set of circumstances. Then there was a state of emergency. This time these men are acting sort of like an international peace-keeping force."

"Your ability to split hairs is beyond all comprehension, Alex. This is illegal and you know it."

"For Christ's sake, Lydia!" he grumbled, apparently giving up on trying to convince her of the rightness of the boarding. "It's only sixty men, and they'll be gone as soon as this UN hearing is over. We're taking a few days, a week at the most."

"Do I get that in writing?" she said, her mouth twisting with distaste.

"Very funny. You just remember that you may be in charge on the station, but the board is still the final authority for the company. You can be replaced."

"I'll try to keep that in mind." The intercom beeped. "Yes?" she said, transferring her attention from the screen.

"Justice Huntington and Ms. McBride are here," her assistant said.

"Good, send them in."

"Lydia, Lydia, what's going on?" Alex demanded. "I will not have company decisions discussed with outsiders—"

"Then maybe you better clear the line because I'm about to make some management-level decisions, and I wouldn't want to offend your sensibilities."

"Lydia, for God's sake just keep things cool up there," Sullivan wailed as she reached out and broke the connection.

"He didn't sound happy," Huntington said, indicating the now-darkened screen.

"He wasn't. He thinks I'm about to do something reckless and foolish."

"Are you?" he asked, dropping into the chair and regarding her over the top of his steepled fingers.

She stared at him rigidly for several seconds, then slumped against the back of her chair. "As much as I want to—no, I'm not."

"Then what are you going to do?" Jenny asked.

"My orders from the board are to welcome the Air Force aboard the station, and to make their stay comfortable."

"Then they're not leaving."

"No. They're here to insure that the course of justice runs smoothly."

"It's been my experience that only tottering political regimes require the presence of armed troops to see that justice is dispensed." Cab shook his head. "It's a sad commentary."

"Isn't there anything you can do?"

"Me? I'm supposed to have sent for these soldiers, remember? As Andy Throckmorton just pointed out, I'd look like an idiot if I started squawking about the illegality of their actions."

"So what do you suggest I do?"

"You could file suit in the Supreme Court, but that would probably result in delaying the UN hearing until the issue of the troops is settled." Huntington paused and looked thoughtful. "Actually, that might be what deBaca is hoping for. If he could get Evgeni Renko out of the public eye for a while, it would quiet things down considerably, and might give him a chance to get re-elected before I can hear this case."

"But meantime we'd have the soldiers here until the Supreme Court acts?"

"Yes."

She shook her head, her silver hair flying about her face. "No, that's utterly unacceptable. Better to just tough it out until you can complete the UN hearing."

"What's the situation on the Reichart station? Do you know how Joe intends to handle this situation?" Jenny asked.

"Joe's gone."

"Gone!" Huntington exclaimed, straightening in his chair. "But why?"

"Joe hasn't set foot on Earth in twelve years. He felt it was best to keep himself beyond the reach of the authorities. I'm sure when he saw those shuttles coming he bolted before they had a chance to take him as well."

"That's utterly ridiculous! DeBaca was after Renko, nothing more. I don't like what's being done anymore than you do, but you're overreacting. This conspiratorial view of the world events is becoming a little wearying," he added.

Anger flared in Lydia's eyes. "You also thought we were wrong to question the motives of the men who had sent you. Then they nuked an innocent community, and suddenly you weren't so sure anymore." Cabot winced. "You may not like it, Cabot, but I'll wager that events will support my assessment of the situation, and you'll once more find yourself reluctantly lining up with us." She rested her hands on the top of her desk, and pushed herself to her feet. "Now, do you want to join the welcoming committee?" Her voice was thick with irony.

"Yes," the judge said quietly. "These actions were taken in my name. I bloody well want to be sure that the commander understands that he'd best not try it again."

There was quite a crowd gathered in the shuttle lobby which Lydia quickly and firmly dispersed. She did allow Muhammid to join them, so it was an odd foursome that watched Captain White emerge from the shuttle access bay. He seemed somewhat taken aback by Cab's presence, and by the cold, arrogant expression on the judge's thin face. He recovered quickly, however, and gave him a sketchy salute.

"Justice Huntington. We have Evgeni Renko as per your orders."

"Quite," Cab said in freezing accents.

"Ma'am," he said turning to Lydia. "Request permission to bring Renko and my men aboard, and get them situated in quarters."

"Ms. Kim Nu will of course handle your quartering as she sees fit, but Mr. Renko will be housed under *my* supervision," Cab said before Lydia could answer.

"I'm sorry, sir, but my orders are to keep Renko under close security at all times, and that'll be a lot easier if he's quartered with my troops."

Cab's nostrils flared, and his eyes glittered beneath his lashes. "I've damn well had enough of hearing orders that supposedly originated with me being thrown back at me as a means to justify blatantly illegal acts."

"I couldn't comment on that, sir. I just follow the orders I'm given."

"Then follow this one! Evgeni Renko is neither a criminal nor a prisoner. He will be treated with the utmost courtesy and housed near me."

White stood silent for several moments then nodded. "Very well, sir, if it's that important to you. But my orders are very clear on one matter; Mr. Renko will be kept under guard for his own protection."

"Protection from whom?" Lydia demanded. "This is a closed community of ten thousand people. I know the backgrounds of everyone on this station. You and your men are the only unknowns, the only potentially dangerous elements on this station. Perhaps we ought to be protecting Mr. Renko from *you*. In fact we clearly ought to. You're the ones who forcibly kidnapped him." White flushed to the roots of his close-cropped blond hair, and his mouth tightened into a narrow line.

"Lydia," Muhammid said warningly, and touched her on the elbow

She drew a hand across her forehead, and sucked in a quick breath. "Forgive me, this has been a somewhat stressful afternoon. Please inform your men that we will have quarters made available for them in the next fifteen minutes. I would prefer that you not come aboard until the arrangements have been made. If your men can simply move to their quarters it will reduce the chances for unpleasantness."

"There won't be any trouble from our end, ma'am," the Captain said with more than a hint of condescension.

"There'd better not be," Lydia warned, and the young man dropped his eyes at the command in her voice.

"There are to be no restrictions on our right to come and go from the station, will there?" Jenny asked.

"Of course not," White replied.

"And the press will have access to our proceedings?"

"Of course. It's still a free country."

"Thank you, you've really put my mind at ease," Jenny said. The Captain grinned at her, missing the irony in her words.

"Well, I'll radio the other shuttle, and get our men ready to come aboard."

"Fine," Lydia said. She watched until he vanished back into the shuttle, then turned to the chief of life support. "Muhammid," she said in an undertone. "Get on the horn and tell them to clear out the farmers' apartments on the edge of the agricultural section."

"Keeping them well away from the rest of the community, I see."

"Like I would with any virus. Also, if they're all in one place they'll be easier to handle."

"Surely you're not expecting trouble? Granted, their presence is an affront, but I'm certain nothing will happen."

"Good. You be confident, Cabot, and I'll be careful," she responded shortly, and turned back to Muhammid. "Also, see if we can find someone in the judge's building who'll be willing to give up their place to Renko. If not, get him in a nearby building."

"Right."

"I guess we're set then." She looked at Jenny. "Thanks for thinking to ask those questions. It's good to know exactly how much latitude we do have."

"I think we've all reacted as if this is the front wave of some sort of invasion. Given the captain's answers, I'm beginning to think that Cab is right and that deBaca was only interested in getting Renko over here," Jenny said soothingly.

Lydia sighed. "Maybe so, but a lifetime of distrusting governments and the military makes it hard for me to take such an optimistic outlook."

"This has been a mess, but maybe it will lead to some real communication between the System and the Earth and start to rebuild that trust," Jenny said.

"Either that or they'll come up with some new abomination," Muhammid grunted as he headed for one of the spokes out of the hub.

"He is up to something, this American president," Yuri Tupolev crooned as he strolled through the central courtyard of the Kremlin and watched the snow flutter lightly onto the sleeve of his overcoat. "But what? What?"

His aide hunched miserably down in his coat, and offered no comment. His nose was red with an incipient cold, and he sincerely wished the Premier could have held this discussion out of the bitter October weather.

Admiral Bulatoff, Supreme Commander of the Soviet Space Fleet, was undismayed by the climate. He scorned both hat and overcoat, and the shoulders of his uniform already held a dusting of snow like a set of crystalline epaulets.

"They have seized the miner and taken him under guard to the EnerSun station. The troops remain," the admiral remarked. His voice was oddly high-pitched and seemed at variance from his heavy, tanklike body.

"Does he seek to make me the villain in this piece?" Tupolev mused. "To point fingers at the barbaric Russians and come away with his own part in this matter unexposed? Well, it will not be so. We will stand or fall together, my so-dear friend and I."

"So what do we do?" the aide finally forced past his sore throat.

"We must not be backward. If the Americans have troops on the station able to oversee the actions of this Fifteenth Circuit, then we must have them also. How many men did the Americans send?"

"Sixty," Bulatoff said.

"Good, then we will send one hundred."

"The people on the station will not accept this," the aide offered meekly.

"They will not have any choice. The station is not armed, is it?" he asked the admiral.

"No."

"There you see? They won't have any choice?"

Chapter Twelve ⎯⎯⎯

There were three Russian soldiers sharing a cigarette on the walkway beneath the apartment. The sight of the olive drab uniforms with their touch of bright red piping brought a gut-wrenching reaction to Evgeni. Fear churned in the pit of his stomach and threatened to close off the air to his lungs. He spun away from the balcony railing, and re-entered the apartment.

How he hated the sight of those men with their broad, flat Slavic faces, and dehumanizing, impersonal uniforms. It brought back memories of Novgorod when he and Irina had first been married. They had shared an apartment with her sister's family, in a big, ugly gray building that sat cater-cornered to the barracks. He had watched the troops march and drill and drill and march each morning as he walked to work. Sometimes he wondered if he had volunteered for the lunar post just to escape the monotonous thunder of boots on hard-packed clay, and the tension of too many people in too few rooms.

It was already too late, but he wished he had avoided such thoughts of the past. It brought to mind Irina, and her absence was like a physical pain. He wondered where she was, but he found he could not conceive of anything beyond the walls of his gilded prison, and the attempt to summon her presence fluttered away like dandelion seeds in a wind.

The door page sounded, and he steeled himself for the inevitable appearance of his guards. Twice daily, at the changing of the shifts, the page would chime, the door would open, and a carefully balanced pair, one Russian, one American, would peer blankly in at him. If he weren't in the living room they would come in search of him. Sometimes he took to hiding in the bathroom or out on the balcony just to excite them.

He suddenly frowned, realizing it was too early for the changing of the cuckoo clock guards, as he secretly termed them. The chime sounded again, and he moved to open the door. It wasn't locked from the outside—there was no reason with four soldiers on guard at all times. He opened the door to find the pretty red-haired American in the outer hall. The four soldiers, Russian and American alike, were eyeing her with interest and ill-disguised lust. She ignored them with the same disdain that a person gives to insects on the sidewalk.

"May I come in?" she asked after he had continued to stare at her for several seconds.

"Oh, oh yes, of course." He stepped back, allowing her to enter the living room. She closed the door firmly behind her, cutting off the encroaching stares from the hallway. She had spoken with him when he had been brought to the EnerSun station, and had promised to try and determine the whereabouts of Irina and Analisa. He hadn't really expected to see her again.

She did not waste time on meaningless pleasantries. "Your wife and child are outbound for Mars with Joseph Reichart."

During the three days since his capture he had been tormented with visions of them trapped by the soldiers and returned to Earth, turned over to the Russians, or perhaps even dead. The sense of relief was so great that the strength seemed to drain out of his legs, and he sank down into an armchair.

"We were lucky to find out at all," Jenny continued. "The Russians have put a block on all communications coming in or out of the station except in a few select cases. Fortunately Lydia is one of those exceptions. She has a daughter who's a research scientist on Mars, and the girl was able to learn of Joe's plans."

Evgeni was confused by all these names of people he didn't know, so he clung to the one piece of solid information he had heard. "They will be staying on Mars?"

"No. Mr. Reichart's plans are to go on to the asteroids."

"So far," he murmured softly. "I was supposed to go to the asteroids after all of this was over," he said, looking up at her.

"And you still will," Jenny said briskly. "We're going to get this thing resolved as quickly as possible."

"But all these soldiers," he protested. "They will never allow you to hold a fair hearing, and they will never allow me to leave this station. Or if they do it will be only to take me to Moscow."

"Don't underestimate the guys in the white hats."

"I beg pardon?" he asked, puzzled.

"Sorry. Old American phrase." She sat down opposite him on the couch, and leaned forward intently. "Look, I know things look pretty bleak right now, but we're all working very hard to get this thing settled. It's sort of funny really," she said with a mirthless smile. "DeBaca didn't see anything wrong with sending occupying *American* troops to the station, but he's screaming like a stuck pig about the Russian landing. The United States has filed a formal protest with the United Nations, the EnerSun Corporation is complaining to anyone who'll listen, and the State Department is exchanging threats with the Kremlin."

"I'm afraid I do not understand any of this."

"Don't worry, I don't think anyone else does either. I think the only people who can really comprehend what's going on are those of us on this station who are living through this occupation." She sighed and looked thoughtfully at her fingernails. "It's not going to be easy, but Cab will find some way to render his decision and get you back with your family."

"Would you like a drink?" Evgeni asked her.

"No, thank you."

He crossed to the kitchen and splashed some vodka into the glass. "It's strange," he said while he carefully replaced the cap. "I am continually finding myself at the mercy of this American judge. First with the U.S. Steel fiasco, and now this. You will forgive me," he said, saluting her with his glass, "if I am less than thrilled with the prospect. How do I know I can trust him any better this time?"

"That's a fair question, and the only assurance I can give you is that he has changed. Cab, whatever his faults, is a very honorable and civilized man. What he didn't understand was that he was dealing with barbarians. He was trying to do his duty as he perceived it, and he thought everyone would play by the rules. When word reached us about your collective he was devastated."

"But what about all these soldiers? They are here to see that I am never heard and that I never get free!"

"No, I don't think that's the case. You got grabbed because your constant exposure in the press was making some very powerful people very nervous. You see, there's a presidential election coming up next month, and your actions may cost the current president his job."

"None of this is making me feel any better."

"I'm sorry, I was thinking aloud. The point is that they may be able to silence the publicity, but they can't silence the court. The hearing will take place, Cab will reach his decision, and you will be allowed to join your family."

"Your optimism is comforting, and I hope you are right. Also, I appreciate your coming here. It gets very lonely."

"I'll try to come as often as I can, or get permission for other people to visit." She stood and smoothed down the fabric of her skirt. "Keep your chin up. This will all be over soon."

"I try to tell myself that, but the time seems endless, trapped in this apartment. I do feel better now, knowing that Irina and Analisa are safe."

"And we're going to keep you safe, too," Jenny said as she walked with him to the door.

"Are all American women like you?" Evgeni asked shyly.

She smiled. "No, of course not. We come in all sizes, shapes, colors, and attitudes. Just like your women do."

"I don't know. You just seem so confident."

"Now, that may be an American trait. We're a pretty independent bunch of people."

"It must be very nice."

"I suppose so, but it can have its drawbacks. You have to take a lot of the responsibility for yourself, and there is a good deal of pressure to live up to the ideals Americans are supposed to embody." She gave him a rueful smile. "As you've seen we don't always succeed."

"At least you make the effort," he said, opening the door for her.

"Hey, we don't have a corner on the ethics market. What you've done took a lot of courage, and proves that honor and justice aren't delineated by national boundaries."

"Thank you, you are very kind to say so. I will remember what you said when late at night I begin wishing I had never started all this."

"Don't look back, it's not worth the effort. Save that energy for the future."

"I just worry about how and where that future will be spent."

"We're going to work to make it a good one. See you in a day or two." She swept past the guards, giving them a cool nod as she passed.

Evgeni closed the door, and leaned his back against the hard surface. Jenny's visit had helped, but now the doubts and fears rushed back, bringing that breathless sickness that had gripped him for days. The woman was nice, but he believed her to be naive. They would never let him leave this place alive. He looked around the pleasant apartment, noting the elegance and luxury of the fixtures and furnishings. Yes, it was a very nice place, but his heart knew it for what it really was: a tomb, a gilded crypt where he would be held until it was time to bury him for good.

Ken Furakawa looked about the cluttered chambers, noting the piles of disc boxes that were stacked next to the reader, and the reams of printout that fell like paper waterfalls over desk, chairs, and sofa. He picked up one page that draped over the back of a chair. *Craig v. Harney,* he read, and the body of the case was scribbled with notes and red underlinings.

"You look tired," he commented as he dumped the papers onto the floor, and took a seat.

"Not tired; defeated. This whole thing is lousy," Cab said, gesturing wearily at the office.

"My emotion at this point would be closer to frustration, but I understand the sentiment. What are we going to do, Cabot?"

"Damned if I know. Technically we shouldn't even be having this conversation. The attorneys for Justice would howl if they thought we were in collusion."

"I would say they have no cause to complain. After all, turnabout is fair play."

"Ouch," Huntington murmured.

"Actually, there are other reasons which would excuse our

meeting," the Japanese hastened to add. "It is probably wrong of me to say so, but given the irregularities of this case to date, and given that these irregularities have been caused by such representatives of the state—fuck them."

Cab jerked upright in his chair. Never in all his years of association with Furakawa had he heard the courtly and elegant Japanese-American utter such a word. He raised one eyebrow. "You *are* upset."

"Have you had time to read the transcripts of the depositions I took, or the answers to the interrogatories?"

"Yes."

"Well?" the lawyer prodded.

"All right, all right. It's obvious everyone is stonewalling and lying through their teeth, but what can I do about it? This is the President of the United States. I can't throw him in jail. Hell, look what happened when I just cited him for contempt. What am I supposed to do? Send some of those troops he so thoughtfully provided for us down to slap him on the wrist?"

"The Russian troops might be more willing to undertake that assignment," Furakawa said with a slight smile.

"Don't talk to me about soldiers. Do you have any idea how nerve-racking it is to be sitting on the bench while armed troops monitor every aspect of your case? Even if we had the evidence to nail deBaca and Tupolev, how could I render an honest decision under these circumstances?"

"I don't know, Cabot. Men have had to reach these kinds of decisions in other times and other countries. If they chose to support the illegal actions of their duly constituted government, who can blame them? They know the alternatives."

"The sound of jackboots in the hall, the knock on the door, and the dark, lonely ride into oblivion," Cab said quietly. "But I can't believe this of *my* country. We're not Nazis. We have the most enlightened political and legal system ever designed. This can't be happening."

"'What country before ever existed a century and a half without a rebellion?... The tree of liberty must be refreshed from time to time with the blood of patriots and tyrants. It is its natural manure,'" Furakawa murmured softly. Huntington grimaced. "It offends you, these words of revolution from the past?"

"It was just that—the past. Surely we've grown beyond the

need to settle matters on the battlefield. We put in place the machinery that would make such periodic upheavals unnecessary."

"But machinery can get old and rusty, and more importantly it can be misused. The killing of those people on the Moon, the occupation of this station by armed troops, is this what the founding fathers had in mind for their beautiful new Constitution? Maybe it's time we did shake the tree just to see what falls out. Myself, I think there are wicked and evil men hiding among the branches, keeping safe and powerful by manipulating a system that should have kept them out."

Cabot shook his head. "I don't know, I just don't know anymore. Once, years ago, it was all so clear. All the philosophy made such sense, seemed so right. Then I left school and saw how the real world worked, and now it doesn't seem so clear. They all talk about honor, duty, service to the people, but I'm beginning to think that at base, the sole function of government is to perpetuate government. The rights and needs of the people aren't worth spit in the wind against that desperate drive to survive."

"I've never before heard you talk about *the people* with anything but the greatest contempt, Cabot," Furakawa said, eyeing him over the tops of his steepled fingers. "You've always been a much better Federalist than a Republican."

Huntington smiled sadly. "I know. Can I blame my upbringing? For seven generations my family has been hard at work making decisions for the *common* man."

"So what's changed?"

He shrugged. "I don't know. Maybe I've realized that I'm one of those common men, too?" He stared thoughtfully down at his hands where they were clasped before him on the desk. "No, it goes deeper than that. I think I've begun to realize that as long as we can restrain men from harming one another, they are perfectly capable of making decisions for their own lives. They don't need an omnipresent state to tell them where and how to work, who to marry, how to live."

"You would be giving up a tremendous amount of power."

"And that brings us right back to the problem, doesn't it? We're sitting here having this discussion because of the actions of two men who don't want to give up that power."

"And since we are back on the subject, I'm going to once

more put you on the spot. What are you going to do, Cab?"

He rose from his chair, and circled around the desk. "I want to see them punished as much as you do, Ken, but I can't do it without evidence. If I did I'd be showing the same contempt for the law that they display. Some of us have to keep the barbarians at bay, and I don't think we should do it by becoming barbarians ourselves."

Furakawa sighed. "You are right, of course, and now I will return home to work."

"I confess, I wish I could go home," Cab said as he walked Furakawa to the door. "I never thought at my age I'd get homesick."

"Perhaps you should make a trip home, then. After all, our dear Russian friends would not stop you. Everyone else on this station may be trapped, but those of us with the dubious honor of being associated with this case can come and go as we please."

"All of us except Evgeni Renko. Dammit! If only we could get the proof we need."

"Care to try infiltrating the Kremlin?" Furakawa joked.

Something in the offhanded remark jogged a memory. Cab grabbed the older man's arm, and stopped him before he could step out of the office. "Wait, wait. A couple of weeks ago I had dinner with Joe Reichart and several station personnel. I was worrying about the lack of hard evidence, and he said not to worry, it was being handled by someone on the inside."

"Do you have any idea who it is?"

"No, not a clue."

"My God, the federal bureaucracy is immense. It would be like looking for a needle in a haystack."

Cab's shoulders slumped. "You're right, it's impossible. Well, maybe the unknown will get in touch with us."

"You are a supreme optimist if you believe that. Surely if the man was going to respond he would have done so by now."

"Unless he was trying to get in touch with Reichart, and of course Reichart's gone."

"And, finding his employer on the lam, our unknown has most likely retreated prudently back into the woodwork."

"There has to be some way to get in touch with Reichart."

"Our friendly troopies, American and Russian alike, are never going to permit you to contact him."

"Not necessarily. They might if they thought I was going to use my influence to try and get him to return with Renko's wife and child."

"Cabot, I think you are enjoying this," Furakawa accused, seeing the delighted smile that curved the younger man's lips. "I had no idea you had such a taste for intrigue."

"Neither did I." He slapped the fragile old man lightly on the shoulder. "I'm learning all kinds of things about myself. Jenny would probably say I'm in a midlife crisis."

"Well, I must leave you or I will miss my shuttle. You seem substantially happier than when I first came in."

"I've got something I can do. It was the sense of futility and helplessness that was destroying me." He shook hands with Furakawa. "I'll be in touch, and we'll get that evidence."

"Business is good," Max, the night bartender, remarked to Artis as she came out of the back room of The White Owl. He was drawing beers and carefully loading a tray for one of the waitresses. The plump women glanced about the crowded room and grimaced.

"I'd rather make less money, and see more familiar faces," she said in an undertone. Here and there, in isolated little knots, a few station dwellers drank and visited, but the room was predominately filled with uniforms, Russian and American. "It's like everyone's got the plague," Artis remarked, turning her back on the room. "The colonists won't sit with the soldiers, and the soldiers won't sit with each other. You could ride a bicycle through the no man's land between each group."

"Maybe it's better that way," Max said, finishing with the tray and waving the waitress away. "Tempers are getting shorter and shorter. So far, everyone's just mumbling into their beers, and nobody's overhearing the insults, but God help us if somebody does." He whistled soundlessly, the air hissing through his teeth. "There'll be a fight like you haven't seen."

"That's why I hired you," Artis said, studying his square, heavy face that bore the evidence of a good many fights. "You're not pretty, and you're certainly not sympathetic like a good bartender should be, but you discourage troublemakers."

"Glad to help out, but when I signed on I didn't know I was going to have to take on the Air Force and the whole fucking Russian navy."

"Look on it as a challenge," she said, patting him on the arm. "And if you should have to break up a brawl, I'll throw in some hazardous duty pay."

"Thanks."

"I'll be in my office if you need me."

He began to fill more orders, keeping a wary eye on the crowded room. There was an atmosphere in the bar that he hadn't felt since a night sixteen years ago in Hong Kong. Then, as now, the room had vibrated with an undercurrent of anger and hostility, fed by the presence of too many men who had lived too long without a woman. He had killed a man that night, but he had managed to elude capture in the teeming streets of Hong Kong, and eventually he had made his way to the System. He had knocked about the Moon and through the asteroids and worked on a smelting crew before he decided the body was getting too old for the life, and had settled down as chief bartender and bouncer for Artis.

"Hey, I'm sorry, I don't understand."

Max's head jerked up from the drink he was pouring, and he looked over to where Bethany Morales was laughing nervously at one of the Russian soldiers. She was one of the youngest waitresses, just earning some extra money before she went Earthside in the spring for college, and was obviously uncertain as to how to handle her amorous customer. The Russian had her by the arm, and was murmuring huskily to her while his friends urged him on. It was clear she was not enjoying the attention.

"Look, you're going to make me spill these drinks. You're a real nice guy, but I really don't understand what you're saying so why don't you just let go," she said, gently trying to disengage herself from his drunken grip.

One of the Air Force men came out of his chair, and jerked the Russian's hand from the girl's arm. "You heard the lady," he said. "Let her go!"

The Russian growled something to his companions, and rose to his feet, kicking the chair away from him. He snatched Bethany back. She gave a wail of protest as she stumbled into his arms, the tray cascading to the floor in a deluge of beer and vodka.

"You mother-fucker!" the soldier shouted, and grabbed Bethany by the upper arm.

A real tug of war was developing between the two men, and there was a rising tide of protests, shouts of encouragement, and curses from the onlookers. Max came chugging from behind the bar as one of the colonists began plowing through the crowd that was gathering around the combatants. Max knew him by sight, and had some vague idea that he worked on one of the station's farms, but for the life of him he couldn't remember the man's name. The man was short and stocky with a shock of carrot-red hair that seemed to grow vertically out of his scalp, and Max could tell by the way the muscles in his upper arms were bunching that he intended to swing.

"Now, let's break it up!" he roared, as he slammed into the wall of backs that separated him from Bethany, the Russian playboy, and her would-be rescuer. The men parted, but sullenly, and Max realized he was too late. The irate colonist had reached the threesome, and with quick, jabbing punches hit first the Russian and then the American. The men fell back nursing their faces, and he caught Bethany in his arms, and began to walk her away.

"Hey! What the hell did you hit *me* for?" the Emergency Force man yelled. "I'm an American like you!"

"You're a goddamn goose-stepping goon. We don't want *any* of you here, so get the hell off our station and leave us alone!"

There was a roar of fury from the soldier, and he lunged at the colonist. His buddies were right behind. But behind them the Russians had gathered their wits, and they fell on the American soldiers like hounds on deer. The room was filled with shouts and screams and the dull, smacking sound of flesh on flesh. Max was hit in the shoulder as one of the few locals charged past him to enter the fray. Somewhere deep within the melee of churning bodies he heard Bethany's terrified scream. He waded in, and the world dissolved into a kaleidoscope of fists and knees and feet.

"Where are you?" Peter asked softly. Jenny turned from her rapt contemplation of the Moon, which was set like a glowing disk against the backdrop of stars and space. Neither one had felt much like dinner, so by tacit agreement they had gone walking and ended up in one of the observation rooms set in the top of the hub.

She sighed. "I wish I could tell you something profound, but I can't. Recently confusion seems to be my primary state of mind."

He cupped her chin in his hand, and tilted her face up. "No need to be embarrassed by that. I don't think any of us feel like we're living in an understandable world anymore."

"I suppose not, but at least you belong somewhere. I feel as if I'm between worlds right now."

"No, you're not. You belong here, with us."

"But do I?" she asked, slipping out of his hold. "I realize now that I never really had very strong beliefs or attitudes. I just drifted along, accepting life as it was, never questioning, and taking the path of least resistance. Now I'm in the midst of a crisis, being forced to make decisions and take stands, and I don't much like it."

"I think you're being too hard on yourself. If you had wanted an easy, mindless existence you would have never left dance and gone into law. You told me you wanted to make a difference. Well, now you have the chance."

"And I'm scared," she said, turning back to face him.

"And you think we're not? Good God, woman"—he took her by the shoulders, and gave her a gentle shake—"who told you you had to be perfect all the time? Can't you leave yourself a little room for improvement? " He pulled her close, and she rested her head on his shoulder. Her eyes remained on the darkness beyond the observation port.

"I wish we could go outside," she said softly, dropping a topic that she obviously had no desire to continue pursuing.

"Why?"

"I'd feel less trapped."

"Being with the court, you have the right to come and go. Maybe you ought to go Earthside for a visit."

"No. It would be too easy to stay."

"There, you see, you have made a decision."

"Only by default. I'm too scared to put it to the test. I might get home and say to hell with all of you up here."

"You'd never leave Cabot," Peter said, turning away to rest his palms on the port and stare out at the stars.

"Why does that bother you?"

"You're right, it shouldn't bother me, and I have no right to put you on the spot."

"What are you talking about?" She tossed back her hair. "What spot?"

He drew in a deep breath and turned back to face her. "All right, I'll ask. Why did you move back with Huntington? You could have stayed with me once you two patched up your differences."

Even in the dim light of the observation room he could see a quick flame of blood on her cheeks. She gestured helplessly, searching for words. "I . . . well, I . . . we had to work together. It was easier if we were closer."

"Oh, come now, Jenny. The telephone has been in service for a lot of years."

"It's not the same. Cab and I are used to working very closely, and . . ." She paused and slapped the wall with an open hand. "And you're absolutely right, you're putting me on the spot."

"Okay, we'll drop it."

They stood at opposite ends of the port and watched as the station's spin carried the Moon out of view.

"Look, I'm not sleeping with Cab, and I am sleeping with you, so what's the problem?" she abruptly demanded.

He held up both hands in a placating gesture. "Hey, there's no problem."

"Good, because I really can't deal with—" An insistent, blaring noise began whooping through the station. "Dear God, what's that?"

"Alarm," Peter said tensely. "I've only heard it once before in five years up here."

"What happened then?" Jenny asked, hurrying after him as he headed for the door.

"Small meteor pierced the skin of the rim."

"How nice," she muttered, and for one wild moment she felt as if the air were becoming progressively thinner in the station.

"Don't worry, they're usually patched long before there's any danger."

"Where are we going?"

"Back to the rim. We may as well find out what's happening."

• • •

"So you see, Captain White. It would be to everyone's benefit if I can convince Mr. Reichart to return to this station with Renko's wife and child."

The officer frowned, and shifted uncomfortably in his chair. "Why didn't you try this before now, and why does it have to be done tonight? Couldn't it wait until tomorrow?"

"I just received new information from Earth that can perhaps be used to convince Mr. Reichart," Cabot said smoothly. "And as for waiting, each hour we delay takes Mr. Reichart farther and farther from Earth." Lydia folded her hands in front of her face, and impassively watched White, trying to judge his reaction.

"I don't know, my orders are to allow only routine radio transmissions, and the Soviets for sure aren't going to like this."

"Captain, I resent your hesitation. You seem to be implying that I cannot be trusted." Cab paused and smoothed the sleeve of his jacket, then looked up and continued. "And, as a close friend to both the President and General Abrams, I can assure you that your attitude will be reported."

White chewed on that bit of information for a few moments, then nodded. "All right, you can make the call, but I want to be present for the conversation, and I'm certain that Commander Sucholevsky will want to be present, as well."

"Fine. Ms. Kim Nu and I will meet you in station control."

White nodded, and left the office. Lydia expelled a breath and leaned back in her chair. "I never thought you'd get away with it, but you combined just the right level of threat and hauteur."

"We haven't 'gotten away' with it yet. We still have to locate Reichart."

"Finding him won't be any problem. He's on one of the standard outbound flights."

"I thought he'd have a ship of his own."

Lydia smiled and shook her head. "Joe's rich, but let's be realistic. An anti-matter deep-space vessel costs *lots* of money. Having one built for personal use would be beyond the realm of reality." She pushed back her chair. "Well, shall we go?" She paused at the door and looked back over her shoulder at Cab. "I hope you're good at riddle games because it's going to be interesting getting the information you want without alerting White and Sucholevsky that you're up to something."

"Just so I can make your day, no, I'm not good at word games. I was rather hoping Joe would be very quick on the uptake."

"Oh, he is, but I rather wish it were something less critical at stake."

Cab caught her by the elbow, holding her in place. "Is it that critical? Or am I just displaying an egocentric view of the world, believing that my little balliwick is so very important?"

"What we do here will have profound impact on the course of future relations between the Earth and the System. There, now don't you feel better?" she asked, giving him a light pat on the cheek.

"No."

"Neither do I."

The communications controller nodded, and Cab slid into the chair before the microphone. "Remember," Lydia warned, taking up a position on his left. "There's going to be a slight delay in communications, but don't let that throw you off."

"Right."

Captain White took a seat and looked bored, while the Soviet commander stood next to Cab, folded his arms across his barrel chest, and glared down at the judge. It was a little like having the Colossus of Rhodes for a next-door neighbor, and Cab resented the physically intimidating presence of the far larger man.

"You're cleared for transmission," came a disembodied voice over the speakers. "Go ahead EnerSun."

"Reichart, are you there?"

"I'm here, Cabot, what do you need."

Cab leaned in, and gripped the mike tightly in both hands. "I am speaking to you in my official capacity." He lightly stressed the word *official* and hoped that Joe would understand and be a little less chummy.

"All right, judge, I'm ready to listen."

Huntington breathed a soft sigh of relief. "I've been reviewing our dealings, Mr. Reichart, and I can't help but think that this situation has been mishandled. I don't know if you remember that dinner party we attended...."

"I remember."

"You said something very interesting that night that could be of use in resolving this matter."

"We said a good many things that night. I'm not precisely certain what you're referring to."

White was beginning to frown in puzzlement and irritation. He rose from his chair and moved in. Cab felt his body trying to shrink to avoid the encroaching presence of the two soldiers. His hands felt slippery on the metal base of the mike, and he took a firmer grip, desperately searching for some clever and obscure phrase that would make everything clear to Reichart.

"We were discussing the problem of *judex debet judicare secundum allegata et probata.*"

"Ah, yes. Now I remember. And you think I can help?"

"I think you ought to return or at least make the information available to those of us here."

"What the hell is going on?" White interrupted. "This doesn't sound like you're trying to convince Reichart to come back."

"Who was that?"

"One of my new associates. He feels we ought to get down to business and stop sparring with one another."

"I'm certainly willing."

"Basically I feel you've overreacted. You've removed a valuable witness when you took Mrs. Renko with you, and this court must have all available evidence if I'm to make a reasoned decision." Cab was babbling, saying anything that came into his head while he worried that he would miss what Reichart said and never learn the name of the inside source.

Suddenly an alarm began bleating through the control room. Lydia crossed quickly to an interstation radio and lifted the small headset. She listened for a few seconds, then looked over her shoulder at White and Sucholevsky. "A fight's broken out between your men, and several local residents."

"What? Where?" White demanded.

"This cannot be tolerated," Sucholevsky said, whirling on White. "Your men have provoked my troops at every opportunity."

"*My* men! What about the high-handed way you people marched in here? You've tried to dictate to my troops the way you do to the colonists."

The Russian began to bluster, and Lydia jumped in. "Goddammit! We've got a crisis on our hands, and all you can do is argue about who's at fault. Now get the hell down there, and *do* something," she said, her arm jerking toward the elevator. "My God, talk about inefficiency, you can't even control your own troops. You better believe this will be reported to your superiors!"

Cab, keeping a wary eye on the two soldiers who were staring with growing anger at Lydia, carefully slid his hand across the consol top and switched off the audio speakers. He then lifted the headset.

"Talk, fast," he whispered into the wire-fine mouthpiece, "while Lydia buys me some time."

"My man on the inside is Taylor Moffit, but—"

"The Secretary of State?" Cab muttered incredulously.

"Yes, but I have a feeling he's backed out on me. He should have had the evidence by now."

"Then he'll have to be reconvinced."

"Talk to him. He'll respond to you. . . ."

"No more time," Huntington hissed, and snapped off the radio. He then leaped to his feet to face the oncoming bulk of Sucholevsky.

"What are you doing?"

"We can continue this conversation at another time," he said with a dismissing wave at the radio consol. "Now where's this fight? We have to get this settled before the entire station blows up."

"You were using the headset," the Russian growled, reaching for Cab's arm. He dodged the heavier man, and raced for the elevator. "Have you sent for station security?" he snapped at Lydia.

"Yes, sir," Lydia said with a wry twist to her mouth as she followed him out of the room. Balked, Sucholevsky lumbered after them.

By the time they had reached the rim, Sucholevsky and White had received confirmation of the fight over their throat mikes, and had gone pelting off toward The White Owl. Cab and Lydia paused at the foot of the stairs leading to the upper levels.

"Thank you so much for taking command for me," Lydia said dryly.

"I'm sorry. I was just trying to deflect Sucholevsky."

"I know, and you're forgiven. Did you get what you wanted from Joe?"

"Yes. Now I have to reach the man."

"Why not just call him?"

"No, this is going to be delicate, and I think it better be handled in person. How soon can I get to Earth?"

"None of the passenger shuttles are running, but..." She closed her eyes momentarily, then nodded. "There's a freight shuttle making a run for Johnson and Johnson tonight. It won't be very comfortable, but they have to let it fly; those drugs decay very quickly."

"Fine. Tell them I'm on my way just as soon as I pack a few things."

Lydia nodded and Cab started back to the AVC stop. She suddenly paused partway up the stairs, and looked back. "Cabot," she called.

"Yes?"

"You're all right."

"Thank you," he said simply, and he found that he meant it.

Chapter Thirteen

"I hope you white people realize that you're in violation of martial law, and if you're caught your asses are gonna be thrown in the slammer," Muhammid announced as the door to Lydia's apartment slid shut behind him.

Tina smiled faintly at his sally. No one else managed to summon even that much enthusiasm. Artis sat huddled in a big armchair, nursing a cup of hot tea in both hands. The jest and vivacity she always displayed was extinguished, and she seemed shrunken and old. Trevor stared moodily out into space, and Lydia, who stood before them like a drill sergeant, looked uncommonly grim.

"Guess it wasn't very funny," the life support engineer muttered as he slid onto the couch. At that moment Flo emerged briskly from the kitchen, carrying the inevitable coffee tray.

"Did you have any trouble getting here?" Lydia asked.

"Nah, hell, there are only a hundred and sixty of them. How thorough can they be?"

"I wouldn't have risked calling you here except that I think it's very important that everyone be brought up to date. Also, because several members of our council have expressed the opinion that it is time to stop cooperating and start retaliating, I naturally feel that such a course would have to be very carefully discussed."

"Well I am unalterably opposed to it! I don't know what

you people can be thinking of," Flo scolded as she poured the coffee.

"Your opinion does not constitute *discussion*," Tina said, her eyes snapping with anger. "And besides, we all know where *you* stand."

"I resent that—"

"Ladies," Trevor murmured. "And may I point out that an exchange of insults also doesn't represent discussion." He followed the remark with a pointed look to Tina. She subsided, but with ill-disguised reluctance.

Lydia sighed, and pushed back her hair with both hands. "Before we get into this, why don't we handle the easy part first. As you all know there was a real free-for-all at The White Owl last night."

"We tried to prevent it," Artis said plaintively, looking up from her tea.

"I'm sure you did, and no one's blaming you for what happened, Artis dear. The friction had been building for days. It could have started anywhere. But to go on. One soldier was stabbed by a local."

"Who was it?" Tina asked.

"Tim Singer, one of the agro workers." Tina nodded. "He's currently being held in custody until a hearing can be arranged."

"Is he being held by local security?" Trevor asked.

"No, under military guard."

"Damn."

"Yes, that sort of sums up my feelings, too."

"Any chance Huntington can get him out or at least get him transferred to our people?"

"I'm sure he'd try if he were here, but he's not."

"Not here? Not here?" Flo echoed, sitting up a bit in her chair. "Why isn't he here, and where did he go?"

"I'll come to that," Lydia said, holding up a hand. "Let me get through the casualties from last night. It has to be said that to Tim's credit he didn't pull the knife at the beginning of the fight. One of the waitresses—"

"Bethany Morales," Artis supplied.

"Was being harassed by several of the soldiers. Tim went in to try and free her, and the fight started."

"So when did the knifing take place?" Tina asked as she

leaned forward and picked up a cup of coffee.

"After Bethany got hurt."

"Now, that I hadn't heard," Trevor said, straightening a bit.

"The fight just sort of rolled over her," Artis explained mournfully. "Apparently she took a glancing blow to the head and passed out. While she was on the floor she got kicked about a good deal."

"Is she all right?"

"She's in the hospital with a severe concussion."

"Oh fine," the chemist muttered, running a hand over his bald spot. "And that's when Singer used the knife?"

"When he saw her go down he totally lost control," Artis said. "That's about the time I came out of my office, so I saw the stabbing."

"Who did he get? One of ours and one of theirs?" Muhammid asked interestedly.

"One of theirs."

"Well, that's something I guess."

"I'd like to shoot them all!" Artis said passionately.

"You may get your chance," Muhammid said with a predatory smile.

"Stop it! Just stop it all of you! I won't listen to this kind of talk!" Flo rose to her feet, her thin hands fluttering agitatedly.

"Fine!" Tina shouted also coming out of her chair. "You know where the door is—walk!"

"Sit down!" Lydia rapped out, laying her words like a stick across the two women's outburst. "And Flo, for God's sake, get control of yourself. I will not tolerate another hysterical outburst from you! I've had just about as much as *I* can take."

She found her voice quavering. Embarrassed by her own weakness she turned her back on her friends, fighting to regain control. She thought of Joe, and for one wistful moment wished she could just drop everything and run away to join him. The moment passed quickly, and she was back in control.

She cleared her throat and swung back to face them. "Now, as a result of the fight Captain White and Commander Sucholevsky have declared a state of emergency and placed the station under martial law."

"This we knew already, Lydia," Trevor said. "They've been putting up handbills, and breaking in on the broadcast system every hour on the hour to announce the rules and restrictions."

She squeezed her eyes shut, and looked pained. "I'm sorry, I don't mean to be repetitive or pedantic. It's just that it's been a very long forty-eight hours, and I'm beginning to notice the lack of sleep."

Trevor stood, and in a totally uncharacteristic show of affection, stepped to her side and gave her an awkward hug. She was touched for she knew how much the gesture had cost this very undemonstrative and private man.

"So, does that bring us up to date?" Tina asked.

"Not quite," Trevor broke in. He looked over at Lydia. "You still haven't told us why Justice Huntington left."

"The administration is stonewalling Ken Furakawa's investigations. Without evidence of wrongdoing, Cabot can't hand down a ruling against deBaca and Tupolev. Fortunately he remembered what the rest of us had forgotten—that Joe had an insider within the administration who was going to get the proof. We got in touch with Joe, and learned the identity of this man. Cab has gone to talk to him."

"And who is he?" Flo asked casually, but there was an undercurrent of intense interest behind the words.

Lydia glanced at her, and felt the prickle of some unidentifiable emotion run down her spine. Her doubts made her feel unworthy, but she hadn't reached her current position without learning the value of caution.

She shook her head. "I think its best that we keep that information as private as possible. It's not that I distrust any of you, it's just that what isn't known can't be told." Everyone nodded except Flo, who dropped her eyes and chewed nervously on her lower lip.

Muhammid shifted irritably in his chair. "I suppose the outcome of this hearing is important to Huntington, but frankly I can't see that it's worth a damn to us. What's relevant to our situation is the presence of those troops, not whether Cabot can slap deBaca and Tupolev on the hands. We've got to do something to show everyone groundside that we won't sit idly while our civil rights are violated."

"So you're going to violate the civil rights of those soldiers by acts of violence," Flo said shrilly. "I can't see that that's an improvement."

"No one's even suggested what kinds of action we would take," Tina said. "Why did you immediately assume that it would be violent?" The engineer's eyes were hard as she stared at the older woman.

"I've listened to things you've said, and heard the mutterings from the community. The mood throughout the station is very ugly, and I'm afraid this could easily get out of control."

"Look, there are ways to deal with an occupying force, short of having children giving them bouquets of flowers with grenades hidden inside," Muhammid argued. "We can limit this thing, and still communicate our outrage at the occupation."

"We can also communicate our outrage through petitions and delegations. Our government provides us with a number of alternatives for seeking relief."

"And all of them take time," Artis said, for the first time pulling out of her depression and taking an interest in the discussion.

"Artis is right. We have to do something to show the authorities groundside that it's not worth it to keep the troops here," Tina said.

"And if we're patient, the troops will be withdrawn just as soon as this hearing is settled."

"How do you know? Can you guarantee that?" Trevor asked, taking his pipe out of his mouth.

Flo looked confusedly from face to face. "Why shouldn't they?"

"I can think of a lot of reasons," Lydia said quietly. "The Earth authorities are desperate to reassert control out here. What better way to insure our cooperation than to leave armed soldiers in our homes? Especially if we meekly accept it without protest."

"But we have been protesting!"

"And they haven't been listening, so maybe we better send a message they can't ignore," Tina said.

Lydia looked around the grim-faced circle of people. "I'll put the question. Should we engage in passive, nonviolent resistance against the occupying troops? Artis?"

The woman briefly gripped the silver ankh that she always wore, then nodded. "Yes, I think we have no choice. And I don't mean in just the political sense. Our people are angry and rebellious. We have to give them some outlet for this anger or it will explode in terrifying and dangerous directions. If we take the initiative, we will at least be able to channel and choose the direction the disobedience takes."

"Trevor?"

"I agree with Artis. I'd rather be in control of the whirlwind than riding it. However, I'm less pure than she is. I want to see these bastards squirm a bit."

"Oh, I do, too, darling. I want someone to pay for what happened to Bethany. But since Flo would object if I cut off their testicles, I'll be civilized and settle for passive resistance."

"Muhammid?"

"You know where I stand. It's Tina and I who came to you about this in the first place."

"I want to make sure you're still committed to this course of action."

"More than ever."

"Tina?"

"Just let me at them. I always did want to be a modern-day Emma Goldman."

"Flo?"

"I am utterly opposed to this madness," she said, and her bony, angular body seemed to curl in distress.

"What about you, Lydia? You know we won't try this if you're against it," Artis said.

The manager smiled wearily. "I may lose my job and find myself back in Corpus Christi, but we'll do it. It's never an easy choice to say "no, I won't," but I think we've been pushed to it. That's what the tyrants have never understood. They can punish you, imprison you, even kill you, but at base no man can force you to do anything against your will."

" 'Freedom—I won't,' " Tina said softly, quoting the phrase coined by the twentieth-century science fiction writer Eric Frank Russell, which had become their motto.

"And I'm going to exercise that right immediately," Flo said stiffly as she rose to her feet. "You may all do what you wish, but I will have no part of it." She started toward the door, then paused and looked back. "And if this kind of unlawfulness and illegality is to be the way this committee does business, then I want no part of the committee either. Please do not call me for any more little meetings. I'm not interested!" The click of the door as it slid shut seemed to echo loudly in the silent room.

"Jesus Christ! What *is* her problem?" Tina exclaimed as she bounded out of her chair, and paced partway to the door.

"Not everyone is as eager to embrace revolution as you are," Lydia said quietly as she sank down on the couch. Artis leaned over and patted her soothingly on the hand.

"Me?" Tina asked. "What about you, Lydia? I didn't notice you holding back."

"One can follow a course of action while still regretting the necessity of the choice. I wish it hadn't come to this. I wish the groundside governments had dealt fairly and honorably with us, and that rationality and compromise could have prevailed." She smiled faintly at the younger woman's shocked and outraged expression. "I'm sorry if I've disappointed you," she said gently. "But when you reach my age, the blare of the trumpets and the calls to glory sound more discordant than inspiring." She shook herself, banishing the momentary depression, and looked briskly at the remaining committee members. "By morning I want your recommendations on how to make life miserable but not threatening for our unwelcome guests. After that, we'll evaluate our people, and begin assigning them to various projects." They all sat silently staring at her, as if comprehending for the first time the magnitude of what they had agreed to do. "Well let's get to it!" she ordered, bringing her hands together sharply. They rose, and made a concentrated rush for the door.

"By *twos*," she stressed, stopping them before they all blundered into the hall. "For God's sake, let's not get arrested for violating the martial law rule on illegal gatherings."

There were sheepish looks all around, and Muhammid shook his head. "Some revolutionaries. Shit, we can't even figure out how to get home without running into trouble."

"I tell you, this situation can't continue!" Captain White said. He tried to force a note of command into his voice, but he ended up sounding rather desperate and harried.

Lydia stared at his worried and frustrated face on the com screen and nodded. "I understand that, but as I've told you our crews are working as hard as they can to locate the problem."

"But it's been a day and a half! Let me tell you, if this is the way you people deal with a crisis it's a wonder you're still alive out here."

"I would hardly classify your toilets as a 'crisis,'" Lydia drawled.

"You come down to these apartments and say that. We have a hundred and sixty men living here with backed up toilets, and the odor is getting pretty incredible."

"I can appreciate how unpleasant it must be."

"Well, don't appreciate it, just get it fixed!" He broke connection, and Lydia leaned back in her chair, her fingers laced behind her head. A soft, almost playful, little smile curved her lips as she contemplated how well this first skirmish in their undeclared war with the soldiers was going. She hadn't heard from Sucholevsky yet, but perhaps a lifetime spent in the workers' paradise had toughened his men.

They might not even have noticed the clogged plumbing, she thought, remembering how, when the Soviet troops had marched into Berlin at the end of World War II, they had thought toilets were a clever new way to wash potatoes. She suddenly frowned when she recalled the adjunct to that amusing story: When the potatoes had disappeared the Russian troops had often shot the families who owned the toilets, believing they had tricked or bewitched them. She hoped they weren't headed for a similar outcome this time. She presumed things had improved over the intervening years, and that the level of sophistication of the Soviet troops was somewhat higher than their brethern of a hundred years ago. After all, she was risking a lot by gambling on their patience and forbearance. If she had misjudged, a lot of people could get hurt—hers and theirs.

It was no good having seconds thoughts now, she decided. For better or worse they were in to it. She leaned over, and called Trevor's lab. He answered almost immediately.

"They're starting to howl and snivel in a most amazing way," she said. "Is your group ready to turn up the heat?"

Trevor chuckled. "I think we can have everything set by lunch."

"Good. That will give them all night to meditate upon their sins."

Trevor signed off with a jaunty little salute.

The community kitchen at the edge of the agricultural area was noisy with the sound of running water and the clash of pots and pans. Dr. Conrad Spector looked about with interest. He had never eaten in one of the kitchens, preferring to take his meals at home with his wife and child, but he knew they were very popular with the younger, unmarried members of the colony. This one had been turned over totally to the occupying troops in an effort to keep them away from the rest of the community.

He spotted Marcia Teadman, and gave an almost imperceptible nod. The nutritionist jerked her head toward the back, and vanished through the double doors leading into the kitchen. Spector quickly followed.

"Got something for me to mix this in?" he asked as he removed a small bottle from his coat pocket.

"Bowls are over the sink," she said while maintaining an unobtrusive watch out the kitchen door.

He emptied the contents of the bottle into a bowl and added water.

"What have you there?" Marcia asked, her deep brown eyes alight with interest.

"Phenopthalin."

"Oh, God," she said with a catch of laughter in her voice. "They're going to be lined up in the bathrooms tonight."

"And with the toilets backed up . . ."

"I'm sure glad I'm not in this man's army," the black woman said. "And I'm equally glad I don't live anywhere near this area. Who cooked this up? Lydia? It's absolutely fiendish."

"Our fearless leader is keeping somewhat aloof from the individual plans, and just overseeing the entire operation," Spector said as he poured the primary ingredient of most laxatives into the large pot of soup that was simmering on the stove. "Each group is trying to outdo the others for level of sheer viciousness and audicity. I hear Artis and her crew were discussing the feasibility of starch in the underwear."

"Is it going to do any good?"

"Who can say? It certainly makes *me* feel better, and who knows? If they get uncomfortable enough up here, and complain loudly enough to their superiors, they might actually be removed."

"That would be a happy day. I just hope nobody else gets hurt while we're levering them out."

"Amen to that."

• • •

"I hear Muhammid dropped operation crapper," Jenny said quietly as she and Peter left the walkway, and headed across the grass toward the dry river bed.

"Yes. He decided we'd, forgive the pun, gotten enough out of that tactic. So the troops now have working plumbing again."

"Everyone seems to be running out of ideas. I know *I* am. Everything I come up with is too rough."

"I know. I think that's why Lydia called this rally. School children singing naughty ditties isn't going to cut it. Whether we like it or not, the time has come to directly confront these martial law regulations."

They were in sight of the rose garden now, and Jenny could see hundreds of people gathered on the grass. Some had spread blankets and were sharing food and drink while others milled about, visiting. There was a gay, almost carnival atmosphere, and still more people flowed off of AVC's and out of buildings to join the gathering. She shaded her eyes against the globed park lights and evaluated the crowd.

"No children."

"What?"

"There are no children here."

"Probably a wise precaution," Peter said, his face suddenly grim. They started forward to join the mob.

"Oh . . . right. I keep reminding myself that things could get rough tonight, but it doesn't seem real, somehow."

"I know. All I ever really wanted to do was build space stations," Peter said a trifle plaintively.

"And all I ever wanted to do was quietly practice law."

"Liar," he said fondly. "You came out here looking for meaning and adventure, and by God, you've found it. You're a born leader."

"Don't be silly," she said, embarrassed. "I'm just Cab's Girl Friday. If anyone's the leader out here it's Lydia or even Cabot."

"True, but don't sell yourself short. I foresee great things for you."

"I hope not." She stopped, placed a had on his shoulder and, stretching up, pressed a kiss against the corner of his mouth. "But thanks for the vote of confidence, it helps to steady my quaking knees."

"Don't worry about being scared. That's the mark of truly

great generals. They're always frightened before a battle."

Jenny turned her head away. "Don't even say the word. We're taking an awful risk here, and it could blow up in our faces."

"You could always go back to the apartment. You're not a resident of this station, even though you do seem to have thrown your lot in with us rabble-rousers."

"And sit home all by myself, worrying about what's happening to you, and where in the hell Cab has gotten to, and wondering if truth and justice are going to prevail? No, thank you. I'll face the troops."

They wandered through the crowd, searching for friends. At last they came across Lee and Diane, a husband-and-wife astronomy team, seated on a blanket with Frank, who worked at the solar smelter, and Kelly, who taught school. Jenny and Peter settled down on the blanket, and Frank, whose hobby was gourmet cooking, produced a large picnic basket.

"I thought this was supposed to be a serious confrontation," Jenny said as she accepted a cracker with pâté and a glass of chilled wine.

"Men . . . and women," Frank said with a nod to the ladies, "can better face the exigencies of life if they have full stomachs."

"You ought to know about that," Kelly said, affectionately punching him in his incipient paunch.

"So, let us eat, drink, and be merry for soon the soldiers will arrive and we're all gonna die," Frank concluded with a comical expression on his wide face.

"Not funny," Lee said quietly, and took a large swallow of wine. A gloomy silence fell over the group.

"Look, let's pretend this is just a normal get-together, and catch up on what we've been doing," Diane said heartily. "Lee and I took some incredible readings off a quasar out in the direction of NGC2535/36."

"Yes, but what's great for an astronomer drives the cosmologists crazy," Lee said with a chuckle. "Everytime we make a new discovery it sends all their carefully constructed views of the universe out the window."

Jenny leaned back against Peter's chest and tried to relax. His arms were warm around her, the wine was sweet in her mouth, and somewhere off in the darkness someone began playing a guitar. It should have been a comfortable moment, but she found her eyes flickering to the edges of the crowd, searching for soldiers, and she couldn't keep her mind off Cab. She wondered where in the hell he had gotten to, and what he was doing. It had been three days since he'd left and she'd had no word.

The night of the brawl at The White Owl, she'd returned to the apartment to find a scrawled note lying on her pillow. "Gone to Earth. On the trail of something important. Keep things running till I get back. Cab." That had been it, and since then—nothing.

She had considered asking Lydia if she knew what was going on, but she was afraid that the manager *would* know more than she, and in some peculiar way that hurt. She had always been closely involved in whatever Cab did, and the fact that he had simply taken off without a word of farewell or explanation left her feeling bereaved. She placed a hand over Peter's, where they lay folded over her waist, and squeezed. He responded by tightening his grip on her, and she felt reassured by the contact. At least it mattered to someone that she was around.

She tried to turn her mind from Cab, reminding herself that he was a big boy and could take care of himself. Somehow it failed to banish the worry. The problem was that she wasn't certain what she was worried about. Was she worried about Cab, for clearly deBaca had to realize that his judge was no longer part of his "team," or was she worried that Cab, once back in his own setting, might abandon the colonists and return to his support of the administration?

Exasperated by her endless, circular musings, she took a gulp of wine and tried to force her attention back on the conversation going on around her. After all, she was several thousands miles from Earth. Whatever Cab was up to she could neither help nor hinder him now.

Chapter Fourteen

It seemed like the cold had been pursuing him across the country. From White Sands Cabot had gone first to the west coast, seized with an overwhelming desire to spend at least one night in his own home. He knew time was of the essence, and that he shouldn't waste it in such foolishness, but it was not something he could resist. He wanted to go *home*.

The Big Sur had been in the grip of a particularly nasty late October storm, so rather than walking the beach and enjoying his first touch of Earth in over three months, he found himself seated in the window seat of the bay window, watching a mixture of rain and hail spatter against the glass, and the ocean, gray and violent, beat against the cliffs beneath his house.

He found the house cold and cheerless after having stood empty for so many weeks, and he found himself thinking about the station, and wondering what Jenny was doing. He realized he had left rather abruptly, and he hoped Lydia would tell her what was happening. In fact, he was beginning to regret not bringing her with him. Jenny had a way with people, and her charm and native friendliness might have been a help when he finally talked to Moffit. Cabot didn't know the Secretary of State, having met him only once briefly at one of the inaugural balls when Tomas had taken office. He knew he was not a particularly warm person, and he had a feeling Jenny could have been more persuasive to a middle-aged politician than he could.

He brushed away a spot of moisture left by his breath on the cold glass of the window, and tried to put thoughts of Jenny aside. It was no good indulging in "if only's." Jenny was a long way away, and he couldn't take the time to wait for her to join him. Also, as much as he'd wanted that walk on the beach, he also couldn't wait for the weather to clear. The next morning he reluctantly closed up his house and headed for Washington.

It had taken some finagling, but he finally got through to Moffit himself. The man had been desperately nervous, especially when Cab had mentioned Joe Reichart, and had not wanted to have Cabot come to his office. Feeling like an extra in a grade-B spy thriller, but figuring it was worth it if it would put Moffit at ease, Cabot had suggested that they meet at the Lincoln Memorial the following morning.

Now as he sat shivering in a bitter wind that whipped down the Mall, he wished he had suggested a truck stop on Interstate 95, a café in Virginia, anywhere but this exposed staircase that led up to the Memorial. Heavy gray clouds swept up the Potomic, dulling the reflecting pool, and lying like cotton batting on the spire of the Washington Monument. The foul weather had one advantage: It meant that very few people were about, leaving Cab and Moffit to hold their meeting in almost total isolation.

That very isolation, together with the obvious fear in Moffit's voice, created a strong sense of paranoia. Cab found himself glancing about, expecting watchers among the trees, or cars that loitered too long at the curbs. He had worked himself up to a near-fever pitch when an electric car pulled humming up to the curb on 17th Street, and Moffit leaped out.

He hurried across the sidewalk and up the stairs, clutching his camel-hair coat tight about his body. Watching him, Cab realized that they were virtual mirror images of one another in terms of dress. Both wore camel-hair coats with soft mufflers folded neatly beneath, brown suede gloves, and dark hats with wide brims.

I wonder if this is the uniform of power? Cab thought. All of us dressed for success, climbing steadfastly up the rungs of prestige and never noticing that the ladder is resting squarely on the backs of the citizens. Dear God, he thought in dismay, I have been infected. Lydia would be amused.

Moffit reached him, and extended his hand. "Justice Huntington."

"Mr. Secretary," Cab responded, shaking the proffered hand. He studied the man from beneath the brim of his hat, thinking that Moffit's hair was grayer than it had been some three and a half years before, and that the man looked as if hadn't slept in weeks.

"You mentioned Joe Reichart," Moffit said, thrusting his hands into his pockets, and pacing toward the entrance to the Memorial.

"He said you had some information for him," Cab said, falling into step with him. "If so, I need it."

Moffit shot him a sharp look. "You're deBaca's man. Even assuming I had such information what makes you think I would give it to you?"

"And I take it your *not* deBaca's man?"

"Not anymore; not totally."

"So you changed?"

"Yes."

"And I submit that I, too, have changed."

They stared in silence at each other. The wind plucked at the brim of Cab's hat, threatening to whirl it away. He reached up and caught it by the crown.

"Let's go inside. It may be a little warmer in there," the Secretary said.

They stepped into the echoing marble interior of the Memorial. The gigantic seated figure of Lincoln stared stonily down the length of the reflecting pool and on into eternity. There was something awesome about the high, vaulted room and that silent figure. Cab shivered a bit, feeling as if the decisions of history were flowing out of the walls and ceiling to lie heavily on his head and shoulders.

He hadn't followed the rest of his family into politics for just this very reason. He hadn't wanted to make decisions that would reverberate down the decades, or be judged by the future generations whose lives his decisions would affect. Now, ironically, he stood in just such a situation. What he did in the next days might very well affect the relationship between Earth and System for years to come. He wanted to tell Moffit to just forget it, and leave. Run home to California, and let others worry about these matters.

His internal struggle must have been reflected in his face, for Moffit took a tentative step toward him saying, "Are you all right? You look frightened."

"I *am* frightened." He turned nervously, hitting a fist into the palm of his other hand. "I've known Tomas C. deBaca since I was an undergraduate at Harvard and took his tutorial in American Constitutional History. He's been a friend, even a mentor, sending lucrative cases my way once I was in practice. Now I'm here, in Washington, secretly trying to find the evidence that will prove that this man—my friend—has, if not authorized, at least allowed a barbarous act. And yet, am I any better than these men I seek to punish? *I* made the decision that led to the act. I'm a fraud. A man in a position of power who knows that inside he's empty, and who's trying so damn hard to keep the world from seeing that emptiness."

"All of us in government are straw men," Moffit said. "The only thing we're really interested in is getting and keeping that power. You've had the strength to walk away from it and you're trying to do something." He gave a snort of disgusted laughter. "Hell, look at me. When those people were killed I stormed home and wrote out my resignation." He gave Cab an ironic look from beneath the brim of his hat. "Seen me resign yet? Then I called Joe. *I* called him. Offered him my help. When he told me what he needed I said sure. And you know something? I haven't done a damn thing about it. Especially after Joe fled his station. I figured, 'Hell, I can't really do anything. Who was I kidding.'"

"So you're scared."

"No. The bottom line isn't cowardice, it's prestige and power. If I had done what Joe wanted, that resignation would have gone through, and I'd be just ordinary old Taylor Moffit back in Wisconsin."

"So you don't have the information?"

"No."

"Can you get it?"

Moffit gave a startled laugh. "Haven't you been listening? I don't *want* to get that information."

Cab gave him a level look. "I think you do. And I think if you know there's someone else out on that limb with you it'll be easier."

"You offering to bring the saw?"

"I'll do even better. I'll *do* the sawing."

"It's going to be a long way down," Moffit said warningly.

"It will seem less bad if we have someone to talk to as we fall."

Moffit smiled, easing some of the lines about his mouth and eyes. "You're much too hard on yourself, Justice Huntington. I would say you're anything but a fraud."

"Thank you for the vote of confidence. But shall we decide on our course of action? Time is not something we have an abundance of right now."

"I'll go over to the Pentagon near closing time and run through the computer."

"They won't think it odd?"

"Not really. I've always believed State and Defense should work closely so I'm a familiar figure over there. My main concern is that the information, if it ever existed, has been removed by now." He thrust his hands into the pockets of his coat, and turned away. "I should have acted immediately after I talked to Joe."

"And I should never have acceded to Tomas's demands. Done is done. We can't dig up dead cats." He balled his hands into tight fists and swung them up over his right shoulder as if he had a deceased cat by the tail. "And drag them around with us for the rest of our lives." He relaxed into a shrug. "Instead, let's try to correct the situation."

"Where can I reach you?"

"At the Mayflower."

Trevor gave a startled laugh. "You certainly believe in keeping a low profile, don't you."

"I refuse to carry this cloak-and-dagger nonsense to an extreme. You'll get back to me tonight?"

"Yes."

"Good. I want to get back to the station—"

"And out of Washington, no doubt."

"Yes, that too. And as quickly as possible."

They shook hands and walked out of the Memorial. A few lazy snow flakes had begun to spiral down out of the gray-white sky.

"Lousy weather," Moffit said.

"Enjoy it. The lack of weather where I'm living is starting to drive me crazy."

"I hear they have tremendous wind storms on Mars," the Secretary said as Cab walked with him to his car.

"I may never get that far. Tomas will probably have me impeached and removed."

"They wanted to impeach Marshall."

"Yes, but the only judge they ever actually removed was John Pickering, who was a drunkard and a madman. Charming company I'll be in."

"Don't be so pessimistic. I'm beginning to think things may actually work out."

"To paraphrase a friend: Good, you be optimistic and I'll worry. See you tonight."

"I'll be there."

It didn't take long for the soldiers to arrive. Frank was killing a second bottle of wine when a sharp *hist* from Peter drew everyone's attention. Behind and to either side of the throng, the Russians were moving in to form a somewhat ragged ring. They stopped about ten yards out from the colonists and assumed a wide-legged, braced stance. There was primitive and awful power about them, like Easter Island statues, and the modern weapons they held waist high also contributed to the hush that began to ripple across the gathering.

Jenny's throat felt suddenly tight, and she set aside her wineglass. She was pleased to note that her hand wasn't shaking, but a cold knot of dread settled into the pit of her stomach when she saw the gas filters hung about the soldier's necks.

About three hundred yards down the central parkway the Emergency Response Force was beginning to move into position. They looked decidedly less comfortable than their Soviet brethern, and they kept a careful distance from the other troops. White and Sucholevsky were pushing through the crowd toward where Lydia, standing apart from most of the people, waited impassively. The light of the globe lamps reflected in her silver hair, and she seemed very regal and commanding as she stood beneath a large apple tree.

"Come on, let's see if we can get close enough to hear," Peter said, jumping to his feet and grabbing Jenny's hand. "Coming with us?" he asked the other four.

"No thanks," Lee said, looking a little queasy. "If I go

anywhere, it's going to be to slip away home. Those guys have *guns!*"

Peter and Jenny wove through the people until they were close enough to hear Sucholevsky's bluster over the background murmur of the crowd.

"You will disperse these people immediately!"

"I think not." Nothing could possibly have exceeded the stately calm of Lydia's reply.

"Look, Ms. Kim Nu, let's just keep things quiet. We don't want any more trouble up here."

Lydia glanced to both sides at the picnicking colonists, and spread her hands questioningly. "Things seem perfectly quiet to me. However, if you and your men feel threatened in some fashion then perhaps you should return to your quarters."

"This gathering is in direct violation of martial law, and I must order you to disband at once." White's tone was still polite.

"Order away. Because I deny your very right to occupy the space you are standing on, much less to impose military law on the citizens of *my* station. Now, take your men and get out of here!"

"You're forcing us to take action against you!" Sucholevsky shouted.

"What action?" Lydia said scornfully. "You're outnumbered almost twenty to one."

"And you are substantially outgunned," the Russian said with a significant glance at his armed troops. "Have you ever seen shotguns fired into a large mass of people at very close range?"

"Since, no doubt, I lack your vast experience in the effects of gun fire on unarmed people, I'll defer to your greater knowledge. I'm sure it must be very unpleasant. On the other hand, before you put too much reliance on your weaponry, may I tell you a very quick story?" She didn't wait for the officer's assent, but plunged right on.

"Back in the 1970's a particularly unpleasant terrorist held a large group of office workers hostage in—I believe it was the Philippines—yes, that's right. No matter. At any rate, this man held these people at bay for three days because he was very well armed. Then he threatened to burn a pregnant woman alive, and his hostages beat him to death with a typewriter.

Granted he killed three of them before they got to him—but they *did* get to him

"Do I need to elaborate on the similarities between that situation and the one we're faced with now?" Her voiced hardened and her eyes took on a steely glint as she faced the two men before her. "You open fire on this crowd, and I guarantee you, I'll send the pieces of you home in envelopes because there won't be enough to fill a coffin."

"Jesus, what a lady!" Peter breathed to Jenny. She nodded, totally overwhelmed by the older woman's power and assurance, but still worried. She didn't consider logic to be a strong point in the military mind, and she could see that Sucholevsky did not take kindly to such a challenge from a woman.

"You make a persuasive argument, madam," the Russian said, baring his teeth and gums in a gaping smile. "But you forget that war is controlled violence. We can use something less than shotgun fire to send you home." He jumped back, muttering a command into his throat mike, and jerked his gas filter over his face. White looked confused. A series of dull thuds were followed by gentle hissing as clouds of choking white gas began to rise among the people.

"Tear gas!" Peter hacked, as Lydia vanished from sight behind a wall of white. Jenny jerked off the scarf she had knotted around her neck, and covered her mouth and nose. The air was filled with screams and harsh coughings as people began to plunge wildly in all directions.

Jenny took a firm grip on Peter's hand, and headed in what she hoped was a direction out of the park. Her eyes were streaming with tears, and her lungs felt as if she had inhaled crushed glass. A uniformed figure loomed up out of the gas, his face alien and insectlike behind the filter. Anger seemed to explode in her head, and she rabbit-punched him in the solar plexus. He dropped to his knees with a groan, and Jenny ripped the filter over his head and pulled it on.

The residue of the gas was still aggravating her eyes and nose, but at least she could breathe again. She took a look around, and realized she had lost Peter. She almost went rushing off to search for him, then realized that was silly. The gloom created by the drifting gas was filled with jumping, writhing, and running figures. It was like a scene out of Dante's "Inferno," and she knew she would never find him in the chaos.

Her hand throbbed where she had punched the soldier, but overlaying the pain was a deep sense of satisfaction. She began to prowl in widening circles, searching for another uniformed figure.

"This is shit. This is absolute shit!" Sergeant Rob Pruden muttered to himself as weeping, frightened people plunged past him. He cast around, turning in small circles, wishing he could locate Sucholevsky and flatten the Russian's ugly, fat face.

These were *Americans* for Christ's sake! he thought. Why in the hell were they letting Russians throw tear gas at Americans while American soldiers stood by and watched?

A pretty young girl, her face red and blotchy from the gas, went stumbling past him. He wanted to offer her his filter, but she was past before he could act. He muttered a few more oaths, then threw down his shotgun, and walked out of the central park.

The air was beginning to clear as the life support system began to scrub the foreign element out of the atmosphere. Pruden continued to walk doggedly back toward their assigned barracks. He received some odd and hostile looks from the colonists, but no one bothered him, and eventually he reached the apartments.

Pulling off his boots, he lay down on his bed and tried to make sense out of what had happened. He couldn't, it didn't, and frankly he was pissed. He knew he would probably be busted for what he had done, but at this point he didn't give a damn. If this was the way the U.S. Air Force did business, he would be just as pleased to be out.

Of course, it was always tough on a man to have a dishonorable discharge on his record. It would hurt his chances groundside. So why stay groundside? he thought, sitting up in bed. He liked it up here, and he had a feeling that the System would be less critical of a man in his situation. Satisfied with his decision, he lay back down, and went to sleep. A man could never get enough sleep.

Jenny dropped her clothes down the laundry chute, and threw the gas filter into the waste disposal. She had toyed with the idea of keeping it as a souvenir, but decided not to risk it.

The filter could link her to the soldiers she had assaulted.

She pushed back her hair, wrinkling her nose at the smell. It, like everything else about her person, reeked of tear gas. She then gingerly inspected the large swelling on her right temple. The last trooper she had jumped had been somewhat more zealous about his own protection than the other three, and he had dealt her a staggering blow with his fist. She was lucky it wasn't any worse, but she was going to have a shiner. In fact, it was already forming.

Her door page sounded, followed by a frenzied knocking. She assumed it was Peter, and didn't bother to throw a robe over the pale peach teddy that she had been wearing beneath her outer clothing. But it wasn't Peter. As Jenny opened the door, Flo Wandall came charging into the apartment. Two hectic spots of color burned on her thin cheeks, and she kept clasping and unclasping her hands as if she were afraid she would lose them if she stopped verifying their presence.

"I must speak to Justice Huntington!"

"He's not here. You know that." Jenny gave the older woman a perplexed look.

Flo took a frenzied turn about the front room, then raced back to Jenny and seized her by the upper arms. "*You* must know where he is. Please, please, call him. Let me talk to him. Someone has to stop this madness."

"That's what Cab is trying to do, but as for talking to him"— she shrugged—"I don't know where he is."

"You can trust me. I know he's gone to Earth to talk to some man who has information that will harm the President, but he must not do it!" She gave her head a violent shake, and a few drops of spittle flecked her lower lip. "He is being used by Lydia—used by her—and she and all the others have gone mad. They precipitated this riot tonight. None of this would have happened if they had done as they ought."

Jenny had about decided that it was Flo who had gone mad with her wild, staring eyes and violent words. Freeing herself from the other woman's grip, she backed quickly away.

"I tell you, I don't know where he is." The telecom began to chime. "Now, if you would please leave, I would like to take a shower and go to bed." The com continued to ring. Jenny gritted her teeth and tried to ignore it. "This has not been one of the best days of my life." Try as she might, she found she couldn't stand it, and she flung herself across the room to answer the summons.

Cab's features stabilized on the screen. He raised his eyebrows in surprise. "That's a fetching outfit, but don't you think you ought to leave the screen off if you're going to run about the apartment in quite so alluring an ensemble?"

"Cab," she breathed, sinking down into a chair.

"Good heavens! What happened to your face?"

"I'll tell you when you get back. You are coming back?"

"Yes, tonight, if there's a shuttle I can catch." His eyes brightened with excitement. "And I got what we needed. We have the evidence, Jenny."

Chapter Fifteen _____

"Cheer down, Cab," Jenny muttered through her teeth as she watched Flo's face take on all the animation and warmth of a death mask.

He looked taken aback by her use of the phrase. He always used the expression when he wanted to indicate to her that she was rushing ahead without adequate thought and about to get into trouble. He seemed to get the message, however, for he subsided.

"So, you'll be back soon?"

"Yes, I have to get over to the Sands and see what's flying tonight." He matched her bland, noncommittal tone.

Flo continued to stare at Jenny with cold, hollow eyes. There was something almost eerie about her expression, and Jenny found herself hunching her shoulders as if in expectation of a blow. Suddenly the older woman whirled and stalked with stiff, awkward strides to the door.

"Flo! Where are you going? Flo?" Jennie cried, half starting out of her chair.

"Jenny, what is going on?"

"Sorry, Cab. Flo came roaring in here just before you called, acting like a hysteric. She was babbling about how we had to stop them—"

"Stop who and from doing what?"

"The group up here. Lydia, Muhammid, Artis . . . you know."

"Jenny, I want to know exactly what has been going on since I left, and I especially want to know how you acquired that black eye."

"I got in a fight with a solider."

"What!"

"Oh, Cab, calm down! I wasn't the only one. There must have been close to two thousand of us out there tonight."

"Jenny, please, my heart can't take much more of this. Just start at the beginning and tell me what's been happening. And please don't spring things on me like that."

"All right." And in a few well-chosen words, she brought him up to date.

"Martial law," he said softly when she had finished. "I better get back up there right away. I don't know how much clout I've got left, but I'm probably the only person who can stop this nonsense."

"Cab, have you given Ken Furakawa the information you received?"

"No, not yet. I thought I'd wait until I was back on the station."

"I wouldn't. Call him now while you have the chance. Things have been such a madhouse up here that I wouldn't count on anything right now."

"All right. I'll transfer the information to him tonight. Take care of yourself, and try to stay out of trouble until I get back. See you tomorrow night."

"Right."

"Captain White, there's a woman here to see you."

White looked up, irritated, at the young airman who had thrust his head into the office. He was trying to cope with the aftermath of the riot in the park, and the last thing he needed was further grief from a colonist.

"Tell her I'm busy, and I'll see her tomorrow."

"She says it's important."

"It always is."

"She says she can help you avoid the kind of thing that happened tonight," the young man offered timidly. White looked up from his terminal, and for the first time actually focused on the man before him.

Nineteen if he's a day, the Captain thought. A year ago his

major worry was getting a date for the high school prom. Now he's thousands of miles from home, being asked to maintain a very harsh level of control over people who, in a different setting, could have been his neighbors. I wonder if he has any idea what we're doing up here? I wonder if I do?

Disturbed by his thoughts, White forced his attention back on the problem before him. "Oh, okay. Show her in, but tell her she can only have five minutes."

"Yes, sir."

He didn't recognize the woman who stepped into his office. Tall and almost painfully thin, she moved jerkily toward a chair. Her hands clasped and unclasped convulsively, and she kept hunching her shoulders, and weaving her head about in small circular motions until he was forcibly reminded of a stork. He pushed the uncomplimentary comparison out of his mind, and politely indicated the chair.

"Mrs. . . . ?" He paused and looked at her inquiringly.

"Miss Wandall, Florence Wandall."

"How can I help you, Miss Wandall?"

"It's I who can help you, Captain," she said, fixing him with a piercing look. He was reminded of his old sixth-grade school teacher back in Detroit, and he shifted uncomfortably in his chair. "I've come to give you the names of the persons who have caused most of the difficulties for you and your men. In return I want permission to make an out-of-station call to Mr. John Malcomb in Washington, D.C."

White gaped at her for several seconds, then shook his head bewilderedly "May I ask how you have access to this information?"

"I used to be a member of a quasi-governmental group called the Committee. It operated outside the bounds of the corporate structure and consisted of people chosen by the community to serve in long-range planning that had nothing to do with corporate policy."

"And now you're going to betray these people?"

"Yes," she said firmly, her lips closing into a prim line. "I cannot condone this confrontation and violence. Whatever our problems with the Earth authorities, there are means available within the system for the redress of those grievances." She paused and stared down at her hands where they tightly gripped the arms of her chair. "These people have organized the resistance against you. If you remove them, the rest of the colony will behave."

White tapped the end of his pen against his front teeth, and thoughtfully regarded the older woman. It seemed almost too good to be true, and he wondered if it were some plan on the part of the colonists to further discredit his troops. The more he analyzed it, however, the less likely it seemed. The woman appeared to be totally sincere. He dropped the pen and nodded.

"Okay, I agree to your terms. You give me the names, and I'll let you make your call. May I ask why you need to contact this man?"

"I'm not certain he can help me," Flo said with a frown. "But he is the only person I know in Washington, and somehow the President must be warned."

"The President!" White repeated, sitting up abruptly in his chair.

"Yes, information that could be very damaging to the country is about to be released." Flo clutched her hands under her chin. "He must stop it."

"Jesus Christ," White muttered. "Maybe we ought to try to reach General Abrams or Secretary of Defense Ryan," he murmured almost to himself.

"I don't care who we call, but we must act quickly."

"Okay, give me those names, and we'll put through your call."

"Tina Duvall, Muhammid Ali Elija, Trevor Martin, and Artis Barnes."

He hurriedly scribbled down the names, then gave her a shrewd look. "Are you sure that's it?"

Her eyes flicked away form his, and she stared at a far corner of the room. "Yes, of course."

"Are you sure Lydia Kim Nu shouldn't be included in this list?"

"Why do you say that?" she asked breathlessly.

He sighed inwardly, feeling somewhat sorry for a group that had this woman as a member. She was totally incapable of dissimulation.

"Please, Miss Wandall, don't lie to me," he said gently.

She hung her head, and nodded. "Yes, Lydia is involved, but I don't think you ought to arrest her, or whatever you're going to do to the others. She's very important to the running of this station, and she is very beloved. An action against her might strengthen rather than weaken the opposition toward you."

White considered, weighing her knowledge of the community against his need to quiet resistance. He decided to go with her instincts. Besides, it would give him a lever to use with Kim Nu. He smiled reassuringly.

"You know, I think you're right. We'll just leave Ms. Kim Nu out of it for now." He rose, and came around the desk to place a hand on her shoulder. "And I want to thank you for coming to me the way you did. It took a lot of courage. And if it's comfort to you—I think you did exactly the right thing." She looked up at him gratefully. "Now let's go make that call."

Cab sank farther down in the uncomfortable chair placed nakedly in the center of the passenger waiting room at the White Sands space port. Feeling the plastic back dig into his neck he straightened irritably, and tried again to find a comfortable position. The room was sparsely populated at this time of night. Most passenger shuttles flew by day with only freight runs taking off at night. Since no passenger flights were allowed in to EnerSun, Cab, by dint of a good deal of bombast and arrogance, the flashing of identification, and a hurried call to Lydia, was once more on a freight shuttle returning to the station.

With a sigh he turned his attention to the beautiful old limited-edition volume he had found in an antique bookstore in Washington. The pages whispered softly beneath his fingers as he read.

An hour passed, and suddenly he felt a prickling along the back of his neck. He closed the book on a slender forefinger, and took a discreet glance over his shoulder. His gut tightened in a nervous spasm.

An M.P. stood in the door, carefully scanning the few people in the lounge. Cab tried to tell himself it was an irrational reaction, but he *knew* that man was looking for him. Without pausing to contemplate the possible ramifications of his action, he rose and walked quickly into the men's room. Behind him he heard the rapid staccato of boots on the tile floor as the

M.P. followed. So, his instinct had been correct.

He stepped into one of the stalls, noticing that the door swung out. He then shot the bolt, and checked his watch. *Eleven fifteen.* An hour and fifteen minutes until his shuttle would fly. He wasn't due to board for another thirty. He wondered if he got there early if he could convince the pilot to let him board?

Worry about that when you get to it, he thought to himself. And since you can't spend the entire night hiding in the john, your first problem is getting past that M.P.

As if in answer to his agitated thoughts, he heard the door swing open. "Hey, mister? Judge Huntington? You in here? I'm from Holloman Air Force Base, and we've got orders to send you back to Washington. The President urgently needs to see you."

I'll just bet he does, Cab thought sarcastically. He didn't know how it had happened, but he could only assume that deBaca had learned of his Washington visit and, more importantly, the results of that visit.

Fear settled into the pit of his stomach like a dull, aching weight, and caused his breath to come in short, agitated gasps. He tried to tell himself that this was Tomas C. deBaca, his old friend and mentor and nothing would happen, but he didn't believe a word of it. They both had too much at stake.

He pressed the side of his face against the stall door, his right hand on the lock, his left hand flat against the metal surface, and waited. He could hear the soldier's footsteps coming slowly down the length of the stalls, pausing occasionally as he peered beneath the doors. Cab felt a momentary surge of embarrassment. There was something terribly undignified about hiding in a john.

But it wouldn't be for much longer. The man had almost reached his door. He murmured a brief prayer that all those years of Tae Kwon Do, which he had taken purely for weight control and to release tension, had taught him *something*. He tensed in readiness.

The man stopped directly in front of the door. "Come on, judge. We've got a copter waiting, and—"

Cab jerked back the bolt, and slammed the door into the M.P.'s face. He had planned to erupt out of the stall and take the man, but his feet became tangled, so his exit was somewhat less dynamic. He lurched and tottered into the open area in front of the basins, but fortunately his opponent was down, nursing a bloody nose.

He spun around, and laid the side of his hand across the man's neck. The result was not profound. He had never in his life struck someone with the intent of stopping them, so he had instinctively pulled back, limiting the force of his blow. The M.P. grunted and staggered to his feet, opening his mouth for a yell.

That provided Cab with the impetus he needed. He spun away from the soldier's groping hands, and brought his hand down in a vicious back swing. The larger man folded up like a paper figure, and hit the floor. Cab leaned back against a washbasin, panting with exertion, and began to shiver with reaction.

He was disgusted with his performance. It had taken him, two hits to subdue the man, and it was sheer luck that the soldier hadn't been able to call for help. That thought brought back the memory of the man's last remark. *We've got a copter waiting,* which implied that there were more soldiers. But where? And how would he get past them? He looked down at the unconscious M.P., and found his answer.

It wasn't like in the movies. It was damn hard to strip the man since he was dead weight, and the uniform was a lousy fit. Cab rolled up the pants legs, and tucked them into the boots. The shirt and jacket swam on his small frame, and the cuffs came down almost over his fingers. He hoped that the darkness would hide the horrible fit. He put on the helmet, but it fell down over his eyes. Pushing it up with one finger he gave himself a sour look in the mirror.

"Some man of action," he muttered. "Two hits to subdue an unprepared man, and now you look like a reject from a costume ball. Hope to hell no one is going to rely on you for anything more."

"Cab!" Jenny cried as the door swung open, and he stepped into the apartment. She flung herself across the intervening space and into his arms. He was somewhat nonplussed by her emotional reaction, but his arms closed instinctively around her, and he held her close.

After a moment, she loosened her viselike grip on his shoulders, and he held her off at arm's length. Her black eye looked worse than when he had called, having reached the ugly yellowish-purple stage. It was badly swollen. He held a hand up.

"Can you see at all out of that thing?"

"A little.

"Have you been to a doctor?"

She shrugged. "It wasn't necessary. It looks worse than it is."

"It looks quite horrible," he said, gently touching her swollen cheek.

"Did you find the man you went looking for?"

"Yes." He placed an arm around her shoulders, and walked her over to the couch. "And it turned out to be Taylor Moffit."

"The Secretary of State?" She looked incredulous.

"Quite."

"And the evidence?"

"Was everything we'd hoped for, and as you suggested I transmitted the information to Furakawa. Good thing I did, too."

She shifted on the couch until she was facing him. "Why?"

He looked rueful, and scratched at the corner of his mouth. "I'm rather afraid I had to assault an M.P. before I could get home."

"What!"

"DeBaca must have found out what I was up to because there were a number of very large M.P.'s waiting at the Sands to 'escort' me back to Washington. I can't imagine how he heard because only you and Lydia knew what I was—"

"Flo," Jenny said abruptly.

Cab looked thoughtful, then nodded. "Yes, it's the only thing that makes any sense."

"What will deBaca do to you?" Jenny asked, reaching for his hand. Her face was grave.

He made a wry face and shook his head. "I don't know, but I do know what *I'm* going to do. I haven't exactly behaved in the most impartial way and judicial fashion," he said over his shoulder as he rose and crossed to the telecom. "So I'm going to call Donaldson and petition the Supreme Court for me to be recused from this case."

"Cab you can't! If you step down, deBaca will appoint some

stoolie who will whitewash what happened on the Moon. They'll get away scot-free!"

He took her by the shoulders and gave her a gentle shake. "Jenny, I'm prejudicially biased in this matter. I can't sit as the impartial trier of law in such a circumstance." His expression hardened. "On the other hand, I'm not about to let deBaca and Tupolev walk away. I'm going to be recused so that I can testify as a witness. I saw that evidence, and I'm going to make certain it's placed before the court."

"Speaking of the evidence, may I see it?"

"Of course. It's a most enlightening example of abysmal bureaucratic stupidity."

"Don't sound so disgusted. You ought to be grateful, otherwise we might never have caught them."

He nodded, and handed her the small computer disc that Moffit had given him. Jenny then went into the study to use the computer while he called the Chief Justice.

"Ah, the military mind," Jenny said, resting one hand on the door frame.

Cab looked up from where he was staring in rapt contemplation of the empty com screen. Donaldson had seemed nervous during their conversation, and Cab had a feeling that deBaca was going to hear about his request for recusal long before the Supreme Court did.

"This once more proves that if alien beings have contacted the Earth and met up with the military they will have left assuming there is no intelligent life on the planet."

Cab leaned back in his chair, smiling in amusement as she paced about the room expanding on her theme.

"Dobson was appropriately vague when he approached General Forbis. Then those idiots at the Pentagon had to get specific. By the time the final order went out to the lunar base they may as well have just said, 'Hey, the President wants to allow this mining colony to be nuked as a favor for Tupolev, so let's all look the other way.'"

"It was an amazing foul-up."

"Did you get hold of Donaldson?"

"Uh-huh, but I have a feeling the next call I receive is going to be from Tomas."

"Are you worried?"

"Not particularly. Confrontations with Tomas are beginning to take on a certain comforting regularity. The time I'll start worrying is when he stops calling."

Donaldson's call woke him. He hadn't had any sleep in almost two days so he had taken a sleeping pill in an effort to relax. Now after only a scant forty-five minutes of rest deBaca felt as if his eyelids had been glued together, and his mouth tasted as if the entire Russian army had been marching through it, wearing muddy boots. He forced his eyes open, and tried to make sense out of what the old man was telling him. When it finally became clear he lost all desire to sleep.

"Under *no* circumstances are you to recuse him, do you understand?" deBaca shouted into the com.

"Yes, but—"

"There are no buts! Just tell him no!" He broke the connection, and sat on the edge of his bed, glowering at the far wall.

It was all slipping away from him. Six months ago, no one would have given Richard Long a snowball's chance in hell of beating him; now he was pulling dangerously close in the polls and the election was three weeks away. And it was all a result of this dreadful Garmoneya affair. Up till now there had been no proof to directly tie him to the killings, and he had been serene in the certainty that any communications which might have linked him to the Russian action had been removed. But he had discovered that that was not the case. Dobson had fumbled the ball. He had ordered the Chief of Staff to remove any evidence, and he hadn't done it. Now Cab, and God knows how many others, held the evidence that would damn him.

If Cab recused himself there was no hope. If, however, he could keep Cab on the bench, there might still be a way to bring him back into line. He reached for the telecom.

Cab answered at once. Almost as if he had been waiting for deBaca's call. He stared resentfully at the younger man's patrician features, and wondered how he could ever have liked him. He was an unbearable little prig with an unwarranted sense of his own worth.

"I'm not going to waste time on the amenities. You're not

getting off the hot seat on this one. You're going to sit on the bench and hear this case."

"Even though I'm hopelessly prejudiced against you?"

"Even so. You're beginning to give me an ulcer, and you've cost me two days' sleep with your little stunt, but I'm damned if you're going to cost me the election."

"That was never my intention."

"Of course not," the President said sarcastically. "You've always been so pure. Politics have always been beneath you. Well, they haven't been beneath the rest of your family so you try this one on for size. If you rule against me in this matter, I swear to God, I'll break your family. You've got two uncles in Congress, your mother is ambassador to Great Britain, and you've got God-alone-knows how many cousins in various agencies. Even if I lose the election I'll still sit in this house until January, and I'll see to it that none of you can get elected dog catcher anywhere in the country." Cab had gone bone-white, and deBaca smiled with vicious satisfaction. "You just think about it." He broke the connection.

Even that small exercise of naked power had given him an adrenal rush that had banished much of his fear and depression. He had broken out of the inertia which had held him prisoner for so many days, and was beginning to plan once more. He had had Malcomb try to get Cab to rule that Evgeni Renko lacked standing to sue when this mess had first surfaced, but Cab had refused. He had then tried to silence the miner by removing him to the EnerSun station, but even that had not succeeded. Well, there was no question that a dead man would lack standing and would be silenced.

DeBaca's lips drew back from his teeth in a particularly unpleasant smile, and he once more reached for the com. Tupolev had gotten him into this mess, so Tupolev could damn well help get him out.

Chapter Sixteen

"If we get any more people on this station we're going to have to start sending to Earth for food to feed them all," Peter remarked as he watched another load of people come streaming off a shuttle into the passenger lounge.

"True, but for my part, I'm glad to see them. At least we're no longer isolated from the rest of the world," Jenny replied.

"Yes, but I keep wondering why. We've got more reporters than a Hollywood wedding, and half again as many UN delegates come to observe the hearing. Poor old Evgeni's even been released from house arrest. DeBaca and Tupolev must know that the hearing is going to go against them, so why this sudden loosening of the screws?"

Jenny kept silent and stared miserably down at her hands. She had a pretty good idea why deBaca and Tupolev had relaxed their hold on the station. She had heard Cab's final conversation with the President, and since that night the judge had seemed anguished, and had been as silent as death. She had no idea what he would do, and she hesitated to question him.

Cab was an essentially private person, but during their years together he had said enough for her to know that his family was very important to him. He had now been placed in the devil's own dilemma, and as much as she wanted to help him she was afraid to intrude.

She sighed and looked up at Peter. "I don't see that fellow we were supposed to meet."

"Yes. Perhaps he'll be on the next shuttle."

"It makes me feel a little strange to be acting for Lydia," Jenny confessed. "It makes me feel as if we've joined the Committee."

"Perhaps we have. After all, she doesn't have anyone else to rely on right now."

Jenny looked glum and nodded, thinking how comprehensive Flo's betrayal and her friends had been. Muhammid, Tina, Artis, and Trevor were all in "protective custody." Only Lydia had been spared, and Jenny had a hunch that was only due to her critical importance to the overall running of the station.

As for herself, Jenny felt as if she had suddenly taken on two full-time jobs. She spent her mornings and evenings researching for Cab. The fact that he still had her searching for precedents encouraged her to believe that he was not going to submit to deBaca's blackmail, but she refused to become too optimistic. She had made that mistake before—with almost fatal results to her relationship with Cab.

Her afternoons were then given over to Lydia. The manager had asked her for help three days ago, and Jenny hadn't been able to refuse. She had been a little nervous about Cab's reaction, but he had said nothing. This day Lydia had sent her and Peter to meet Alex Sullivan, the President of EnerSun, but he hadn't appeared. Either he had missed the shuttle, or he had decided against becoming too closely identified with the events that were taking place aboard the EnerSun station.

Peter had turned away and started back for the spoke when Jenny's attention was caught by two men who were just emerging from the shuttle access tunnel. They were big, hard-faced men who handled their magnetized boots with an ease born of long experience in low gravity. They each carried computer cases which had become the trademark of journalists in the field, but there was something wrong with the picture. To Jenny's mind neither one of them looked much like journalists.

"Hsst," Jenny whispered, and caught Peter by the arm. "Who are *they?*"

Peter frowned, and studied the two new arrivals who headed off without a sign of hesitation for one of the access spokes. "Damned if I know. They do look sort of . . ." He hesitated, groping for an appropriate word.

"Yeah." Jenny nodded. "That's how they struck me."

"Let's get back to Lydia. Maybe she'll be able to check the passenger roster, and see who our two mystery men belong to."

"Dear God, what paranoids we've become. Checking up on every stranger as if they're going to be a threat to us."

"I wouldn't call that paranoid, I'd call it prudent, after what we've been through. After all, when you've been kicked in the face you start to look out for men with hobnail boots."

"Your Honor," Furakawa said in his soft, dusty old voice. "My next witness was to have been Michael Dobson, the White House Chief of Staff, but Mr. Dobson has ignored the subpoena and refuses to appear."

Cab squinted into the brilliant television lights that ringed the small courtroom. The powerful lights together with the crush of bodies made the room unbearably hot. They had been here for only an hour, and Cab was already beginning to feel faint. He briefly wondered how much of it was physical discomfort and how much was emotional anxiety. If he passed out on the bench they would have to postpone the hearing, and he would have found an honorable way to avoid the decision that was haunting him. Unfortunately that would be only a temporary solution.

"Can you establish the link between the White House and the Pentagon without Mr. Dobson?" Cab asked.

Furakawa inclined his head. "Yes, your honor. General Abrams will be able to testify as to his and Mr. Dobson's conversation."

"Then please proceed."

General Steve "Skip" Abrams made an excellent witness. Like all military men he was desperately anxious to protect his service, so he almost fell over himself trying to throw the blame squarely on the politicians. The effect on the spectators was electric. Cab assumed that the reaction in the VIP suites, where closed-circuit televisions carried the hearing to those people unable to obtain a seat in the small courtroom, and to those watching back on Earth, was the same.

As for himself, he tuned out most of Abrams's testimony, and continued worrying with his own private problem. After all, none of this was new to him. He had read the transcripts of the meeting between Abrams and Dobson, and he had seen each of the orders as they went down line from the Pentagon to the lunar base.

Of far more importance to him was the vise in which deBaca had placed him. If he acted according to the dictates of his conscience, his family would suffer. He didn't for a moment believe that deBaca had the power to totally bar them from public life, but he could make it very uncomfortable for the Huntington clan.

Cab had considered calling his mother and pouring out the whole story into her sympathetic ear, but that had seemed childish and cowardly. He would have been, in essence, asking for permission to ruin the family, and by receiving such approbation would have been relieved of responsibility.

No, this time, the decision and the responsibility rested squarely with him. He realized with a sense of shame that in his whole life he had never taken a risk. He had never stood up and committed himself without the protective buffer of his name and his wealth, and where was the risk in that?

He looked down to where Evgeni Renko sat impassively at Furakawa's table. He had not yet been called to give his testimony. That would most likely come tomorrow, and when it did, Tomas could kiss the election good-bye. Tomas had given him an impossible task, Huntington thought resentfully. There was no way he could stop the hearing now, and even if he refused to censure deBaca and Tupolev it would make no difference. The world would have heard the testimony and drawn its own conclusions. *So, it's damned if you do, and damned if you don't,* he thought wearily.

Cabot wondered how the miner felt. He was one small man who had set in motion world-shaking events. As a result of his actions, governments would most likely fall, and in the end what would he have to show for it? The satisfaction of seeing justice done? But nothing would bring back the lives lost at the Garmoneya Mining Collective, and so much misery would result from this hearing. Was it really worth it?

Coward, Cab thought savagely, swinging his chair around until his back was almost to the courtroom, and covering his eyes with one hand. This man has had none of your advantages or privileges, yet he's willing to risk everything in the service of a principle. How can you do less?

But I'm frightened, another part of him wailed miserably.

So frightened. We stand to lose so much. It's easy for a man like Renko. He had nothing to begin with so he can afford to be heroic.

There was a featherlike touch on the sleeve of his gown. He opened his eyes and looked down into Jenny's concerned and questioning face. "Cab? Are you all right?" she asked in an undertone.

He looked up, and realized that the cameras were fixed on him like curious robotic eyes, and there was a murmuring from the spectators. He flushed and shook his head, waving a hand dismissively in the air. "Yes, yes. I'm fine. It must be the heat." She stared at him oddly, and he wondered why. He had no way of knowing that in that moment he looked very young, very vulnerable, and very lost.

"Maybe you ought to recess for a little while. It is becoming like a sauna in here."

"Yes, yes." He seized eagerly on the excuse. "That's a good idea. When Abrams finishes, we will take a break." She nodded and patted him on the hand before returning to her chair.

Late that night the com chimed. Tossing aside his book, Cab swung out of bed and, jerking on his bathrobe, hurried into the living room. Jenny was already asleep, and he was anxious that the delicate rings not disturb her. He couldn't imagine who would be calling at this hour, and even in his wildest imaginings he would never have expected the person whose face appeared on the screen.

"Mr. Renko," Cabot said faintly. He had never spoken with the Russian; first out of embarrassment, and then because he wished to maintain some semblance of impartiality during the duration of the UN hearing.

"Please forgive me for calling you so late, but I have to talk to you." The Russian's face was a sickly shade of gray, and his words tumbled over each other in an agitated staccato.

"This is most irregular, Mr. Renko. If it should be learned that you and I were in contact during—"

"Irregular? I will tell you irregular, Mr. Huntington. There are men on this station who have been sent to kill me!"

Cabot coughed, and traced his forefinger along the edge of the desk. "Come now, Mr. Renko. Surely—"

"You think I'm lying! I tell you it is not so. You come here, and I will show you these men. They are waiting. Waiting to kill me." His accent had become so thick that Cab was having a hard time understanding. He held up a placating hand.

"All right, all right. I'll come, if only to reassure you that you're in no danger."

He broke the connection and hurried into his room to dress. Jenny was standing blearily in the door of her bedroom when he emerged into the living room.

"Where are you going? Did I hear you on the com?"

"Yes. Evgeni Renko called. He's got it into his head that assassins have been sent to kill him. I'm going over to his apartment to try and calm him down."

"You don't think they have been?"

"Of course not," he said impatiently. "Tomas will play hardball politically, but he's no murderer."

"How about Tupolev? We know for sure he's a murderer, and deBaca has demonstrated an amazing capacity for looking the other way."

"What are you trying to do? Scare me?" Cab said lightly. "I'll be back in thirty minutes or so. Don't wait up."

He made the walk to the neighboring apartment building in minutes. The soldiers had been pulled from Renko's door when martial law was lifted, and he was now free to wander about the station. Cabot, too, had wondered at the sudden relaxation of the stranglehold the troops had maintained on the station, but he had assumed that deBaca and Tupolev were responding to public pressure, and trying to repair their images.

Renko must have been waiting at the door for he flung it open on Cabot's first knock. Pulling the judge into the apartment, he slammed and locked the door behind him. There was no doubt that the man was badly frightened. His hands were shaking, and his Adam's apple bobbed convulsively.

"All right, Mr. Renko, I'm here. Now please show me these phantom assassins."

"First I tell you what happened earlier this evening." He moved jerkily across the room, and peered out from between the curtains. "Yes," he almost said to himself. "They are still there." He looked back at Cabot. "Tonight I go for a walk. I think maybe I will go to the hub and swim. I am in the locker room changing when someone grabs me from behind. Another man breaks a vial under my nose and I start to pass out.

"But they have misjudged. They do not realize that the pool is very busy at night. I hear voices, and they drop me. The next thing I know I am sitting on the floor with my back against a locker, and a crowd of boys around me. I tell them I fainted for I do not wish to frighten them, but *I* know different. If they had not come in when they did I would now be a new satellite in orbit around this station. There are many convenient air locks in the hub. The men trailed me back here, and even now they are waiting, like shadows in the trees, for a chance to take me. Come, I show you."

Cab joined Evgeni at the window. He followed the direction of the other man's pointing finger, but saw nothing. He held his breath, and looked again, and this time he saw a flicker of movement among the trees. It was definitely man-shaped. Cab felt his mouth go dry.

"But why," he said in a whisper to Evgeni, as if afraid the man in the darkness would hear him.

"Tomorrow I will testify. My wife, who is the only other person who saw the attack on the collective, is somewhere in the asteroids. Without my testimony what have you got? Only that the Americans agreed to allow a Soviet boat to fly over their air space and fire a missile. Only *I* can establish that that missile struck the collective."

My God, Cab thought. I've answered my own question. I wondered today what deBaca thought he could hope to gain by forcing me to render a decision favorable to him. After all, Renko would have testified and that together with the orders to the Air Force would have damned him with the American people even if my decision didn't. But with Renko removed, and if I were to submit to his blackmail, he might very well walk away from this with his image only somewhat tarnished. He might even manage to keep his grip on the White House.

Fear rose up and grabbed him by the throat. He turned his head to look at Renko. "Dear God, those men saw me come here. They must know that you are telling me everything, and that means that they're going to have to act—and quickly," he concluded, flinging himself away from the window, and running toward the com. "I'll call station security—" he began, but it was too late.

The lock clicked, and the door swung quietly open, revealing two large, hard-faced men. Cab began to back away. Evgeni had already placed the sofa between himself and their two assailants. One of the men pushed the door shut with a negligent gesture.

"It really is a shame that you chose this particular time to come calling, Justice Huntington," the fair-haired man said in a soft Russian accent as he dropped a lock-picking device back into his pocket. "Because now we are going to have to kill you, too." His dark-haired companion muttered something inaudible and looked glum. The Russian laughed gently. "My friend is somewhat dismayed by this prospect, and I have convinced him that we have little choice."

Cab continued to back away until he was brought up short by a small table set at the side of a chair. His heart was hammering in his throat, and he wondered if his terror could be plainly read on his face. He reached back to steady himself, and his hand came in contact with a heavy china vase. He closed his fingers about the vase, and brought it down behind his back.

He glanced at Renko, and was dismayed to see the man looking like an ox on its way to slaughter. All animation had vanished from his face, and he stood with slump-shouldered resignation while his killers approached.

Cab murmured a brief prayer, and flung the vase with all his strength at the silent one of the pair. It took the man neatly in the temple, and he staggered as the white-and-lilac-colored shards rained down around him. But Cab hadn't waited to see the result of his throw. The moment he released the vase he had launched himself for cover behind a large chair. The Russian whirled, his attention shifting from Evgeni for the moment, and his hand plunged beneath his coat.

"Run!" Cab shrieked at Evgeni. The miner shook himself out of his trance, and pelted for the door. The Russian assassin dithered between his two intended victims, and Evgeni managed to dodge past him and reach the door. The second killer was still stunned by the blow. His hand was up at his temple, and blood welled from beneath his fingers.

Evgeni yanked open the door, and vanished into the hall. The Russian whirled and started in pursuit. Without stopping to think whether he was being brave or foolish, Cab flung himself on the man's shoulders, and tried to pull him back. His only conscious thought was that he had to give Evgeni time to escape.

His opponent growled deep in his throat and, reaching back, seized Cab by his coat collar. Cab's fingers clawed at the Russian's brawny shoulders as he struggled to hang on, but he was jerked loose, and thrown like a rag doll into a corner of the room. He slammed into the wall, and the air went out of his body in a great *whoosh*.

He lay on his side, gasping like a fish, and slowly his eyes began to focus again. What he saw sent him into an agony of terror. The assassin had pulled out a large-bore pistol with a silencer attachment, and was leveling it on him where he lay helpless on the floor. He struggled to rise, to roll, anything, but his battered body refused to obey his frenzied commands. There was a dull *phut,* and a crushing blow as the bullet slammed into his chest. Fire lanced through his body, and something warm and sticky began trickling over his hand which rested beneath him.

Consciousness was beginning to slip from him as he heard a decidedly American voice saying, "Come on, he's dead, or he will be soon. We've got to find that Russian before he raises the alarm."

Jenny, he thought as his eyelids fluttered closed. *I hope you waited up....*

Evgeni darted through the dark and empty central park using every available piece of cover. He considered racing up to one of the silent apartment buildings, and hammering on doors, but he decided with bitter hopelessness that it was useless. The only man with the power to protect him was either dead or in the hands of his killers.

Behind him he heard the thud of running feet, and he realized with a burst of panic that they were closing in on him. Even if he had wanted to, there was no longer any time to call for help.

He flicked mentally through the station, trying to find a place to hide. Nothing presented itself, and then it struck him. *Outside.* He had spent the past seven years in one-sixth gravity. He was fully trained in zero gee. Out there he might stand a chance against his Earthbound pursuers. He redoubled his efforts, heading for the nearest spoke.

Jenny glanced at the clock on her bedside table. It had been far more than thirty minutes, and Cab still wasn't back. She knew it was foolish, but a nervous agitation had set her stomach to jumping, filling her mind with an irrational dread. She flung back the covers, and padded into the front room, where she quickly dialed Evgeni's apartment. The phone chimed endlessly, and no one answered. She frowned at the receiver. It didn't make any sense. She couldn't picture Cab and Evgeni going off together for a companionable drink. She hung up the phone, went back into her bedroom to dress, and hurriedly left the apartment.

The door to Evgeni's apartment was partly ajar. Hesitantly Jenny reached out and pushed it open. And gave a muffled scream when she saw Cab lying in a widening pool of blood on the white-carpeted floor. She ran across the room and dropped to her knees next to him. The front of his shirt was soaked with blood, and there was an ugly hole where the bullet had penetrated. She was afraid to touch him, but she forced herself to reach out and lay the tips of her fingers against his throat. There was a flutter of pulse, and she gave a sob of relief.

Leaping to her feet she ran to the com and called the emergency access number, then returned to Cab to wait. She was gently brushing the heavy dark hair off his forehead when his eyes opened. He gave her a confused look.

"Jenny?"

"Hush, Cab. Don't talk. I've called for help."

"Evgeni. You have to find him. They're going to kill him if they can."

"Cab! I can't leave you like this."

"Please," he whispered. "I'll be all right."

Suddenly the room was filled with people. Gentle hands pried Jenny away from Huntington, and a stretcher was placed next to his prone body. She watched as two emergency medical crew members lifted him onto the stretcher, and she winced when he gave a cry of pain.

"Jenny," someone said, then repeated it with more force when she failed to respond. "Jenny! What is going on here?"

She slowly turned to face Lydia. The older woman took her by the shoulders, and gave her a shake. "Come on, girl, get a hold of yourself. Communications paged me as soon as they got your call. Now what happened?"

"I'm not sure. Cab got a call from Evgeni earlier this evening. Evgeni said there were people outside who had been sent to kill him, so Cab came over to try and reassure him."

"Looks like he was right, doesn't it? Only they got the wrong man. Come on, we've got to find Evgeni before they do. Let's get back to my office where I can better monitor things."

"But Cab," Jenny said, hanging back.

"Will either recover or die, but either way you can't do anything to help him. While I, on the other hand, badly need your help, and can benefit by your presence."

Green eyes met black in a desperate plea for understanding. The black eyes didn't waver, and with a sigh Jenny nodded. "All right, I'll come with you."

"Can you use a gun?" Lydia threw over her shoulder.

"Yes. Cab taught me."

"Good. Because I have a feeling you're going to need to."

They paused in Lydia's office while she brought up a schematic of the station on her computer. She leaned back in her chair, and thoughtfully knuckled her chin while staring at the bewildering array of lines and levels that formed the EnerSun station.

"It doesn't seem very big until you start looking for a single person. Then it suddenly becomes enormous," she said to Jenny, who perched on the corner of her desk. "Do you have any idea where Renko might have headed?"

"I'm afraid not. I've only talked with the man a couple of times. It wasn't enough to learn how his mind works."

"Did Cab indicate how many men there were?"

"He just said 'they.'"

"Which implies more than one, and, one hopes, fewer than ten. I think it might be nice to have a little more firepower on our side," Lydia said as she reached for the phone. "I'm going to call Peter."

He was asleep when Lydia called, but it didn't take him long to grasp the situation, and he promised to be over in minutes. Lydia then began taking reports from security as they fanned out and started through the station.

"This is going to take forever," Lydia muttered. "They've just started on the rim and that still leaves the hub, the spokes, and all the maintenance conduits."

She leaned back in her chair and chewed nervously on a hangnail. Suddenly her phone chimed, and both she and Jenny jumped to reach for it. Lydia beat her to it, and hit the accept button.

"Lydia, this is Ralph Miller. I'm the second-shift relief man in suit storage. I've just found Tony out cold on the floor and three suits are missing."

"Thank you, Ralph, you're a lifesaver, and I mean that literally." She cut the connection, and gave Jenny a triumphant look. "That's it then. They've headed outside, and we now know how many there are. You better stay here," she tossed over her shoulder as she headed for the door. "Null-gee is no place for beginners."

"But I know how to handle myself in zero-gee. Peter taught me," Jenny said, charging after Lydia.

"Fine, then come along. Just be sure you know the risk you're taking." The door slid open and they almost ran down Peter, who had just reached the office. He caught Jenny by the shoulders and steadied her after she slammed into his tall form.

"Hey, what's going on? Have you found them?"

"Don't talk, just follow and listen," Lydia said, never breaking stride. Peter shut up, and he and Jenny jogged quickly after her.

When they reached suit storage they found Ralph helping the groaning Tony into a chair.

"I've sent for medical," Ralph said, "but they haven't arrived yet."

"They're having a busy night," she responded shortly. "We need three suits and pistols, and quickly." Ralph hesitated, looking down at his injured friend. "He'll be all right for now," she said with a jerk of her head at the hapless Tony. Ralph nodded, and vanished among the lockers.

Lydia crossed to the desk, and called Sammy Hong, the head of security. "Break off the search, and get a team over to the hub and suited up. The men we're looking for have gone outside."

"On our way."

Ralph returned with the suits, and the three quickly dressed. Lydia handed Jenny a large-barreled, bulky pistol. She hefted it gingerly.

"Null-gee pistol," Peter explained. "The shell has it's own booster."

"Then I don't have to do anything special?"

"No, just aim it and fire the way you would a regular pistol. The booster will automatically kick in after the shell leaves the barrel. Oh, yes, you've got seven rounds, and trying to reload in free fall is a bitch, so use them wisely."

"Ready?" Lydia asked as she holstered the pistol, and tucked her helmet under one arm.

"Aren't we going to wait for security?" Jenny asked a bit timorously.

"We've wasted too much time already. For all we know, it may be too late for Renko."

Jenny nodded, and followed Lydia and Peter to an airlock. They fitted on their helmets, and Lydia started the cycling sequence. Jenny's gloved hands fluttered restlessly from the butt of her pistol to the flight controls for her maneuvering unit, which rested on her back over her oxygen unit.

She realized that her teeth were chattering, and she clamped her jaw shut. Those times spent space-walking with Peter had been pure larks, and he had always been on hand to rescue her when she had misjudged the amount of thrust from her MU and sent herself spinning and tumbling through space. This time there would be no help if she found herself in trouble, and one miscalculation could cost her her life. The men they were going up against were utterly ruthless. They had proved that when they had brutally shot Cab, and they wouldn't hesitate to use any error on her part to kill her.

It was a kill-or-be-killed situation, because she had a hunch the men they were hunting weren't going to quietly surrender. The thought sickened her. It was one thing to placidly fire rounds into a stationary target out at the shooting range; it was quite another to shoot a living human being. She wondered if she could do it, and she decided that she couldn't. She chinned on her radio ready to tell Lydia to let her out, that she couldn't go through with it, but it was too late. The outer door of the lock swung open revealing the icy stillness of space.

Lydia and Peter kicked off, and floated out of the lock. Jenny placed both hands against the sides of the lock, and held herself in place. Fear filled her throat like a choking miasma. She watched the bright flare of a jet as Peter fired his MU, and came into position next to Lydia. Their white-suited forms were retreating from her, becoming smaller by the moment. She gave a little sob, and kicked out after them. These two people had become very dear to her. She couldn't allow them to go up alone against a pair of trained killers.

Jenny fired a quick burst, feeling the thrust against the small of her back, and went scooting soundlessly through the vacuum to where Lydia and Peter were holding stationary in space. The sunlight glinted brilliantly off their white suits, and Jenny thought with consternation what wonderful targets they all made.

"If I were Renko I'd try to hide among the debris," Lydia was saying when Jenny arrived. Her voice sounded odd and tinny through the suit radio.

"There's a whole tangle of old fuel tanks that were used to house the workmen when the station was built. That's where I'd head. We can reach them quickly by going up the length of the hub and cutting sunward across the rim." Peter's arm arced out slowly indicating the direction.

"Lead on," Lydia said. "You've been out here a lot more than I have."

As they skimmed over the top of the rim, Jenny stared down in fascination at the aluminum plate that formed the torus ring, and the fused bricks of undifferentiated lunar soil held together by mechanical fasteners that formed the outer shield. After all these weeks on the station she had begun to view it as an extremely well-planned, if somewhat remote, model city. Now with the stars glittering against the backdrop of darkness, the sun flaring gold and orange before her, and the blue-green globe of the Earth floating serenely to her left, she realized how fragile and tenuous man's hold in space was.

They shot over the rim, and there before them, like a dinosaur's graveyard, lay the tangle of giant fuel tanks. From their perspective they had a clear view of the entire dump. Then, off among the tanks on the right, Jenny saw a familiar white glitter. She boosted forward and touched Peter on the arm, pointing silently at that telltale glint. Seconds later they saw a pinprick orange flare as a booster shell fired.

Lydia swung her arm, indicating that they should fan out and try to come in from above. Peter nodded and, firing his MU, went gliding off to the right. Lydia peeled off to left, and Jenny, holding motionless in space, suddenly realized that there was no way to distinguish between the six people who were about to begin playing a deadly hide-and-seek among the rubble of booster tanks.

Evgeni huddled at the base of one of the fuel tanks, and worked frantically to seal the small tear in the arm of his suit. Fortunately the sealing system in these American suits worked much better than the suits he had worn at the collective.

The tear closed, he leaned his head back against the metal tank, and wondered how much longer he could hold out. He had made a serious miscalculation. He had assumed he could outmaneuver his pursuers in the free fall of space, but that was not the case. The men who followed him were experts in null gravity. In fact, they were better than he, as evidenced by this most recent of his narrow escapes. He had managed to avoid being struck by the shell, but it had torn a hole in his suit as it passed. It would't take too many more such "escapes" before his air supply would bleed away into the vacuum, and he would be dead.

He thought he saw something out of the corner of his left eye. He jerked his head up, and began looking nervously in all directions, but there was nothing there other than the seemingly endless labyrinth of metal cylinders. Still, he had remained stationary for too long. He had managed to steal a suit from the storage area, but the weapons had been tightly locked away, and unfortunately his assailants suffered from no such handicap—they were all too well armed. Given the unequal contest, his only safety lay in constant movement. Otherwise they would find him, and take him like a badger in a trap.

Jenny wove through the tumbled fuel cells. She had long since lost sight of Lydia and Peter, and the feeling of abandonment made her skittish and jumpy. She kept releasing the right flight stick to touch the holstered pistol, and each time she made the maneuver she was threatened with an eminent loss of equalibrium. She knew it was foolish, but she couldn't help herself. She was certain that at any moment one of the assassins would appear from behind a tank, pistol out and leveled squarely on her. In that event, she wanted to have at least a chance to fire back.

She found herself straining to listen as if she would hear the dull roar of a maneuvering jet being fired. *Too many science fiction movies,* she thought hysterically. *You know there's no sound in space.* And indeed the only sounds she could hear were those self-contained noises from the suit itself: the occasional crackle from the radio, and the nervous exhalations of her own breathing.

There was a flash of movement off to her right. She grabbed for the pistol while her left hand tightened convulsively on the flight stick. There was a burst of fire from several of the jets, and she went spinning and tumbling through space. Fortunately she managed to keep a grip on her weapon. No propellant shell came out of the darkness to kill her, so she calmed down enough to reholster the pistol, and halt her wild tumblings. She then cautiously approached the area where she had seen the movement.

She stopped at the end of one tank and held her breath, trying to sense if there was another person on the far side of the metal cylinder. Some sense beyond the normal five told her that there was. She felt her muscles tighten with anticipation, and she fired the jets that sent her flying up the side of the tank to a position where she could shoot down on the person who waited on the other side.

A white-suited figure was huddled against the fuel tank. Jenny's finger tightened on the trigger, and as she felt the trigger pull home she realized that the person below her was unarmed. She jerked her arm up, and the booster shell went whizzing off at a forty-five degree angle from her original target.

Evgeni lifted his head to stare up at her, and the dark, blank faceplate added to the terror that she felt emanating from him. She held out a hand to try and reassure him, but before she could chin on her radio he had fired his MU and gone skittering off among the maze of fuel tanks. She cursed aloud, and went flying in pursuit.

They came skimming around a large knot of tanks, and suddenly there were *four* white-suited figures gathered in a clearing in the midst of the dump. There was a moment of consternation, where they all regarded one another, then Jenny fired a forward burst, and went backpedaling toward the cover of the nearest tank.

Two of the men pulled pistols, and shots were exchanged. It was like some sort of surrealistic nightmare. The eerie silence added to the sense of unreality, and everything seemed to be moving in slow motion. There was a brief gout of fire from the muzzle of the pistols, then the tiny rockets in the shells caught and sent them traveling with ever increasing velocity toward their intended targets.

One hit. The body of the man was thrust backward from the impact of the shell, and he seemed to fold in on himself as if trying to protect his vulnerable flesh from the icy cold of the vacuum. There was a fountain of blood from the front of his suit that quickly froze into ice particles that formed a red halo around his now limp body.

The impact of the bullet had sent the body drifting slowly toward Jenny's hiding place. As it began to drift past, she reached out and caught it by the tool belt, pulling it in for a closer look. Peter's face, white and still, like a stone effigy on some medieval tomb, stared up at her. A scream was torn from her throat, and she thrust the body wildly away. Tears filled her eyes and streamed down her face. The moisture began to cloud her faceplate, and she fought for control. Slowly a murderous rage began to replace the blind terror that had filled her at the sight of Peter's body.

Peter's killer was still in view, moving cautiously toward the place where Evgeni had vanished among the tanks. Jenny fired a short burst from her maneuvering jets, and came drifting out of her cover. It was a risk. If the man were to turn she would be an easy target, but by the same token, he, too, would be open for a clear shot.

Seconds passed, and she wondered how he could be so oblivious to the danger that was approaching from behind. Perhaps he had mistaken her for his companion, she thought, and she prayed that was the case.

She put the shot right into the back of his helmet. *It isn't so different from the range*, she thought unemotionally while she watched the bits of helmet, blood and brain form an undifferentiated cloud around the shattered remains of the man's head. *You just have to keep it in perspective*.

Evgeni stuck his head cautiously around the end of a tank,

and stared at her. She thrust the pistol back into it's holster, and chinned on her radio.

"Evgeni." Her voice sounded old and rusty, and she coughed once to clear her throat. "It's me, Jennifer McBride. You're safe now."

They met Lydia and several of the security personnel on the outskirts of the tank dump. The manager stared silently at Peter's body, which Jenny and Evgeni had towed between them. Jenny couldn't bear to leave him in the cold and the dark like some gruesome miniature satellite, so Evgeni had helped her bring him home.

"Did you get the other one?" Lydia asked at last.

"Yes. He's back there somewhere," Jenny said with a jerk of her helmeted head. "It's a pity the cavalry couldn't have arrived a few minutes earlier," she added bitterly, looking at the three security people.

"They did the best they could, and they certainly saved my bacon. The other killer got the jump on me, and when they arrived he was trying to beat my faceplate in with a tool from his belt."

"Is he..."

"Dead? No, at least not yet. He took off when he saw reinforcements coming. He'll either have to come in, or die slowly as his oxygen runs out. Either way, I'm not going to lose any sleep over it." She turned her head and looked at Evgeni. "Well, Mr. Renko, it looks like you're going to be able to testify tomorrow as planned." She paused and reached out to touch Peter's helmet. "I only hope it was worth all the pain," she said softly.

"He's not going to be able to testify to anything unless Justice Huntington is able to take the bench," Sammy Hong said, drifting over to join the conversation.

"Cab," Jenny whispered. "Oh, my God! Cab!" she wailed and, firing a long burst out of her jets, went flying toward the hub.

"Someone go with her and make sure she gets in all right," Lydia ordered. "The rest of you help me take Peter home. This has been a hell of a night," she added almost to herself. "Hope I don't have to live through another one like it."

Chapter Seventeen

"All rise. The court of the Fifteenth Circuit, acting for the International Court of Justice in the matter of Renko, the Right Honorable Justice Cabot Huntington presiding, is now in session."

Cab pressed his hand against his chest, and made his slow way toward the bench. He was moving as if he were ninety, and he felt as if he were a hundred and fifty, but he was grateful to be ambulatory.

The day before, the Justice Department, together with their Soviet counterpart, had tried to have him replaced, citing ill health and delay of justice as grounds for the removal. He could just imagine the kind of toady who would have been found to replace him, so over the strong objections of his doctors he had left the hospital and heard Renko's testimony, the final testimony in the case.

He was determined that the matter would be settled today, so he and Jenny had spent the better part of last night in a frenzy of research and writing. He tightened his grip on the sheaf of papers that contained his decision, and prayed that his family would understand. He believed they would, and even if they didn't, there was nothing else he could do. Some things transcended family loyalty, and perhaps even self-preservation.

He began the laborious climb up to the bench, and from somewhere in the back of the crowded courtroom someone began to clap. He was quickly joined by more people, and soon the room was filled with a deafening round of applause. Cab felt his face growing warm with embarrassment. He patted the air in front of him, trying to stem the uproar.

Everyone, except the attorneys for the U.S. and the Soviet Union, was standing by now. Old Furakawa beamed and nodded to him from his position at the advocate's table, Evgeni smiled shyly at him, and from far back in the room Lydia gave him a respectful salute. Finally the tumult died, and he gave a self-conscious little cough.

"Thank you for that totally undeserved accolade." The only sound in the room was the hum and whir from the press cameras. "By now all of you have heard about the events of two days ago. My only contribution to Mr. Renko's rescue was that I managed to get shot. The people who truly deserve your praise are Lydia Kim Nu, Jennifer McBride, and Peter Traub, who tragically lost his life in that rescue. Now please be seated, and I call this court to order."

Those who had chairs muttered and grumbled their way back into them. The standing-room crowd positioned themselves more comfortably against the walls, and an expectant hush fell over the room. Cab spread his papers out in front of him and, taking a deep breath, began.

"The matter now before this court arises out of the alleged violation of the United Nations Nonmilitary Lunar Pact, Treaty number 2323. To briefly review the facts: Evgeni Feodorovitch Renko, acting as a private citizen, alleged a violation of the UN treaty, claiming that the other members of the Garmoneya Mining Collective had been killed due to an attack upon their home by a patrol boat belonging to the Union of Soviet Socialist Republics. This complaint was further extended to include the United States of America without whose tacit cooperation the Soviet boat could not have reached the collective. This allegation was directly contrary to the official explanation of the tragedy, which maintained that a meteorite had destroyed the Garmoneya Collective.

"The presence of a possible eyewitness to a violation of the Treaty 2323 brought the case before this court, which by agreement of the United Nations has been empowered to act as an auxiliary arm of the International Court of Justice.

"After hearing testimony from experts who have made an onsite inspection of the impact crater, after reading transcripts of orders issued from the Pentagon to the American lunar military base, such orders by the Soviet Union being unavailable, and after hearing corroborative testimony of those orders, it is clear that the destruction of the Garmoneya Collective came not from an errant meteorite, but from the calculated actions of men of power in the capitals of the two most powerful nations in the world.

"It is apparent to this court that a violation of United Nations Treaty number 2323 has occurred, and this court therefore recommends that the UN General Assembly meet to censure the United States and the Soviet Union for their actions."

There was a murmur from the spectators, and several reporters jumped up and began heading for the door. Cab held up a restraining hand, and silence returned.

"However," he continued. "This sterile pronouncement of a violation of a military nonaggression pact fails to capture the full scope of the tragedy in terms of human loss, or the level of sheer barbarism indulged in by so-called 'civilized' nations.

"As Burke wrote, 'Law is the great standing policy of civil society, and any eminent departure from it, under any circumstance, lies under the suspicion of being no policy at all.' And that is the situation we are faced with today. Two great and powerful nations under the leadership of what can only be described as immoral men committed an act of butchery that has no place among the concourse of civilized men. If we require obedience of the law by simple people, how much more must we require from the governments sworn to uphold those laws?

"But what was the act committed by the fifteen people of the Garmoneya Collective that caused so violent a reaction in the capitals of power? Simply this: They had sought to build a better life for themselves and their children by engaging in the marketplace of free trade.

"That brings us back to the Charter of the United Nations under whose auspices this court now sits. That charter states that among the main purposes of the United Nations is cooperation in promoting and encouraging respect for human rights and for fundamental freedoms for all. . . .

"What then are these freedoms that this august, if sometimes ineffectual body, has sworn to uphold? President Roosevelt elaborated upon these rights in his Four Freedoms message to the Congress of the United States on January 6, 1941. Among those freedoms he spoke of was the freedom from want, which was all that the inhabitants of the Garmoneya Collective were pursuing. During that address he also spoke of the freedom from fear, and it is to that end that this court and the international law, which it applies and interprets, must be directed. It is our duty to work for a time when the people of the Earth and the System will live in freedom from the fear brought by the midnight knock on the door, the concentration camp, and death at the hands of a coercive government.

"In the past, it was generally considered that the treatment given by a State to its own subjects did not come within the purview of the international law. Even the most outrageous violations of human rights committed by a State toward its nationals could not have formed the subject of an application to a judicial organ. Fortunately such a narrow interpretation of international law has long been rejected, leaving this court free to act upon such wanton violations of human rights as is now before it.

"As was written in *McKinster versus Sager,* 'Justice is the end of government.' I would modify that statement to read; 'Justice *should be* the end of government. But to continue from the case. 'It ever has been and ever will be pursued until it be obtained or liberty be lost in the pursuit.'

"The events of the past weeks have brought home to us how fragile is that liberty that permits us to strive for justice." He looked down at Furakawa, and gave a small smile. "Recently I was reminded of the words of Jefferson when he wrote, 'The tree of liberty must be refreshed from time to time with the blood of patriots.' Two days ago such a sacrifice was made by a young man who gave his life to insure that truth would be heard in this courtroom, and that justice be done.

"Therefore it is the ruling of this court that the destruction of the Garmoneya Mining Collective was a foul and barbarous act, unworthy of the two great nations who participated in this act, and therefore this court orders that restitution be made to the families of the slain inhabitants of that collective. Such restitution shall be borne equally by the Union of Soviet Socialist Republics and the United States of America. It is so ordered," he concluded, and brought his gavel down with a resounding rap on the top of the bench.

• • •

"Justice Huntington, Justice Huntington!" yelled a journalist as he emerged from the courtroom in the company of Jenny and Lydia. "Did you know that impeachment proceedings have been brought against you in the Senate?" Cab paused and looked at the young man who stared at him with eager eyes ready to capture any reaction or nuance which might cross the older man's face.

Cab gave a small and ironic little smile, and said quietly. "I suppose one can't blame Tomas for wanting to get even." He then moved serenely away, to the vast annoyance of his questioner.

Andy came oozing out of the crowd, and joined the trio. His fat face was set in grim lines as he put a hand on Cab's shoulder.

"You know about this?" Cab asked.

"Yeah, but I was going to wait and break it to you a little more gently."

"That's all right. I really didn't expect anything less. When did you hear?"

"The news was released just after you finished delivering your decision."

Cab sighed. "Tomas never did have a sense of timing. Now it will look like just what it is—sour grapes."

"We're all headed over to my apartment for a celebration," Lydia said. "Want to join us, Andy?"

"Sure. God knows we've got enough to celebrate, what with the troops being removed, and the wicked having been brought low."

"There's also plenty to mourn," Jenny added quietly.

Lydia put an arm around the younger woman's shoulders. "Don't think we've forgotten Peter. We haven't, and I'm sure he'd approve of our little celebration. He always said he found the idea of an Irish wake very appealing, so let's remember him with love and gratitude, and give him a rousing sendoff."

"Excuse me," Cab said, noticing Evgeni, who hovered near the mouth of the spoke, gazing intently at Cab. "There's someone I must speak with." They approached each other cautiously, and stood staring silently at one another for several moments. "Well," Cabot said at last. "Are you satisfied?"

"Yes. It will not bring them back, but at last justice was done."

Cab winced and looked away. "Ah, yes . . . well, as to that. We've never exactly gotten to know each other, but I'd like to say now that I'm sorry about that earlier hearing. Given the terrible consequences that came out of that decision I'm sure you can never forgive me, but it comforts me that you think justice has finally been done, and I hope that it will in some small way expiate that earlier action."

"It has helped, and that helped more," he said, pointing at Cab's chest. "You came close to dying for my sake."

The judge made a dismissing gesture. "So what now, Evgeni?"

"There is a shuttle leaving in two hours for the jump point. I will be on it, and from there I go to the asteroids to rejoin my family." He smiled. "Mr. Reichart still owes me that stake."

"I'm sure you'll get it. Mr. Reichart is an honorable man."

"And so are you, Mr. Huntington. You have lost quite a lot, I think, by this action."

Cabot shrugged and immediately regretted the action for it sent a stab of pain through his chest. "Before my ancestors became proper, wealthy, and conservative they were quite revolutionary. Maybe I'm a throwback."

"We can always hope," Lydia said coming up behind him with Jenny and Andy in tow.

Cabot turned slowly to face her. "I've wanted to say this ever since I met you, and now I think I can. Lydia Kim Nu, you are a truly dreadful woman."

"Why, thank you, judge," she said with a slight bow. "I have been cultivating it for over fifty years. Mr. Renko, we are having a party, which will no doubt quickly deteriorate into a drunken brawl, at my apartment. Would you care to join us?"

Renko smiled guiltily and nodded. "Soon I will be back under the watchful eye of my wife, so while I have the chance I think I will join you. Women are not very understanding about this sort of thing," he confided to Cab and Andy.

"And what are we?" Jenny demanded. "Boys in drag?"

"Different." Renko scratched at his head. "You're not wives," he then added by way of enlightenment.

"A subtle distinction," Lydia said and, linking her arms through Cab's and Renko's, began marching them toward her apartment.

The noise level at the apartment had already reached amazing proportions when they arrived. The front door stood open, and people were spilling out into the hall. It looked as if half the residents of the station were trying to cram themselves into Lydia's home. They tried to move through the throng, but their progress was impeded by people who pushed forward to shake their hands or pound them on the back. Cabot's smile took on a sort of fixed rigidity as he felt the newly closed wound pull open and begin to bleed.

He began to think longingly of bed, but he couldn't leave now. He had come among these people with disdain and arrogance, and had been offended when they had rejected him. Then as his respect and affection for them had grown, their attitude had begun to shift until now he had finally been accepted. Given that victory he was, by God, going to stay at this party rather than creeping home to bed. A man could always sleep. It wasn't often he was given a second chance.

They finally reached the living room, and the round of congratulations began all over again. Artis waved enthusiastically from where she was holding court on the couch, and Muhammid came bursting out of the kitchen with a cocktail shaker in his hands. All the familiar faces were present with one notable exception. Florence Wandall was conspicuously absent.

Cabot put his mouth close to Lydia's ear and asked, "Where's Flo?"

Lydia looked sad. "She decided that retiring back to Minnesota was a good idea, and I agreed. A number of our people wouldn't be as forgiving as I am."

"You've never struck me as particularly forgiving."

"Sometimes emotion plays a large part in our decisions. I've known Flo for twenty years. She was my friend. We all knew she was never as critical of the Earth authorities as we were. When the confrontation came, she was placed in an intolerable position. She acted with honesty and as her own sense of integrity dictated. I can't condemn her for that." Lydia smiled sadly. "You see, she still believed that the system provided a means for change."

"And I have to agree with her. In the hands of the right people this system can work."

"Replacing the deBacas and the Tupolevs won't change anything."

"Then you don't think it's over?"

"Oh, God, no. This has just been the beginning. You're in for some rough times out here, judge."

He gave a twisted little smile. "If I'm still out here. As Tomas reminded me, he's still in the White House until January. More than enough time to push through my impeachment and removal."

Much later he found himself seated with Lydia, Trevor, Muhammid, Tina, and Artis. Someone had captured Evgeni, and trundled him off to catch his shuttle, and the party had begun to wind down. Muhammid took a reflective sip of whiskey and squinted up at the ceiling.

"So what are you going to do now, Cabot?"

"Go back home, I guess. I really shouldn't hear any cases during the duration of my impeachment hearings."

Lydia regarded him over the top of her wineglass. "Why don't you stay here?"

"Yes," said Artis eagerly, laying her hand over his. "We've grown accustomed to having you about. Besides, you can't take Jenny from us."

Her remark reminded him that he hadn't seen his law clerk for several hours. He frowned, wondering where she could have gotten to.

"And look at it this way," Tina said. "You'll be in position to head out to Mars once this mess is settled."

"You're very optimistic, but I'm afraid I can't share in it." He pushed painfully to his feet. "And now if you'll excuse me, I'm going to find Jenny and go to bed."

He found her sitting in darkness in their living room. He sat on the arm of the couch, and studied her shadowed profile. "You left early," he said at last.

"I couldn't stay there any longer. I kept thinking back to that other party . . . other times, and thinking that he should have been there."

"Did you love him?"

She shook her head, her hair cascading forward to half cover her face. "Not in the way you mean—no. But I did love him. He was my friend."

"Do you want to go home?"

"No. I want to stay with you."

"I can't offer you much of a future. No practice left, probably no judgeship, either."

She shifted on the couch to face him. Her face was a white blur in the darkness. "It doesn't matter. Whatever *they* decide"—she made a contemptuous gesture Earthward—"won't alter the fact that you belong here."

"Doing what?" he asked gently as he slid down onto the couch to join her. She moved in closer and rested her head on his shoulder. He forced himself not to flinch.

"I don't know, Cab, but I just don't think you can go home and quietly pick up where you left off."

His arms went around her, and he laid his cheek against her hair. "You may be right."

They sat in silence while he stared out the sliding glass door toward the empty river bed. Night lay serenely across the station while thousands of miles away the Earth continued spinning along it's frantic course with seven billion people aboard, and fearful, directionless men at the helm. And all of them—people and leaders alike—were dependent upon the System if they wanted anything more than subsistence living.

He was suddenly seized with the fear that Lydia was right. That this had been only the beginning—that the Earth governments would continue their policy of coercion against the colonists, and that the System would stubbornly refuse to compromise and negotiate with the home planet—and the final result could only be open conflict.

He decided that the power to determine such an outcome didn't belong in the hands of some toady sent up from Washington. It belonged in *his* hands, and he was going to see that he kept it, by God. He had planned to remain aloof from the impeachment proceedings—telling himself that the outcome didn't matter—but it did matter and he wasn't going to sit quietly by while he was crucified to satisfy deBaca's need for vengeance.

He would return to Earth, but only to fight the impeachment. And then someday, if justice still meant anything to the men and women in the Senate chamber, he would return to the System and complete his circuit.